Heart of Lohikärra

L. L. Nelson

Nelding & Michcomb Publishing

To my husband - For always supporting me, even when I doubted myself. You are more amazing than you know.

To my kids - For inspiring me to be a better mom and showing me what it looks like to have limitless confidence in yourself.

To my sisters - For inspiring me and just being plain awesome. You all rock!

To my dad - For always believing I was an amazing writer and being my cheerleader.

A mysterious young woman, an elven invasion, and the tokens of the High King

Haldrek Rodreksson has known his entire life where his future lies and what is expected of him. But on the eve of battle, soothsayers show him three visions of a different future: a mysterious young woman, a new invasion, and theft of the High King's tokens. Visions which make him question his future and that of his homeland, Lohikärra.

When the capital of Lohikärra falls, Haldrek's world is thrown into disarray and he must scramble to keep the young woman from his visions safe.

Injured, weaponless, and with little support, will Haldrek be able to save the woman and change the visions he was given? Or will he, his homeland, and his loved ones fall to their enemies?

Get a free copy of the prequel
Visions of Lohikärra here:

https://www.llnelsonauthor.com/newsletter/

Contents

Chapter 1

I hated feeling like a beached whale. And a tired one at that. The only upside to not sleeping as much was my ability to spend a few extra moments with Haldrek in the quiet early hours of the morning. Though the past few months had been relatively peaceful, they had been busy with advisors, hersirs, and messengers alike demanding our attention. But right now? It was just Haldrek and me, nestled within our four-poster bed. He was currently curled up on his good side, hand beneath the bedsheets, applying a salve that was supposed to make childbirth less painful and strenuous. While I was skeptical of those claims, I didn't complain when he applied it.

He seemed to enjoy it as well.

"Ina?" His voice, still husky from sleep, made me open my eyes.

"I'm awake." A nerve in my leg began to tingle, and I shifted to remove the pressure. Haldrek took it as a sign to apply the balm more thoroughly. He moved closer to me, navigating around my enormous belly and kissing me on the forehead.

"How did you sleep last night?"

"Same as usual. A few hours of strange dreams, interrupted by the urge to pee, and then kicking at the top of my belly."

Haldrek slipped his hand from between my legs and gently stroked the top of my belly. "Our child seems to know exactly when I'm trying to feel him or her kick. They stop moving like they're trying to hide from me."

I laughed as he moved his head down and started making some sounds into my belly. It tickled until the baby shifted and head-butted me in the crotch. I groaned and Haldrek pulled back in surprise.

"Did I hurt you?"

I shook my head. "You made the baby move, though. Did you feel it?"

He nodded. "A little." As his hand drifted back down below my belly button, he asked, "Have the midwives said how much longer until...?"

"Whenever my body decides, but they think within the next week. Apparently, I'm showing signs of imminent labor. At least according to them."

"Like what?"

I shrugged, wondering how much Haldrek wanted to know. "They didn't tell me much, but I guess the body has ways of showing. Like supposedly there's a line on my butt telling them I'm about to give birth."

Haldrek started laughing loudly and pushed his head into the pillows to smother the sound. When he came up for air, I frowned at him.

"If you don't believe me, go talk to the midwives yourself."

Another kiss on the forehead, then he whispered, "I believe you. And the midwives. I've just never heard a description like that before."

The world around us stayed quiet as his hand made its way back to my belly, a comforting pressure.

"Part of me is scared for when it happens. Like, how painful will it be? And...what happens after?" I thought back to my dragon ring pendant. Senja had promised protection to both me and my child while I was pregnant, but what happened after the child was born? Would Rorik come after both of us? What if I couldn't stop him? And even more terrifying, how would I react to being a mother? Would I love this child or be like my own mother, who had openly talked about how she couldn't find the desire to bond with me after I was born? I still remember hearing her talk about how she'd had my father and the nurses deal with me while she recovered from childbirth.

Haldrek's voice was soft. "What do you mean?"

I blinked a couple of times to clear my thoughts. "I'm afraid of what Rorik might do once the baby is born. And I'm afraid... am I going to be a good mother? Or am I going to be like mine?" My throat tightened up. "She barely tolerated me after I was born. Until my father convinced her to hold me for a little while and she deemed me cute enough." Tears poured down my cheeks, and I felt silly for my fears about motherhood. Rorik was the much bigger threat.

"I think you will be an amazing mother. You've already shown how much you care for children, even before you were with child. I barely met your mother, but I'm betting she wasn't creating orphanages or aiding them? You might be her offspring, but that doesn't mean you will be like her."

A wet, teary laugh erupted from me. The thought of my mother doing what I'd been doing since my arrival in Lohikärra was unfathomable.

"Plus," he tugged at the dragon ring necklace, "I spoke to both Paavo and Senja about creating a token or some kind of item to protect our child once they are born. They are already making something to keep the baby safe from Rorik after he or she is born." He paused to kiss me again, this time more urgently on my cheek and down to my mouth.

"I've had my own fears, not that I wish to burden you with them. The dragons have calmed most of them."

"What..." I hesitated, wondering if Haldrek's worries would increase mine. "What worries have you had?"

He sighed, pulling back a little. "There are some women who do not survive childbirth. Or die soon after. Like..."

I immediately knew where his fears were coming from. "Like your mother. But wasn't that... wasn't her death because of some kind of illness? Not childbirth?"

He nodded. "Despite all the cures my father could find, and even the dragon water from Mirratoft, the illness that ravaged her was too much. She lived only a short time after I was born, but I've always feared my birth brought on her death." He shook his head. "Not that it is the same situation, but all the dragons have told me they protect female haldragas during childbirth. Senja and Paavo spoke firmly, promising you would be safe during your labor. I know better than to not trust them. I only say all of this because I want you to know you aren't alone in your worries. Everything will be fine." He kissed me once more on the forehead as he stroked my hair away from my face.

I smiled, knowing he was trying to be confident for my sake. Strangely enough, though I worried about how painful labor would be and how I would handle it, I had no fear of dying. Whether that was from Rhaegos's comfort and the confirmation I would be fine, or from my connection to the Realm of Ghosts, I didn't know.

Not knowing what to say, but wanting this moment to last as long as it could, I leaned forward, pressing my lips against his. He eagerly responded, intertwining his legs with mine and squeezing me as close to him as possible.

After a moment, he whispered, "No matter what happens in the future, as long as you are by my side, everything will work out. I would fight the dragons themselves to keep you—and our child—safe."

When we finally did wake up and prepare for the day, our first meeting was with a handful of hersirs and new counsellors Haldrek had hand-picked after the debacle with the imposter. Men like Thoreg and Gizur had been removed from the palace, replaced by other men and women from Drattüjert and the surrounding areas. People who were open to change and understood the dangers we faced from Rorik and others like him.

Meetings were easier now, and I attended enough for the times when Haldrek had to leave and I needed to know what was going on. That said, my back and legs already hurt as I waddled into the room, behind him. The counsellors stood around a table overflowing with parchments and maps. As soon as I spied a high stool near the table, I sat down, in time for the top of my belly to squeeze tight like the baby was pushing against it. I tried not to grimace as I looked up at the counsellors.

"High Queen," said one of the new counsellors, a man by the name of Aleifr. "If you need to rest..." He faltered, glancing up at Haldrek. I waved off his concern.

"I'm fine. The child is active and so all is well. This has been going on for the last few days. He or she is restless, I guess." I laughed.

Haldrek placed his hand comfortingly on my shoulder, then focused on Aleifr and the other counsellors. "If the High Queen says she is fine, I trust her. Speak. What news have you heard today?"

Another counsellor stepped forward. "More refugees arrive in the city every day. Instead of Etelaranikä, however, the majority are coming from Bragidrattür. It sounds like Rorik's men have been causing mayhem in the border villages, knowing there is little Thegn Bragidrattür can do right now."

Haldrek grimaced. "I asked Gunner if he needed aid. He told me he had the situation handled." He glanced around the room, looking for Gunner's hersir, his nephew Bjornulf. The man was scribbling away on something in the corner. After a moment or two, Haldrek cleared his throat. "Bjornulf?"

The man jumped to attention and smiled. "Yes, my king?"

"Any word from your uncle? I asked him not long ago if he needed warriors to protect Bragidrattür. Last we spoke, he said all was well. Have you heard anything from him to confirm what these refugees are saying?"

Bjornulf gaped for a moment, then nodded. "Last night. As I was composing my most recent ballad, he spoke to me using the illustrious dragon magic within these pendants we wear. He spoke of troubling news in Bragidrattür and told me to speak to you when I next sat in one of these meetings."

Haldrek's jaw tightened slightly. Bjornulf wasn't a bad hersir, nothing like Kamira or Lady Drifa, but it was clear Gunner's nephew was more interested in writing his ballads than speaking on behalf of his uncle.

"Did he say anything else? Specifics about what is going on or what aid he might need?" I spoke up, hoping to ease more information out of Bjornulf. In all my interactions with him, he seemed to enjoy playing the part of a lyrical bard. If given the right chance—

He stood up and bowed. "My fair queen, it is grim news indeed. I fear the words my uncle spoke might break your heart, knowing how tender you are toward the people of

Lohikärra." He glanced back at Haldrek. "The refugees' pleas are truth, my king. My uncle confirms attacks along the border with Etelaranikä are increasing. At first, he thought it might be little more than skirmishes between the kin who have always squabbled there, but now he knows the seriousness of the rumors that have been brought before him. Dark rumors."

Haldrek frowned. "Dark rumors? Explain."

Bjornulf stiffened up. "Some of the refugees who have made their way to the thegn hall, they speak of the dead rising again and fair maidens being spirited away to the dark forests of Etelaranikä. Some of the necromancer's men, who upon capture swore curses upon their captors, spoke firmly of a wrathful dragon demanding these women as sacrifices."

The counsellors began to murmur, and I looked at Haldrek in surprise. His jaw clenched tighter, and I tried to sense Rhaegos in the periphery of my mind. She nudged me, but said nothing. There was no sense of calm in her presence. Something was up, even if Rhaegos wasn't going to talk about it.

There is nothing you can feasibly do in this situation. Haldrek and Teminth are dealing with what needs to be done.

I grumbled in response. How was I supposed to be a good queen and wife if I didn't know how to support Haldrek? As if on cue, my stomach tightened again, until I nearly gasped with pain.

Support Haldrek by taking care of yourself and the babe. Comfort him, reassure him you will be fine. Then he will focus more of his attention on the issues at hand.

"How many warriors does your uncle need, Bjornulf?" Haldrek's voice interrupted my conversation with Rhaegos and I looked up. He was staring the hersir down and for a moment, I struggled to believe Haldrek was the younger of the two.

Bjornulf dusted off his tunic and looked nervously at Haldrek. "He requested at least two sattars of men, my king."

Haldrek sighed. "I will send two sattars of men from Drattüjert. And I will speak to the Thegn of Heidrunefoss about sending warriors as well. Rorik's actions will eventually affect her, if they haven't yet."

Bjornulf and the counsellors all nodded in agreement and one began writing down something on the parchment he had. Bjornulf cleared his throat and then asked, "My king, I will let my uncle know of our decision. Should I also... Should he also prepare a place for you at the thegn hall?"

Haldrek turned to me, concern etched across his face. I could guess what he was thinking. As High King he needed to go to Bragidrattür and show solidarity. But the last thing either of us wanted was to be separated right before I was about to give birth.

I smiled, trying to reassure myself with Rhaegos's words. "Mattie and Llamryl will arrive in a day or so from Andrattür. You should go support Thegn Bragidrattür and his people. I'll be fine."

He squeezed my hand and shook his head, returning his focus to Bjornulf and the others. "Tell Thegn Bragidrattür I will come to support him, but the sattars of Drattüjert will arrive before me. While I trust my queen," he squeezed my hand once more, "I could easily see Rorik doing something through his cursed magic before the child comes. Plus, it is tradition that the High King be witness to the birth of his aethlings. There is also the naming ceremony, which must be done before I can leave. Since Teminth tells me no living dragon has willingly allied themselves with Rorik, I will go to Bragidrattür once I have completed all that."

I opened my mouth to rebut Haldrek as the fear of the counsellors and Bjornulf seeing him as weak for staying washed over me. Haldrek had mentioned the naming ceremony before, but I was under the assumption it was a formality. Despite getting along more amicably with the new counsellors, I still remembered how the former ones had acted. Instead, the men all nodded again, and this time Aleifr spoke up. "A wise decision, my king. It has been too long since an aethling lived within the palace walls. Ensuring the safe arrival of yours and the High Queen's child will do much to raise morale in the upcoming months."

I blinked for a moment, stunned by the lack of contention. Haldrek smiled, encouraged by this news, and began issuing orders to the men.

Is this the right decision, Rhaegos? I don't want the people of Bragidrattür to think Haldrek doesn't care about them.

The feeling of soft laughter filled my mind. *Are you telling me you don't want Haldrek by your side when you give birth?*

Both Rhaegos and I knew that was a lie. But I didn't want people to think he didn't care. Not because of me.

Be calm, little one. Haldrek is doing well. There is no harm in him leaving for Bragidrattür a few days after the child arrives. A wave of concern washed over my mind. *Teminth is correct. No living dragon allies with Rorik. Yet there is corrupted dragon magic rotting away at the heart of Etelaranikä. A magic I haven't sensed since the time of Bjornulf and Freya.* She paused once more, and I felt her presence wrap around me protectively. *No. It is wise for Haldrek to wait until the babe is born. Not because any harm will come to you before that, but because both of you will need a source of joy to buoy you up in the months ahead.*

Chapter 2

R haegos's words did little to comfort me. Haldrek seemed lighter and happier, knowing he wouldn't have to leave until after the child arrived, and I tried my best to match his cheerfulness, despite worrying about the storm clouds on the horizon.

The day after our meeting with the counsellors and Bjornulf, Haldrek and I found ourselves in the throne room with Ingrid Niemi. I tried to make myself as comfortable as I could while staying dignified. Ingrid confused me as much as her daughter, Sibila, did. On the one hand, Ingrid had been married to the man who'd tried to kill me, but then again, she had been quick to send messengers of peace after Rorik had begun his shenanigans. Sibila seemed to think highly of her mother, as did Lady Salla and Lady Taimi.

It still came as a surprise to find her bowing before Haldrek and me on this warm summer morning. Haldrek stood with the Staff of Tenelth in front of her as I sat, trying to ignore the aches and pains in my belly and back.

"Do you swear, by the dragons and to the dragons, loyalty to myself, High King Haldrek, and to my wife, the High Queen?" Haldrek lowered the staff to where Ingrid knelt.

She placed her hand on the top of the staff. "I swear, by the dragons and to the dragons, loyalty to the rightful High King and Queen of Lohikärra, Haldrek Rodreksson of Andrattür and Maja Ingmar Svanunge of Svartån."

Haldrek raised the staff and beckoned for her to stand. She did so, then bowed to both of us. "It may not be much right now, but given the circumstances, I want you to know where my loyalties lie. Etelaranikä needs Lohikärra, just as Lohikärra needs Etelaranikä."

Rhaegos's presence swirled around in the back of my mind, a pleasant, peaceful sensation washing over me.

"We accept your loyalty, Lady Ingrid of Etelaranikä. May peace come to your lands swiftly."

Haldrek's choice of words surprised me. Technically, with Rorik's revolt, the title of thegn should have gone to Sibila, right? As Gustav's only other heir? She was certainly old enough to be thegn.

Gustav and Rorik's actions have caused much upheaval in Etelaranikä. Ingrid is trusted among those still living there. One day, Sibila will take over as the thegn of Etelaranikä, but for now, it is safer for her to reside in Drattüjert. Just as it was safer for you to stay in Fargo for a time.

Rhaegos's words unsettled me. I still didn't agree that I was ever safe in Fargo, but I knew better than to argue with her.

I never said Fargo was a safe place, only it was safer than living in Lohikärra while you were a child. Many of those who have challenged you since your arrival would have taken no issue with getting rid of you as a child.

"Ina?"

I looked up, cheeks flushed with embarrassment as I realized Haldrek and Ingrid were staring at me.

"Sorry. Rhaegos was speaking to me."

Haldrek nodded, and Ingrid grimaced. She cleared her throat. "As I was saying, Etelaranikä is still in dire need of aid. It need not be warriors, either. I know you have sent men and women to Bragidrattür to aid the thegn there in foiling Rorik's schemes. But we need food, clothing, medicine. Even just weapons. There are plenty of people still defying Rorik."

That's why they had been staring at me. Even though it wasn't an official task of the High Queen, I had developed a knowledge of the resources Drattüjert had at its disposal and what could aid those in need.

"Of course. I will have to double check the city's supplies, but this spring and summer have been bountiful. I expect there will be plenty of foodstuffs and supplies to aid those fighting Rorik in their backyard."

Ingrid frowned in confusion for a moment, then shook her head. "I thank thee, High Queen. You have been merciful to me and those I speak for." She twisted one of the rings on her fingers and smiled nervously. "That is all I had to say concerning official business, though I have a question of a more personal nature, if you will oblige me."

Haldrek nodded once more. "You may speak your question."

"I wish to know how Sibila is doing. As a hersir and in general. With the fighting as it has been, I have not had a chance to speak to her in many months. A mother always cares for her children, even when they are adults."

The comment tugged at my heart, touching on my own pain and fears. Anger displaced the peace I'd just felt, and I muttered, "That hasn't been my experience."

Haldrek cleared his throat and looked back at me.

"Sorry." I straightened up, adjusting my belly to feel more comfortable. "I haven't been feeling great for the past few days. Sibila has been doing well, however. She, Salla, and

Taimi have been pleasant companions for the last several months. I'm surprised I haven't seen her today yet."

Lady Ingrid waved away my concern with a smile. "It is understandable. I, too, had a difficult relationship with my mother during the time she was alive. It wasn't until I spent time with Lady Salla that I learned what it was like to have a good mother/daughter relationship. I certainly had fears of becoming my mother before Sibila's birth."

I stiffened up, wanting to say something about how I doubted that, but Rhaegos's presence squeezed tight around me, as if to comfort me.

Ingrid and you share much in common. Listen and know she is not your enemy.

I nodded, more in reaction to Rhaegos's words, but Ingrid continued.

"Before Sibila was born, I vowed not to be the mother I had had. Even with Rorik, I tried to be more like Salla than my own mother." Ingrid sighed. "It appears there were other things in play while he was growing up, however."

My heart squeezed tight at the same time as my stomach did, and I took a moment to compose myself. I sensed from Rhaegos that Ingrid was being honest. When my body relaxed, I smiled at Ingrid.

"Once again, I apologize for my sharpness. Um, if you haven't seen Sibila yet, I'm sure she would be happy to see you again. You could go to her quarters if you wished." Those felt like the right words to say, but it also felt strange imagining anyone excited to see their mother. I glanced over at Haldrek, who nodded.

"Of course." He turned back to Ingrid with a warm smile. "Since you have sworn your loyalty to us and petitioned us for more aid, unless there is anything else, you are free to visit Sibila."

Ingrid bowed deeply. "I will take my leave. I bid the dragons be with you both in the upcoming days and months."

She left the throne room, and Haldrek gestured for one of the servants to walk with her.

I closed my eyes as a wave of both hunger and nausea washed over me. The imagined image of Ingrid and Sibila reuniting joyfully after many months made my chest squeeze tight once more. I took a deep breath, wondering if there was anyone else we had to meet with today.

Haldrek's hand brushed against mine. "Should we return to our quarters for the midday meal? We could have some privacy. I know you're not fond of crying in public."

I made a gasping laugh and nodded. More tears fell from my eyes as I opened them. Haldrek helped me up and wrapped his arm around my shoulders.

"Thank you." I leaned into his shoulder for comfort, despite today feeling warmer than normal. As soon as we were out of the throne room, I whispered, "I hope one day I'll be able to have a relationship like Ingrid and Sibila." I rubbed my belly, trying to ease the tightness in it. "With this one or any others we may have. Having that kind of relationship feels like fantasy, though."

Haldrek squeezed me tight. "I think you will. Lohikärra was once a fantasy to you, but now it's real. Why not anything else?"

The next morning, I sat reclined against the cold stone wall in my favorite alcove within Haldrek's and my quarters. Haldrek was downstairs dealing with our daily tasks as I tried to stay cool and ignore the nausea and cramping. The sunlight and air in our room had felt more intense today, so I stayed in just my knee-length under tunic instead of getting fully dressed. When Haldrek had asked if I was all right, I told him I was fine, just hot and tired. Not that he believed me. Soon after he went downstairs, the trio of midwives who had been tending to me interrupted my solitude. They checked me and told me the same thing as before—I was near delivery, but not quite there yet.

It hadn't helped my growing sense of unease and misery.

Pulling at the collar of my tunic and letting some cool air near my skin, I sensed Rhaegos rustle in the back of my mind.

There is good news and good company coming. Sivath sends his greetings. There was a peal of laughter after that statement.

"Mattie's here?" I shifted to get up and felt a weight on my shoulder.

Relax. Save your energy for the next few days. Haldrek has already greeted her and her family.

My mood improved significantly at the thought of seeing Mattie once more. She'd been busy dealing with both internal and external Andrattüran affairs; it had been months since I'd seen her.

A few moments later, the door to our antechamber creaked open and one of the female servants squeezed in with a low bow.

"My queen, you have guests—Thegn Andrattür and her family. The High King has already greeted them."

"Let them in." Excitement flushed out my previous anxiety and I shifted around to face Mattie and Llamryl as they entered, Geirny holding tight to Llamryl's collar.

"Ina!" Mattie wrapped her arms around me, giving me a firm hug. It was good to see her again. I went to stand up as soon as she stepped back, but my stomach squeezed tight once more and I paused to take a breath.

Llamryl waved me off. "Relax. You look like Mattie right before Geirny arrived. She was in nothing but—"

"Llamryl!" Mattie glared at him and he closed his mouth, an impish smile crossing it.

"I was only going to say you were more comfortable in just your night tunic. If my sisters are to be believed, they also preferred to be in less clothing as their birthings neared."

"You think I'm about ready to pop?" I grimaced through another squeeze.

"If you mean you look about ready to give birth, then yes." Llamryl batted away Geirny's hand as she attempted to grab his nose. "What have the midwives said?"

"Some time in the next few days. I'll be ready for the backaches and squeezing to go away. It's gotten worse with every day. I can barely sleep now." Random tears filled my eyes, and I brushed them away. "I'm ready for this baby to arrive, but I'm scared too."

"Scared of what?" Llamryl wrangled with Geirny as she squirmed to get down. As soon as she was on the ground, she was crawling around. I smiled in spite of myself.

"Scared of becoming my mother. Of not having any attachment to this child. I mean, I love him or her right now. Every time I felt a kick or the baby moving around, it made me happy. What if the baby arrives and all of a sudden, I feel nothing? What if I hate the child?"

Mattie sat next to me, wrapping her arm around my shoulders. "I highly doubt that will happen. You have more maternal love and instinct in your little toe than your mother had in her entire body. Are you going to be exhausted and emotional after the baby comes? Absolutely. I was, and so were Thandes and Meri, after their babies were born. That'll ease after a week or two. And you'll have people to help. I told Haldrek I planned to be here for as long as you need me. Sivath has been pestering me about some prophecy involving the Heart, Strength, and Foreigner of Lohikärra. I told him I'd visit your library while I was here. But that's not the most important part. First and foremost, I'm here to support you. Plus, there will be plenty of servants, midwives, and nursemaids to take care of everything else."

Her words comforted me, even if they didn't take away all my fear. Even as some subsided, others rose.

"I'm also afraid of Rorik. As soon as the baby is born, I know he'll try something. He tried attacking me early on in my pregnancy, but the dragons protected me." I played with the dragon ring around my neck. Rorik had attempted the same kind of attack that had ended my first pregnancy. This time, an invisible barrier had blocked his magic, one that injured him each time he attacked it. Only once he'd collapsed was I pulled out of the

Realm of Ghosts and back into the Realm of the Living. Despite Rhaegos's assurances that the baby and I were fine, I hadn't been able to sleep for the rest of the night.

Mattie squeezed my shoulder, and I looked over at her. As she went to speak, the door to the antechamber creaked open and three women came walking in solemnly. The atmosphere in the room changed enough for everyone to notice. Llamryl ducked in front of the women and scooped up Geirny.

"The dragons have many plans for you and your descendants, Maja Ingmar Svanunge." The woman in the middle spoke and the sensation of cold water made its way down my spine. "Rorik the necromancer will have no lasting effect on you or your loved ones."

The younger woman to her right smiled. "Our entrance confused you, but there should be no alarm. The dragons bid us to come and your husband, the High King, has already welcomed us. He wished to be here with you, but as we arrived, so did a messenger from Heidrunefoss."

I tried to feel around for Rhaegos, wanting to know her thoughts. There was no ill will that I could sense from these women, but I wondered who they were and why they had walked in here with no introduction.

They are the Vollr, and they speak for my kin from time to time. The young woman is honest. You—and Haldrek—are on the edge of changing fates, much as you were when you arrived here from Fargo. They bring no harm, only tidings of possible futures.

I nodded, trying my best to be polite and calm. "Welcome. Rhaegos tells me you are the Vollr. You are here to bring tidings of possible futures?"

The eldest of the three, an ancient woman with wrinkles covering every inch of exposed skin, laughed. "You are wise to listen to Rhaegos. Yes, we come to bring tidings of the future. What may be is due to what once was." She waved a hand, and one of the servants scurried away. "Many different stories will vie for that which is to come. But it is up to you—and the High King—which ones will come true."

The servant returned, and I watched as he fiddled with a bowl and pitcher. Another servant brought a small table before me as I looked at Mattie and Llamryl.

"If it brings you comfort, the Thegn Andrattür and her family may stay." The middle Vollr spoke again. "Their presence won't affect the ceremony."

"What kind of ceremony is this?" I stared at the bowl of clear water in front of me. Mattie slipped away from where she sat as the three women created a circle around me, one set of clasped hands settling on my spine.

"A ceremony to see a potential future. The dragons know of yours and the High King's concerns, both personal and that of Lohikärra. They wish to aid you in bringing forth the best future for all."

I nodded, not knowing what to say. Instead, the eldest Vollr cleared her throat. "Place your hands in the bowl of water, that you may connect with the flowing tide of fate. It is also easiest to see visions of the future when your eyes are closed."

My cheeks warmed up with embarrassment as I placed my hands in the bowl. The chill water was a welcome relief from the day's heat. As I closed my eyes, the Vollr began chanting, and the child shifted within me.

I gasped as an image crossed my mind and I watched it like it was a movie. To my left, both Haldrek and Henry stood ready to fight. Their rage emanated throughout the vision. To my right, Rorik stood elevated, draped in robes and covered with black feathers and scales. He held a staff that glowed with a green gem at the top. A great power flowed outward from him, and fear overwhelmed me. Tears dripped down my face as helplessness washed over my entire body. Once I thought I couldn't stand another moment, the vision changed.

Now I sat in a familiar place: The Realm of Ghosts. Rhaegos stood near and a Lohikärran man held his hand out to help me stand. As soon as I did, a ghostly scene in my periphery caught my attention. Haldrek and Henry were bent over something and their grief made its way from wherever they were to where I stood in the Realm of Ghosts.

You have a decision to make, little one.

I had no idea if the Rhaegos I heard was from the vision or from my own connection with her. Before I could ask, that vision washed away and I found myself back in the throne room. Haldrek and I sat on our thrones and there were dozens of children, ranging from newborn babes to men and women in their twenties.

Your progeny.

That was Rhaegos's voice in the present. A sense of warmth and comfort wrapped around me.

Then the vision disappeared and the Vollr's chanting stopped.

I opened my eyes to see the Vollr, as well as Mattie and Llamryl, watching me. The only person who didn't seem concerned was the eldest of the Vollr.

"You have seen the visions of the most probable future. Rorik has seen these as well, though through a more vile source. He seeks to keep any of these visions from coming to pass."

I thought back to the visions. The only one that seemed pleasant in any capacity was the last one, with Haldrek's and my descendants around us. The other two were grim and full of sorrow.

"If the visions I saw don't come to pass, will worse things happen?"

The middle Vollr nodded her head. "You and the High King are at a crossroads, not only for your personal fates, but for that of Lohikärra and all of Sethys."

The servants took away the table and I shifted as my stomach tightened once more, harder than it had before.

I took a deep breath and, once it passed, I smiled as best I could. "Thank you for letting me know."

The three women nodded, and I rocked forward to stand. As soon as I stood, water flowed down my legs and a heavy weight dropped into my hips.

Before I could say anything, the youngest of the Vollr nodded.

"And so the future of Lohikärra arrives."

Chapter 3

L abor sucked.

As soon as my water broke in front of the Vollr, they made their departure and Mattie sent Llamryl to get Haldrek and the midwives. Within a few moments, the antechamber was filled with people. Some cleaned, some brought food, and others brought runic ribbons to dress my belly with as I fought the overwhelming sense of panic threatening me.

Once Haldrek arrived, he was immediately by my side. I could still sense his anxiety. The tension and worry lines in his face were visible as the midwives checked me and recommended I begin what they called the 'laboring walk'. As I paced, he paced as well. Every time I stopped and gritted through a contraction, he stopped as well, letting me grip his hand tightly and trying not to look worried. He fussed over me with food, insisting I eat after Mattie told both of us labor would last a while and I would need energy for pushing later.

At a certain point, as the contractions became regular and irritation replaced my anxiety, I told him to check on the hersirs and counsellors or *something*, that I would have someone grab him once the baby was almost born. He seemed disappointed in my words, but didn't argue.

I felt bad as he left the antechamber, but Mattie and the midwives both told me this was a normal part of laboring. Many women would push their husbands out of the family bed or home for a time while birthing their children. The midwives assured me there were certain parts of childbirth which only women could partake in. I didn't believe them fully, but as I sat down on the 'birthing throne' that they had brought up, I tried to brush my worries from my mind.

Now, hours later, I was even more miserable. My body ached, and I wished for comfort in some form. Nighttime had already fallen outside, and the midwives had confirmed the baby was descending with every push. They had sent a servant to retrieve Haldrek, and I knew he would be here soon. Despite focusing on one of the carved dragon heads on the antechamber ceiling and trying to breathe through the contractions, the pain and pressure only got worse and more exhausting. It felt like the worst case of constipation I'd ever had. I leaned against the back of the birthing throne and pushed once more as my belly tightened. As soon as it relaxed, I took a deep breath and steadied myself as the midwife applied whatever balm or salve was supposed to be helping me.

The contractions seemed to rise as soon as they fell, despite pushing when the midwives told me to and resting in between. I began to wonder when the baby would come and if we'd both survive this.

How many stories had I heard of women in labor for days only for them and their child to die? What if the visions I'd seen this morning were already gone? Never to happen? What if the person I saw on the throne wasn't me, but someone else with Haldrek and I had seen their kids who would keep Lohikärra safe? A particularly difficult contraction pushed my insides apart, and I screamed, letting out my frustrations.

You saw your children in that vision, Ina. The Vollr could not have shown you it if there was no chance of it happening.

Rhaegos's presence wrapped itself around me and my fatigue lessened. I closed my eyes as I pushed through another contraction. In my mind, I could see her wrapped around me as I labored, leaning against the softer scales of her belly. While her dragon form protected me, I noticed her watching something in the distance, and the hairs on the ridge of her back looked as if they were lifted or larger than normal. She was comforting me and aiding me, but she was also watching for something.

"The babe is almost here, my queen! A few more pushes and the head should be out!" One midwife spoke, but she sounded far away. In fact, the pain and pressure of the contractions lessened while I was in this realm with Rhaegos. Every time I felt the urge to push, I could with little exhaustion. The labor still wasn't pleasant, but it wasn't as arduous as before, and I could sense the baby progressing down through me. I didn't feel stuck anymore.

I give you my strength, as all dragons do their haldragas. Both you and this child will survive this birth. All will be well if I have anything to say about it.

Someone placed their hand on my shoulder and I opened my eyes as a particular intense contraction tore through my body. I gasped and cried out as the sensation of something pushing out of me sent pain up my spine and down my legs. I couldn't see beyond my belly, but something firm and wet rubbed against one of my thighs.

"The head is out!" The midwife in front of me looked up in triumph. "You are almost there, my queen! Just a few more pushes!"

I smiled as someone led my hand down between my legs and I felt the child's head. Wet hair brushed against my fingers and I made a laughing gasp as another contraction pushed the baby further. Glancing up at Mattie, I said, "Is Haldrek near? He'll want—" I gritted through another contraction and Mattie nodded, disappearing from my view.

Close your eyes and return to my side, little one. Your babe is safe and will soon be delivered. You will need more of my energy now.

I closed my eyes again, letting the pain and contractions fade into something less exhausting. Instead, I leaned against Rhaegos and let her energy sustain me as the rest of the baby pushed out between my legs. Soon a squalling cry broke through, loud and clear, and I laughed in relief.

Looking up at Rhaegos, I noticed she was still on alert. "Rhaegos—" Before I could say anything more, a searing pain in my belly made me double over, both in Rhaegos's realm and the real world.

"Ina!" Rhaegos's voice and Haldrek's voice blended together as I opened my eyes to see blood pouring onto the floor. I toppled forward. Just as I hit the cold stones, a dark presence washed everything out. My throat squeezed shut as the presence began to choke me.

"You think you can outwit me? You think you can just use the dragons' magic to hide from me?" Rorik's voice echoed in my ears. The presence wrapped itself around me, squeezing me until I gasped, then rolling me over onto my back.

I screamed as I saw Rorik standing over me, clothed in the feathered and scaled robes from my vision. Black etchings like claw marks swiped out from his eyes and a large inked dragon body covered the middle of his forehead to his chin, making his eyes a bright, almost toxic-looking green. He held the staff and the gem on it glowed brightly, the same color as his eyes. A sense of doom and powerlessness sunk into my skin and bones. Images of my loved ones torn asunder forced themselves into my thoughts, my child screaming in terror echoed in my mind. Regret flooded me, the sense that I'd done something incredibly stupid and would now be punished for it. Weakly, I reached out for Rhaegos, but she was nowhere to be found.

Instead, Rorik floated down to where I lay, getting mere inches from my face. A wickedly smug grin crossed his face and the gem's light grew as he spoke, blinding me.

"Ryluth demands a sacrifice. I will destroy you and all you love to please him. Not even the other dragons can save you and your child from me now. I am Ryluth's Heir."

Pain exploded out from my gut, overwhelming me as I passed out.

"Ina! Hold on! Focus on my voice!" Mattie's words entered my mind and I could sense people rushing around me, but I had no control of my body. I couldn't open my eyes, nor could I move my hands or feet. Strangest of all, I didn't even feel any panic or fear. I could only feel my chest go up and down as I breathed, feeling myself fade away from my body. Some kind of magic entered and attempted to keep me awake, but there wasn't enough power in it. Instead, another force pulled me away and I fell.

When I hit the ground, I was more aware of my surroundings. No longer numb to the world or realm around me, though everything was dark, I could sense someone was watching me.

I slowly brought my hand to my face and felt my way down from my neck to my chest, my under tunic still damp with sweat, and then to my belly and legs. There I stopped. My belly was soft and sore, no longer round with child, and my legs were sticky with some kind of residue.

That's when the panic kicked in.

"Rhaegos?" I choked out, hoping she was somewhere near, able to hear me.

I'm here, little one. Rorik has played a foul trick on you, finding a break in the barrier that was mine and my kin's magic. Your son is safe, but Rorik plans the demise of your soul as we speak. You must battle your way out of this place, at least until I can reach you.

I nodded, Rhaegos's words echoing in my mind. My son. There was a small bloom of hope in my chest. I needed to fight Rorik not only for myself, but for my son.

A weight fell on me in that moment, and I collapsed to the ground with a grunt. As I stood back up, I felt armor on me, as well as a blade at my side. Touching it, I realized it was Freya's Menace.

"If the dragons think a few pieces of armor and a sword will protect you, they are stupider than I thought."

I ducked to the ground as a ball of magic flowed over me. It left toxic green shadows in its wake and I turned around to see Rorik, still floating. His legs didn't move as he made his way toward me. Without thinking, I pulled out my blade and rolled to my feet. My body was still weak and unstable from childbirth, but I did what I could as I dodged another greenish orb, slicing at it with my blade. A whistling sound and light exploded from the orb, making it easier to see.

"Is that all you have?" The words flew out of my mouth before I could think, and a deep scowl covered Rorik's face.

"Do not mock me, half-breed!" He cast another spell, this time with the staff, and I moved just in time to avoid being hit. The heat from the spell and a smell like rotting corpses made me gag. Out of the corner of my eye, and behind Rorik, flashes of green light illuminated the shadows of two dragons fighting. My gut told me one of them was Rhaegos.

"What are you looking at?" Rorik's shout brought my attention back as he swung his staff. I bent backwards to dodge, only to feel my stomach muscles spasm and my legs give out. He stabbed down at my exposed flesh and I rolled away, frustrated at my weakness. I knew I'd have to recover from being pregnant, but I wasn't expecting to fight this soon after giving birth.

Knowing I'd have to change my tactics, I swung my blade as he stepped toward me. It bit into his leg and cut through the tendons behind his kneecap, then exited upward. He howled as he tumbled, crashing to whatever surface we were fighting on. The space grew lighter, lit up by greenish light, and I watched as his leg grew back, causing the old leg to flop uselessly from the point where I'd cut it. Rorik scowled and pulled off the offending appendage as if it were little more than some ripped fabric.

"What the hell?" I whispered, staring at him in disbelief. I wanted to gag again as the leg flopped away. Was that because we were in some alternate realm, or was he able to toss away body parts like some zombie or freakish lizard?

Or undead lizard? Undead dragon? I focused on Rorik as I tightened my grip on my sword.

"What were you expecting? A necromancer who can't regrow his own limbs? Especially in a realm he created?" He gestured and the space grew lighter once more. What I saw made my stomach sick. It was a crude recreation of the throne room at Drattüjert. Instead of being inside a palace, we were inside a cave-like expanse with shadowy bodies hanging from the ceiling and bloodied dragon scales scattered across the floor. Despite my better judgement, I imagined those dragon scales had been used for darker purposes.

Rorik stumbled toward me proudly, a smirk plastered across his face. With every step, his gait became more normal. "I have done something no other necromancer in the history of Lohikärra has done. I have brought Ryluth back from the dead. The texts said it was impossible. My dragon, before I cast her away, said it was impossible. But I did it, and I have reaped the benefits. Ryluth has made me powerful beyond measure." Rorik began swinging his staff around, making figure eights in the air. "I am the Heir of Ryluth, a title last held by Ryluth's own seed. Only the most powerful can wield the power I have. Killing and raising people, dragons, worlds." His expression darkened. "There is only one thing stopping me from having all of Ryluth's power..."

I tipped my sword into the ground and tested my weight on my legs. They felt better, and I stood up, facing Rorik. If I could keep him talking, I might be able to buy some more time, at least enough to put him on the defensive.

"What's keeping you from having all of Ryluth's power? Me?"

Rorik laughed and lunged at me. I twisted away from his spear staff and slammed the blade of Freya's Menace down on his wrists. Despite my weakened nature, the blade cut through his wrists cleanly, sending them and the staff skittering across the floor.

Almost as soon as I did, he screamed, his hands growing back as mangled stumps. He slammed them into my face, knocking me to the ground and sending Freya's Menace spinning away.

Punches rained down as I tried to block him with my arms. My dragon ring, which should have been around my neck, weighed heavily against my thumb. Something hit the ground near us, making everything shudder, and I used the distraction to shove my hands into Rorik's eyes. As he screamed, he pulled back, holding the stumps to his face.

I scrambled away, my back knocking into a firm, scaly surface. Claws locked around me as something pulled me into the air.

Hold on, little one. I will free you from this realm yet.

A flash of bright light blinded me as Rorik's howls faded and I passed out, exhausted, in Rhaegos's arms.

Chapter 4

I woke up to Haldrek and Mattie's angry voices in the antechamber. Keeping my eyes closed for a little while longer, I listened to them over the soft hum of whoever was touching a damp washcloth to my head.

"... you know what I fear, Mattie. It's not that unreasonable. The dragons promised—"

"You're afraid that you're going to end up like our father. That if something happens to Ina, you'll have the same urge to run off and leave Lohikärra. Here's the thing. You aren't our father, and both Teminth and Sivath have said Ina will be fine. She's still alive, and no one is forcing you to abandon your son."

Flashbacks to Svangendom popped into my mind, and I laughed tiredly. Some things never changed.

"My queen?"

I opened my eyes to see the servant staring at me in surprise. "I'm alive." My voice sounded terrible. Hoarse and raspy. "Go get Haldrek and Mattie."

The woman stumbled over herself as she ran. Opening the door, she said, "The queen is awake!"

Before she could move, Haldrek pushed past her and was at my side. His eyes were red and face blotchy as he wrapped his arms around me, pulling me into his embrace. My abdomen muscles spasmed, and I groaned, feeling soreness and bruises from my ribcage all the way down to my legs. I wondered how much was from childbirth and how much was from my fight with Rorik.

"I'm so glad you're awake. It was terrifying seeing you like..." Haldrek shuddered, then pulled away to give me some air. He looked down at my dragon ring and whispered, "I thought that was supposed to keep you safe?"

"It did. Rorik... Rhaegos told me Rorik found a way through the dragon's magic right as I was giving birth. Something about a barrier going down. But he... I'm safe. For now."

Haldrek squeezed me once more, and it felt good to be in his embrace. "Did he pull you into the Realm of Ghosts again?"

"No. I could have handled myself in the Realm of Ghosts. Or at least I think I could have." I thought back to the one vision of Rhaegos and the Lohikärran man trying to help me there. That hadn't happened yet, but now I wondered what would trigger that if Rorik wasn't tormenting people there anymore. "Rorik pulled me into another realm. One I think he created." I shuddered this time. "It was terrifying—some dark, distorted version of the palace, but within a cavern of some kind."

"Was this place in Lohikärra? Or somewhere else?" Mattie's voice was soft, and I looked up to see her at the foot of the bed. She crossed her left arm over her chest, gripping her right arm with it. She seemed to be squeezing herself to stay composed.

"A different place. Rhaegos was fighting another dragon in the background. Rorik said he'd brought Ryluth back to life. Called himself the Heir of Ryluth as he tried to kill me."

Mattie grimaced. "That's why Sivath has been restless. Probably why he's been pestering me about that prophecy, too." She sighed. "What happened to Rhaegos?"

"She fought off the other dragon, and then rescued me. That's how I escaped whatever realm Rorik created. It was terrifying being there." Tears flooded my eyes suddenly, and I burrowed my head into Haldrek's chest.

"You are safe now. I... I already spoke to Paavo and Senja about our son."

I sat back up. "He's fine, isn't he?" It was then I realized I didn't hear the sound of a baby anywhere. "He's okay, right?"

Haldrek nodded and gestured to a little alcove a few steps from our bed. I didn't know what previous kings and queens had used it for in the past, but we had made it into a sleeping space for the wet nurse who had been chosen to help me a few weeks prior. I guessed she was tending to him as we spoke. "He's sleeping right now, and one of the nursemaids is with him." A smile crossed Haldrek's face. "He was big and loud, too. Mattie had him wrapped up against me while they took care of you. Said it was something the Hethurin taught her."

Mattie shrugged. "Thandes and Meri both swore up and down that swaddling babies on your chest after they're born helps them." She glanced up at Haldrek. "Kept him calm too. It's hard to panic when you have a baby on your chest."

Haldrek nodded. "It was strange, but good. He seemed to snuggle right up on top of my heart. Literally."

I smiled, but part of my heart twisted inside. What if my only chance at bonding with the baby had passed? I tried to move past where Haldrek sat on the bed, my muscles still throbbing. "I want to go see him. Make sure..." Tears bubbled up once more as both Haldrek and Mattie moved to stop me.

"You need to rest, Ina. Your body has been through a lot." Mattie stopped next to my feet. "I was exhausted after Geirny was born and I didn't have to deal with half the stuff you just did."

"But... what if... what if I don't bond with him?" I tried to wiggle some more, but exhaustion washed over me as Haldrek pulled me back to where I'd started.

"You'll be able to bond with him." Mattie smiled. "You've been bonding with him for the last nine months. A day or so isn't going to hurt you." She paused, glancing at Haldrek for a moment. "You're about as likely to be like your mother as Haldrek is to be like our father. Which is to say you're going to be fine."

I nodded, tears still flowing down my cheeks. For some strange reason, loneliness washed over me along with the exhaustion. I leaned my head against Haldrek's chest.

"Do you want me to rest with you right now? You can curl up next to me, if that helps you feel better."

I nodded, rubbing my face into his undertunic.

"Then I will stay with you until you feel better." He kissed the top of my head, then stood up.

Mattie had already disappeared, and I could hear her in the antechamber talking to someone as Haldrek curled up on my left side. He pulled me close, wrapping his arm around my back. Despite the fact that it was warm enough to be midday, it felt lovely being curled up next to him. My body relaxed and I fell asleep to the rhythm of his breathing.

A few hours later, I woke up to the sound of a baby crying. At first I was confused, wondering where I was and what was going on. As soon as I opened my eyes and saw Haldrek laying next to me, everything hit. I was in the palace and the baby...

I sat up and groaned as my abdomen muscles complained fiercely. A grunt popped out of my mouth as I curled back over on my side. I knew I'd be hurting after the baby was born, but my desire to get up and hold my son made me frustrated with how my body was acting.

"Haldrek..."

"Hmm?" He looked at me sleepily and I realized he'd dozed off, too. As the baby fussing continued, I rolled over, attempting to get off the bed, impatient to see my son no matter what condition I was in. I could deal with pain and soreness. Haldrek grabbed my wrist gently, stopping me.

"You need to rest. One of the nursemaids will bring him into you."

He sat up in bed and gestured to someone by the alcove. Once they slipped inside, he helped me settle back into a sitting position.

The fussing grew louder. By the time I was comfortable, the nursemaid was by my side, a little bundle wriggling and crying in her arms.

"Let me see him." I reached out as Haldrek pulled my undertunic's collar loose and over my shoulder.

"This is what Mattie was saying the Hethurin do to bond with their children." He murmured, ignoring my grumbles as he helped me pull the tunic under my armpit. As soon as my left shoulder and arm were free of the tunic, leaving me half-naked, the nursemaid handed me the baby, unswaddled. I pulled him to my chest and chin. The warmth and softness of his skin melted away any remaining irritation. He stopped fussing for a moment, but continued wriggling around on my chest, as if he was trying to get comfy. I imagined he had done the same before he was born, and I couldn't help but grin.

"He might be hungry," the nursemaid whispered. "If you'd like, I can fetch the wet nurse to feed him and bring him back once he's full."

I shook my head. "I can feed him. Right? This is the first time I'm seeing him and I want every moment I can get with him."

The woman glanced at Haldrek, then nodded. "Some abthanry women aren't very fond of nursing their children, but if you wish, I can show you."

I nodded and Haldrek sat back as the woman helped settle the baby on my chest and got him attached to me. As soon as he started to nurse, I laughed through my sudden happy tears. My heart and lungs squeezed tight, as if they were about to burst. "I can't imagine anyone not wanting this with their child." Even as memories of what my mother had said about my birth returned to my mind, I tried to focus on the baby now on me. My baby. My son. The little one I'd fought to come back to. Even though Haldrek had said he'd been big, he felt so tiny in my arms as I brushed my thumb over his fingers and hand.

"How are you feeling now?" Haldrek gently scooted over to my side of the bed and watched as our son shoved his face into my breast repeatedly.

"Better. I'm glad he's safe. And I'm glad I feel this connection to him, like I never want to let him go. I would fight Rorik and Ryluth and anyone else who tried to hurt him." My vision blurred as more tears filled my eyes. Stroking the soft hair on his head, I laughed. "I can't imagine not doing everything in my power to keep him safe, you know?"

Haldrek nodded and brushed a couple of tears from his eye. "I was terrified that I might lose both of you. He came out crying, but as soon as you fell forward, he went quiet. That's when Mattie ordered one of the nursemaids to do the Hethurin thing, putting him on my chest. I could feel him breathing, and that made things less scary. I mean, I was still afraid I'd lose you, but..."

"You were glad he was safe."

Haldrek nodded. "Losing either of you would have broken me. But both of you?" He shuddered. "I look forward to cutting Rorik down and knowing once and for all he's dead."

Memories of being sucked into Rorik's realm and the attack afterwards came back vividly, and I tried to push them away. "Does our son have a name yet? I know there were many we were thinking of."

Haldrek laughed. "I know what name I'd like to give him, but it didn't feel right to name him without you. Especially after everything you went through."

"Which name were you wanting?" I knew of a few, family names mostly. Part of me hoped he didn't still want Bjornulf. That name came with a lot of weight and I didn't want that kind of pressure on him. I already saw how people perceived Thegn Bragidrattür's nephew.

"I was thinking Eero. It's a powerful name, and there have been a few aethlings and thegns who bore that name as well."

I frowned. "Arrow, though? Like the weapon? How is it spelled? Like bow and arrow? I don't want him being teased for his name."

Haldrek shook his head. "E-E-R-O. It means strong ruler." He stroked our son's cheek. "After everything Lohikärra has been through, it will need a powerful ruler. It will need peace for many generations."

"Are you sure that won't be a heavy burden for him? I... I don't want him to feel like... I dunno."

"Is there a name you'd prefer?" He continued to stroke our son's face, brushing the fine strands of dark hair around.

"Part of me would still like Ingmar, seeing as it is a family name. And more common."

Haldrek laughed. "Three generations of Ingmars from Svartån? That's a weighty name in its own right. Especially with everything you and your father have done for Lohikärra."

I sighed, frustrated with the fact that Haldrek had a very valid point. Our son popped his head away from my breast and stared at me wide-eyed. I laughed a little and shifted him to lie vertically. Haldrek gently covered him with the edge of my tunic, so only his head was visible.

"Though... Eero Ingmar Rodreksson has a nice ring to it. If he feels one name is too heavy, he can always go by the other one." Haldrek kissed me on the temple, and a light buzzing of pleasure went through my body.

"Eero Ingmar Rodreksson... That does have a nice ring to it. I supposed that could work." Cocking my head to the side to watch Eero as his eyes fluttered closed, I tried to imagine what he would look like as he got older, and wondered which one of the children from my vision he was.

"Then are we settled on it?" Haldrek stood up. "I only ask because I know people will want to know for the naming ceremony and beyond. As well as dragons." He angled himself on the bed to watch Eero as he slept. "Paavo and Senja have already asked. They spoke of a gift they wish to bestow on him, but it requires his name to complete."

I laughed softly, wondering what kind of personalized gifts dragons gave babies.

"I think we are." I stared at our son for a moment longer, mesmerized by how his little body curled up on mine. "Welcome to the world, little Eero."

Chapter 5

As eager as I was to recover and get back on my feet, I had to admit I still needed rest. A couple of days after Eero's birth, I finally got out of bed. Haldrek and Mattie helped me get into a tub full of gloriously warm water to cleanse myself. It did wonders for my aches and pains, but as I sat there with a servant to ensure I didn't injure myself further, I saw bruises and welts on my arms and legs my tunic had hidden. Injuries that couldn't have come from birthing Eero.

Your physical body may not have been in Rorik's realm, but his magic stuck to you in the places where you got injured, bringing those injuries with you.

I shuddered at Rhaegos's comment and slipped my leg back under the water, not wanting to remind myself.

He's still coming after us, Rhaegos. And what can Haldrek and I do to keep Eero safe? Keep ourselves safe? Especially if he has brought Ryluth back from the dead. Unless he's bluffing.

There was a huff of annoyance from Rhaegos, but I wasn't sure if it was fully directed at me.

Do you think Rorik is the kind of human to bluff? He has brought Ryluth back from the dead. While you were fighting Rorik, I was battling my uncle. Ryluth is still weak, which is why Rorik has been causing mayhem in the lands surrounding him. And why he came after you.

My skin grew cold at the thought and I felt vulnerable at that moment. I slipped the rest of my body under the water to hide, and to comfort myself, but the water had cooled and did little to help.

Raising my hand, I gestured for the servant to help me get out. After a few minutes, I was dressed and resting comfortably in bed once more. Though my body was still tired, my mind was too awake to let me rest. Rhaegos's presence nudged my mind and the image of me being in a soft nest like bed came to mind. Much like when I'd been laboring, Rhaegos's dragon form wrapped around me, and my mind seemed to slow down.

I did not mean to frighten you, little one. Despite Rorik's growing power, any of the dragons are still more powerful than him.

A thought popped into my head. Rorik had said something about casting out his dragon. If he was no longer a haldraga, wouldn't it be a simple thing for a dragon to just swoop down on him and gobble him up? That would make everyone's lives so much easier. I imagined a dragon dive bombing Rorik as he went to the bathroom outside. In a split second, he was gone, a tasty snack for one of the dragons.

Rhaegos laughed in my mind. Apparently, the thought amused her as much as it did me.

I wish it was that easy. Unfortunately, when he ripped his dragon from him, it was to replace her with Ryluth, so Rorik is bonded with him instead. Even in Ryluth's weakened state, he's still formidable. Not as formidable as a living dragon, but he was strong enough in life to require my father's sacrifice. Rhaegos was quiet for a moment. *You do remember the story of how Bjornulf became a haldraga, right?*

I groaned sleepily, trying to remember. *The video games made it sound like Tenelth was on the edge of dying and gave his spirit to Bjornulf to keep it from being eliminated.*

Rhaegos huffed. *There is much more to it than that. Svante would have known better than to change the story that drastically.*

I could be remembering it wrong. It's been a long time since I played that storyline. My eyelids grew heavy, both in Rhaegos's realm and in my physical body.

Sleep for now, little one. I shall have Haldrek tell you the true story of how my kin, Bjornulf, and Freya destroyed Ryluth. It shall make Rorik's actions clear.

When I woke up, Haldrek was next to me. His breathing was regular enough that I knew he was dozing, but he hadn't begun snoring yet. I opened my eyes to see Eero curled up on his chest, just beginning to rouse. I couldn't help but laugh as Eero grabbed a fist full of Haldrek's tunic and tugged, eliciting a grunt from him.

"I think he may be getting hungry again." Haldrek murmured, opening one eye. "I'll go grab the wet nurse."

Shaking my head, I sat up, trying not to make my body ache any more than it already was. "I can feed him. I enjoy doing that." Over the last few days, a pattern had emerged—Eero fed from me when I was awake and fed from the wet nurse at night. As much as I enjoyed my rest, I took the times I did get to nurse Eero with pleasure. They were quiet moments, ones where I knew he was safe and secure. I felt closer to him during and after those feedings.

Haldrek helped me with my undertunic and settled Eero on my chest. "I think it is safe to say you have bonded with him. You are most certainly not your mother."

I nodded. "I hope so. Still, I don't know if it's me, though, or just this period after him being born. You know? Mattie said my hormones would be all over the place and they have been. You've seen how much I've cried, but what if that is causing this, too? What if, once my hormones settle, I won't feel such an attachment to him?"

Haldrek raised an eyebrow. "I don't know what these hormones are that you and Mattie speak of, but I think I understand what you mean. If you are concerned about whether you'll still be protective and maternal toward Eero in the future, just think of the times you were maternal before being with child. I remember a certain time in Svartån when you risked your own life to keep a child safe."

I frowned in confusion.

"Aldinnvollr? When the Shrine of Rhaegos exploded?"

The memory came back in an instant. The little girl had nearly been swallowed up by the avalanche, and I had grabbed her with mere seconds to run. Haldrek had been pissed, but the mother's gratitude and the girl's safety had been worth it.

"Remember Solvange? Her orphanage? Or when you took that child who was in peril of dying? Or when you created the High Queen's Home and fought to keep those people safe?"

"That was my duty as a thegn and queen," I mumbled, focusing on Eero as he ate vigorously.

"Solvange, perhaps. But most would not have criticized you if you ignored her pleas, given that her orphanage had been your father's project. The High Queen's Home, however..."

I looked over at him, and he wore an impish grin.

"You are more maternal than you give yourself credit for, Ina. I have no doubt about that." He stroked a finger across Eero's sole, making the baby kick and lose his focus on his meal. I laughed at the small interaction, allowing myself to enjoy the moment.

"I will say these are some of my favorite moments. Hormones or not."

"Agreed." Haldrek sighed. "Which is why I'm not thrilled to be going to Bragidrattür so soon."

My heart sank. I'd forgotten about that in the chaos of Eero's birth. As much as I wanted Haldrek here, he had a duty to those people as well.

"When do you plan on leaving?"

"In a few days, but not until after the naming ceremony. I am still preparing and resources are being bundled up for those who are in need of aid. I plan on sending a handful of men, and Ingrid, with supplies to the thegn hall in Etelaranikä for those who are suffering there. Then I will go with the larger group to the thegn hall in Bragidrattür. I'll find out where Rorik is attacking exactly and take the fight to him."

Rorik's power in his realm had frightened me. I was used to being dragged into other realms and having to fight there, but now I worried about Rorik doing the same thing to Haldrek.

"You won't be able to fight him like you normally do. If he's got the power of Ryluth with him…"

"I know. I've dealt with necromancers before." Haldrek hesitated. "Well, would-be necromancers. Lesser necromancers. But I'm familiar with many of their tricks. And I have Teminth with me, remember?" The gentle nudge from Haldrek made me smile.

"I know. But I know Rorik isn't just in this realm anymore. He's created his own, and if he drags you there, he'll have the upper hand."

Haldrek's expression turned somber. "Teminth has told me the same. He will protect me with all his might, but I still shouldn't do anything rash." He snorted lightly. "Sometimes Teminth thinks I am still ten years old."

I laughed, trying to keep some lightness in the conversation. My eyes started to well up again, thinking about how long Haldrek might be gone this time. He'd been able to stay in Drattüjert during my pregnancy, recovering from the injuries that the imposter had given him, but while I felt safer and more welcome here in the palace than I did last year, I still wanted Haldrek by my side.

"How long do you expect to be gone?"

"However long it takes to kill Rorik. It could be a few weeks, or it could be a few months. I want it over as quickly as possible." He pulled my head close, kissing me tenderly on the forehead. "I don't want to be away from you and Eero for too long, but this needs to be dealt with now."

"I know." An intense desire to fix the situation, to make things easier for Haldrek, came over me. I hated feeling helpless.

"I'll keep you updated on my progress through our pendants. As usual."

"I know. I'll still miss you." The vision of Haldrek and I returned to my mind as he wrapped his body next to mine and put his hand on Eero's back. The baby made a soft grunting sound and I smiled. If the Vollr had given me that vision, it was still highly likely, right?

You are correct, little one. But you can't rely on the visions alone. Especially as Rorik actively seeks to change them.

I shuddered at the thought and snuggled up closer to Haldrek. In a few short days, this moment would be just a memory, and I was going to treasure every moment I could.

That night, I found myself in a lightless place. Though I wasn't cold, the place felt chill and ominous, a heavy pressure weighing everything down. I wasn't in the palace anymore, that was for sure. Despite the surrounding darkness, I felt like I was in a barrow, though not even Ottkatla's Barrow had felt this bleak when I was in it. Far away, the sound of chanting and drums caught my attention and made every muscle in my body freeze.

Then a voice, much closer, began chanting in what sounded like Lohikärran, but it was nothing I could understand. As soon as it stopped, a higher pitched, yet muffled, voice began to scream. I jumped to my knees, trying to think of the light spells Mattie had taught me when we first got to Lohikärra.

As soon as I cast the spell in my mind, an orb of light burst from my hands, just in time to see Rorik raise a blade over a person bound and gagged on a bloodstained stone altar.

"Stop!" I cast the light at him, knowing it wouldn't do anything, then a charge of lightning. Both hit him as he plunged his blade into the person's chest, their screams echoing throughout the chamber.

Rorik fell to the ground as I began running and everything went dark again. I cast the light once more, along with a fireball, but it only served to illuminate the now-dead woman on the altar, fresh blood staining her dress. She looked familiar, but before I could take a closer look, the light went out. Something moved toward me in the shadows.

"How dare you interrupt the sacrifice!" Rorik lunged and I threw the fireball at him. He dodged away, then his cold, clammy hands locked around my neck.

I pulled more fire into my hands and grabbed his face. He howled, squeezing tighter.

"You really think you can destroy me here?"

I pushed my thumbs into his eye sockets and he howled once more, this time releasing me. He staggered back as I gasped for air and tried to get myself into a defensive position.

"Who is that?" The words caught in my throat as my heart threatened to beat out of my chest. No matter how much I tried to breathe, my throat couldn't expand enough. Panic and rage welled up inside of me.

"No one of importance to you. Ryluth demanded her essence, and who am I to deny him?" Despite garish burns and chunks of skin hanging from his face, Rorik seemed to be in little pain. He brushed a hand across, removing the errant skin and revealing a new face, completely healed.

"Ryluth demands more and more, and I will give it to him until all of Lohikärra bows before me in fear."

Forcing back my revulsion, I patted my hips for a weapon, but found none.

"Your pathetic dragon can't help you here. Ryluth has blessed this realm for my use." He reached out his hand and the front of my tunic twisted tight. The next thing I knew, I was flying toward him with barely any time to cast a spell.

I crashed into a rock outcropping face first, then spun around, Rorik pulling me back toward him. He opened his mouth to speak and the reeking stench of rotted flesh hit me in the face.

"The only thing stopping me from gaining all Ryluth's power is the Heart of Lohikärra. Something you are somehow tied to. I will have it if it's the last thing I do."

He threw me onto the altar, now devoid of a body. My hands and feet were bound by something invisible as I twisted around, trying to escape. I tried to speak, but my mouth refused to move.

"You really think Rhaegos or Haldrek can save you now?" A new blade, sharp and clean, appeared in his hand along with a wicked smile.

As he raised the blade above me, I shouted *Too-Salpama* as loudly as I could in my mind and yanking my arms up. A bolt of lightning missed the blade, hitting the rocks above us. Rorik jumped out of the way, dropping the blade as rocks tumbled on me, turning my vision black, and I heard a child's scream.

I jerked awake, my face buried deep in my pillow and my arms tucked under me. Eero's cries woke me further as I struggle to right myself. There was a panic in his voice I'd never heard before. My feet were still caught in something as I jumped out of bed and tumbled to the floor with a painful gasp. As soon as I got loose of whatever held me, I pulled myself up on one of the bedposts.

"Ina?"

Ignoring Haldrek and the few servants who had rushed in from the antechamber, I ran into the small alcove off our room.

Inside, the wet nurse was trying to soothe Eero. His cries were getting more and more frustrated. She stood up, and I stumbled to take the chair she had been sitting in.

"He woke up screaming like this just now and—"

"Give him to me!" I tried not to sound too sharp, but my heart was still racing from the nightmare. I was desperate to hold Eero.

As soon as he was in my arms, both of us calmed down. His cries became more muted as he stared at me, unblinking, until they turned into soft breathing noises.

There was a groan from the archway and I looked up to see Haldrek disheveled and sleepy.

"What happened, Ina? I've never seen you rush out of the bed like that before."

Tears welled up in my eyes, my chest wet and aching as Eero grunted against it, obviously hungry.

"I had another nightmare…" Pulling one of my breasts out, I let Eero latch and relaxed. The wet nurse walked over to the archway and lit a lantern, allowing light to spread through the small alcove. It was warmer and more comforting than the light of my nightmare.

Had it been just a nightmare? Or something more?

"Tell me what happened." Haldrek gestured for the wet nurse to leave the room and she slipped out behind him.

"Rorik pulled me back into his realm. Maybe? I don't know whether it was on purpose. It was terrifying and confusing." The tears which had been threatening to fall earlier tumbled down my cheeks, and I brushed them away. "He was sacrificing a woman. On an altar. She was screaming, and I tried to save her, but I couldn't. I hurt Rorik with a lightning spell and he attacked me. Said something about the Heart of Lohikärra. He almost killed me, too. But I brought some rocks down on top of us and that pulled me out."

My stomach spasmed and I groaned. I was exhausted, but I was afraid to go back to bed.

Haldrek pulled a stool next to mine and wrapped his arm around me.

"I wish I could do something to protect you." He touched the dragon ring still hanging on a chain around my neck. "Where was Rhaegos? Did she try to help you at all?"

I shook my head. "Her presence was nowhere to be found. Rorik said something about Ryluth blessing his realm and keeping the other dragons out of it."

Haldrek shuddered and pulled me close. "All the more reason to bring the fight to him. I'm glad you were able to protect yourself tonight."

I am glad as well. Rorik's sacrifices bring Ryluth more power, I'm afraid. This barrier is new, but my kin and I fight against it as we speak.

Rhaegos's words did little to comfort me. I looked down and watched as Eero sucked hungrily with his eyes closed.

"At least he's safe." I whispered. "I woke up to him screaming, and that's what sent me running. He… I was afraid Rorik had hurt him as well." More tears welled up in my eyes. I wished there was something to protect Eero like the jewelry I had.

"I will speak with Paavo and Senja in the morning. The gift for Eero should be done by now. They said it would keep him safe with their magic, but I don't know exactly what they are giving him."

I nodded, letting my attention wander around the room as I grew sleepy again. By the door, a trail of blood drops made their way to me, and I realized the layers of linen rags that had been used to soak up my birthing blood must have gotten dislodged when I ran out of the bedroom, leaving a trail of blood behind me. Normally gross but, given my dream, it now felt like an ominous fortune.

Chapter 6

The next morning came too early for me. I had reluctantly given Eero back to the wet nurse when I began dozing off on the stool. Haldrek had helped me back to bed, and I'd slipped into a heavy, dreamless sleep for the rest of the night.

As soon as Haldrek left the bed, I was awake. Sore and cursing my actions from the night before, but I was awake.

"Go back to sleep, Ina. You need your rest and I would never leave without a proper farewell." His voice was soft outside the drapes of our bed. "The naming ceremony is today. I won't be leaving until after that. My plan is to leave tomorrow."

Given how we had performed our farewells in the past, I didn't know if he could give me a proper farewell with the state my body was in. I wanted to savor as much time as I could with him.

"I have no idea how long it'll be before I see you again. You think I'm just going to fall back asleep?" I rolled my body into a sitting position, taking care not to bruise it further. My chest felt heavy, and I wondered if Eero would be awake soon.

As if on cue, a hungry cry broke the early morning silence and the sound of footsteps told me Haldrek had slipped away to get Eero.

A few moments later, Haldrek pulled one of the curtains back and popped his head in, along with the arm holding Eero. Without a second thought, I took our baby from him and smiled as Eero began nursing hungrily.

Haldrek slipped back into the bed, closing the curtain behind him and sighing. "If I didn't have to leave for Bragidrattür, I would stay by your side for as long as I could. That said, I think this skirmish will be quick and I'll be able to rid this world of Rorik and his evil."

My encounter with Rorik from the night before was still fresh in my mind. "Why do you think it'll be quick? If he's got Ryluth bonded with him..." My gut told me this wasn't going to be as simple as Haldrek seemed to think.

Haldrek shook his head. "If he's coming after you, he's on the defensive. Things aren't going the way he expected, and he's having to make himself more terrifying. He came after us as soon as we became High King and High Queen, tormenting you with nightmares and more. But when that imposter came, he drew back, thinking the imposter could deal with us. When that didn't happen, he probably tried again, but couldn't hurt you or Eero because of the dragon magic." Haldrek touched the ring around my neck.

Things still didn't add up, but Haldrek's words brought another question to my mind. "Why me, though? Why not you? He's spent all this effort coming after me, but you're the High King. I mean, if I was a bad guy, I'd want to go after you first, because you're more of a threat to me. If I, Ina of Svartån, die, you're still the High King and you can still go after him. Unless something more is going on?"

Haldrek frowned. "That's something I never thought about before. If he hurts you..." His expression darkened, and he shook his head. "I will find out more once I'm in Bragidrattür. At least I hope so. Either way, I want you and Eero to be safe, so I'm going to do what I can to take Rorik's attention off you."

I sighed, still not feeling content. As much as I loved spending time with Eero, I was also itching to get back into fighting form so I didn't feel so vulnerable. In a perfect world, Haldrek wouldn't be the only one to take down Rorik. After everything he'd put me through, I wanted to fight him myself.

"When you do find him, let me know. I want my own revenge for what he's done to us."

Haldrek raised an eyebrow as he looked up at me. "The midwives told you that you'd need to rest from fighting and training for at least six weeks after Eero's birth."

"You think you will have defeated Rorik before then?"

"That is my goal." He kissed me on the forehead. "If you are awake for the day, I suppose we should get ready. There will be many people here for the naming ceremony."

My eyes widened. "How large is this ceremony going to be?"

"Not as large as our coronation. Even so, there will be many people. An aethling is a sign of stability and people will want to see Eero once I've proclaimed him as my son and heir to the title of High King. Also, once people see the three of us together, they will know that all is well in Drattüjert."

I grimaced, trying to ignore the aches and pains of my bruises, reluctant to end this quiet, intimate time. It meant things were moving faster than I wanted and Haldrek would be gone soon. "I suppose we should get ready." Once he had finished feeding, I handed Eero off to one of the nursemaids and let Haldrek help me out of bed.

The throne room was bright and airy as we arrived. Dozens of people stood around the room, waiting and watching us. After so many days of near privacy, it felt overwhelming to be in public again, so I did my best to focus on the task at hand. Eero was swaddled tightly in my arms as I walked closely behind Haldrek. As soon as he stopped in the middle of the dais, I handed him Eero. A smile crossed my face as I watched how gently he carried our child, and an intense feeling of love and pride washed over me.

As Haldrek sat on his throne, I did the same, welcoming the ability to sit and survey the crowd. Among the many faces were a few familiar ones—Mattie, Llamryl, and their daughter stood next to Paavo and Senja, while many of the other thegns and hersirs stood near the front of the crowd.

Haldrek straightened up in his seat. "As High King of Lohikärra, I introduce to you all, my son, my heir, and the High Aethling, Eero Ingmar Rodreksson." Haldrek raised Eero above his lap and I watched as Eero began wriggling, awakened by Haldrek's voice. "May he one day rule over the mightiest kingdom Sethys has ever seen."

The crowd cheered and Eero began to cry. Haldrek bounced him for a few moments before bringing him over to me. Without thinking, I took him and nestled him in my arms, covering his ears and trying to soothe him as the nearest thegns began the procession of gift-giving. Gold, perfume, and trinkets of all kinds were offered, and I let Haldrek give our gratitude as I tended to Eero.

After some time, Senja and Paavo walked up to the dais with a small silk-looking purse. While both dragons looked pleased, Senja especially looked happy.

"Senja and I have a gift for the new aethling as well." Paavo nodded to both of us as Senja walked over to me with the little purse. She opened it with one finger and pulled out a tiny bracelet. At regular intervals, there were polished stones that I knew were made from dragon scales. Carved on each one was a different protective rune. In the center was a larger stone, carved with an unfamiliar rune. However, it looked similar to Haldrek's runic signature, so I assumed it was as much.

Paavo's voice boomed throughout the room as Senja gently helped me put the bracelet on Eero's tiny arm, tightening it so it wouldn't fall off. "We offer the new aethling the protection of the dragons. As we all know, there are many dangers he may face now and in the future. This bracelet will protect him and his heirs for as long as Tenelth's descendants reign."

Senja gestured to hold Eero, and I gave him to her with no hesitation. I trusted her implicitly to keep him safe.

She turned around as he squirmed, flailing his arm with the bracelet on it much to the amusement of the crowd. After a moment or two, Senja turned back around and gave him to me.

"Thank you," I whispered.

"You're welcome. We know your concerns and believe this will help soothe them." Her smile made me happy, and I was grateful for all she and Paavo had done. Rhaegos's presence shifted around in the back of my mind and her gratitude also emanated from her.

Senja laughed softly. "I'm glad Rhaegos is pleased as well." She stepped back and returned to the crowd with Paavo.

A few more people offered their gifts and once all was said and done, Haldrek stood.

"My gratitude goes out to all of you who have received our son, Eero, as the new aethling. In this spirit of celebration, I now offer an invitation to share in the bounty of this day. Please join us in the feasting hall for more celebrations."

People cheered and began moving out of the throne room. As the place emptied, my heart began to grow heavy, knowing Haldrek would likely leave soon. Even in our joy, Bragidrattür still needed him, and as far as I was aware, everything was ready for his departure. Haldrek placed his hand on my shoulder and kissed the top of my head.

"How are you feeling? Should we join the celebrations upstairs?"

I smiled sadly. "We can. But I'm going to have a hard time celebrating knowing you'll be gone soon."

He went quiet for a moment. "I'm not leaving today. The sun may still be high, but today is a day of celebration. Thegn Bragidrattür knows I won't be starting out until the day after tomorrow." Haldrek's mouth quirked up. "He sent his congratulations on Eero's birth and told me I should take my time to celebrate."

"What? Why?"

"I think he may be a little embarrassed at having to ask for my aid. Bragidrattür isn't necessarily known for its warriors, but the people aren't weak fighters by any means. I believe he thinks he can still handle Rorik's incursions on his own, with the addition of the warriors I have already sent."

"I was about to say…" My heart lightened some, grateful for the extension of time with Haldrek.

"So today is a day of celebration. Of Eero and of the future we will have together." He offered his hand to help me up. "Let's enjoy ourselves and take it as an omen of future times."

We enjoyed ourselves that night. The palace kitchens had outdone themselves with more food and drink than I could imagine. It was dark by the time I retired to Haldrek's and my quarters, still recovering from everything. Haldrek slipped out with me and we relished our quiet time together, even as the rest of the palace and the city celebrated well into the night.

On the morning of Haldrek's departure, I woke to Eero's fusses and fed him as Haldrek tested out his armor once more, then made final preparations for his journey. I tried not to cry as I thought about what had happened the last time I had watched him prepare for war.

"Ina?"

I looked up, my vision blurred with tears. "I'm sorry. You know me. I hope…" My throat tightened as I attempted to compose myself.

Haldrek gently squeezed me and kissed the top of my head, ruffling my hair with his nose and mouth. "This will be a quick trip. I promise."

I started bawling, unable to control myself. "You had better keep yourself safe or else."

"Or else what?" There was humor in his voice and I gently punched his armor, eliciting a laugh.

"Or else I'll go to the Realm of Ghosts and boot you out myself."

He laughed and kissed me again. "So that's how things are going to happen." There was levity in his tone, but immediately I knew he was referring to something I wasn't aware of.

"What are you talking about?" I pulled back to stare at him, concern filling me. Was something going to happen to him in Bragidrattür?

He still smiled, but it changed to a more somber smile. "The Vollr gave me a vision as well before they visited you. Different from any other vision I've ever received."

My choked cry bubbled up, and I looked up at him. "What vision was that?"

"The youngest Vollr, guardian and keeper of future things, came up to me and pressed her thumb into my forehead. I didn't know they could give visions that way. She told me the vision I would see was already set in stone, regardless of anyone's actions. As she said those words, everything darkened and then a vision of the throne room appeared before me. I was an old man, but there were many children around, both young and old. She told me that these were my descendants and they would bring worlds together. Worlds that had never joined before."

Another sob burst through my mouth, and I tried to brush my tears away. I was glad he would survive, but a noticeable absence in his vision worried me.

"Was I there with you?"

He paused. "I didn't physically see you, but your presence was there. You were still around, if that makes sense."

My chest tightened with a sense of doom. As soon as it arrived, Rhaegos swatted at it as if it were an annoying horsefly. *Don't forget your own visions, little one. Don't jump to the worst-case scenarios.*

Another kiss, this time by my ear, brought my attention back to Haldrek. "There is no one else I would have be the mother of my children except you. If it is set in stone that I have many descendants, they will be with you."

"Then why wouldn't I be in your vision?" I whispered softly.

"I don't know." His voice was softer now, more contemplative. "I think there is a reason you should stay at the palace. I want you by my side for years to come and both you and Eero will be safest here." He tugged at Eero's bracelet as the door to our antechamber creaked open.

We looked up to see a servant at the door. He bowed and said, "My king, your men wish to know when you are to set out."

Haldrek grimaced. "I will be down soon." He turned back to me. "Are you feeling well enough to walk with me?"

I nodded, my tears overflowing. "We shouldn't leave your men waiting."

Without another word, he helped me up, and we left the antechamber with the servant.

In a matter of moments, we were outside facing half a sattar of mounted warriors ready to go. As soon as Haldrek and I arrived, they nodded to us.

Haldrek put his arm around my waist and kissed me again. I tried to savor the moment, the feeling of his touch. He then bowed down and kissed Eero on the forehead, trying to be as gentle as possible. When he straightened up, he put his helmet on and said, "This will be a quick trip, *mine drawing*. I look forward to returning home victorious and spending many a day and night with you two in my arms."

That set off my tears once more.

"I will hold you to that promise. In this life and the next."

He smiled, squeezing my hand before walking down the stairs and saddling up with his men.

As he headed out, Eero began to fuss and a heaviness settled into my chest. Not just the feeling of missing Haldrek already, but the feeling of doom had returned, along with some vulnerability.

How much should I be worried, Rhaegos? Are these feelings just my hormones?

Rhaegos swatted at the sense of doom once again and wrapped her presence around me, lessening the feeling of vulnerability.

It is mostly your body and mind adjusting to its new normal, but you and Haldrek must stay vigilant until Rorik is well and truly dead.

Rhaegos's words didn't comfort me much, and as Haldrek and his men disappeared out of the eastern gate, my gut told me it would be awhile before that happened.

Chapter 7

That night, my dreams took on a very different vibe. Instead of the darkness that had seeped into many of them with Rorik's attacks, this dream was vibrant and beautiful.

I was in an incredibly green, lush forest. It was high above everything else and even though my feet were solidly on the forest floor, I still felt like I was flying above the world. Most of all, it was peaceful. As I wandered around the forest, I tried to remember if I'd ever been to this place before. It didn't feel like Svartån or any of the other parts of Lohikärra I'd been to. It didn't even feel like the video games. But I knew for a certainty I was in Lohikärra. I just couldn't figure out which part or at what time in history.

Ina.

A cool breeze brushed across my shoulders and cheeks, pulling some of my hair forward as I tried to make out the voice. It was soft, but I couldn't tell if it was male or female, young or old.

"Hello?" I continued to walk, enjoying the dream, but also trying to figure out where the voice was coming from.

Ina.

The voice sounded closer this time. More urgent. It had to be someone in front of me, right? I quickened my steps, taking care to jump over bumpy roots and logs. The wind grew a little stronger, as if pushing me now, toward a spot where the trees were thinner. If I was on top of a ridge, I could probably make sense of where I was and what was going on.

"I'm coming, whoever is calling me..."

The forest remained quiet except for a few bird calls. I slowed my pace as I got close to the edge of the tree line. With how the foreground lay, I knew I was coming up to a cliff of some sort.

Ina.

A final push from the breeze made me grab onto a branch, stopping my forward momentum. Below me lay a beautiful valley, green all around except for a sizable stream meandering through it and a handful of buildings with brightly colored roofs. Farms, I guessed. In the distance, more mountains rose up tall. Halfway up one of them, a large, dark hole gaped. I definitely wasn't in Svartån anymore. There were no mountains like this anywhere in Svartån. Where in Lohikärra was this place? An urge inside me grew, pushing me to take one more step and peer over the edge to find more clues. I tugged on the branch, testing its sturdiness, and then took a step forward.

Much to my surprise, a gust of wind pushed me back, into someone's arms. They wrapped around me tightly, pulling me back as an ear-splitting scream echoed through the valley. All peace and serenity was gone, the absolute terror in the scream making me sick to my stomach.

Hold on to me, little one.

Rhaegos's voice rang through my head and I squeezed myself tight against her as another gust of wind tried to pull us apart. As it raged, pulling leaves and small branches off the surrounding cliff, another scream boomed. This time it was more like a dangerous howl, and I thought I heard a hint of maniacal glee in it. I shuddered and Rhaegos pulled me further into her chest.

When the sound stopped, I stared up at Rhaegos, terrified, as I tried to calm my beating heart.

"What on... What was that?" She was in her human form, and the firmness of her embrace was comforting.

"Something I'd hoped I'd never have to hear again." She grimaced, and I began to worry. "The first sound was a human being sacrificed. I have heard too many of those in my many lifetimes and I had hoped never to hear one again."

I glanced over my shoulder to look at the cave. Even though it was on the opposite side of the valley, I got the sense the sounds had emanated from there. "But there's no one around, Rhaegos. Where did the sounds come from?"

"All of this is an illusion, little one. We are not outside the cave, but in it. Or at least, a realm made to look like the cave." I frowned, and she shook her head. "It's not important. The second sound was of Ryluth regaining his physical form. I've heard that sound before, too."

"Wait. I thought..." Hadn't Rhaegos already fought Ryluth? I thought he'd already come back.

"Rorik brought Ryluth back to the Realm of Ghosts. There he and I fought when you and Rorik fought after your child's birth in the realm Rorik created. But he was still weak and unable to rise up once more in this realm."

"Is that why Rorik has been coming after me? To bring Ryluth back to this world?"

Rhaegos nodded. "But Ryluth accepted another offering. He received his first 'Bride', much as he did in Bjornulf's and Freya's time. That gave him enough power to create a body in this realm."

"What do you mean, received his first bride?" For some reason, I had a sinking feeling about what that meant, but I knew it'd be better to ask than to assume.

"It is a twisted belief some dragons have. Ryluth in particular. He has always believed he can gain power quickly through consuming human souls." Rhaegos sighed. "And some souls are more potent than others. Usually those who are untouched by others."

I groaned, definitely feeling sick now. "Virgins, you mean."

"In a sense, yes. Ryluth certainly enjoys those who have not been touched by other men, but many of his past brides went through a vile ritual involving men loyal to him. Another thing he believed gave him and his followers power."

I felt gross just thinking about that. And it made me wonder... "How? How do you know about those rituals?"

"I know my uncle. He rarely changed from lifetime to lifetime. I would often pretend to be loyal to him in order to keep the human 'brides' as safe as possible. Other humans as well. Anyone who was offered up to him. His actions and beliefs are not common among the dragons, I promise."

Rhaegos was one of the few people—creatures?—I trusted implicitly. If she said Ryluth's behavior was abnormal for dragons, I believed her. Plus, I remembered Ryluth being a villain in the Lohikärran video games. Bjornulf and Freya had fought him and his followers on a regular basis in the first game.

"Why does Ryluth still want me, then? If he can eat and consume the energy of anyone and he prefers 'untouched' victims?"

Rhaegos grimaced. "Freya was the one bride who escaped Ryluth's clutches, and he never forgot that. You carry her blood in your veins, so that is one reason Rorik seeks what he does."

"But so do Rorik and most people in Lohikärra. Freya was the mother of Lohikärra, right?"

The world around us shuddered, and I buried myself into Rhaegos's embrace.

"Ryluth senses my presence here. We have little time. You are partially correct, though." She wrapped her arms around me and picked me up as if I was a little child. She then jumped up into the air as I tucked myself against her chest. "We must flee. The longer we stay here, the more danger we are in. The longer you and Haldrek take to destroy Ryluth, the more terrible his destruction will become."

I woke to Eero's cries. The sound of frenzied terror in them made me shoot up out of bed and stumble over to the alcove. Pulling the curtain aside, I saw the wet nurse on her hands and knees, searching for something as Eero lay on a pile of bedding, swaddled, but fiercely crying and rocking back and forth as if he was trying to escape his bindings. One arm had already escaped, and he was flailing it as hard as he could. I scooped him up quickly, unwrapping the tight fabric.

"What in the name of the dragons is going on?" My heart still raced, and I tried to calm it as Eero's cries turned into whimpers.

"I'm sorry, my queen." The wet nurse grabbed something in the shadows and sat up, huffing. In the dim light of the lantern next to me, I could see her face was flushed. "Sometimes babes cry uncontrollably, whether it be day or night. When he started crying, I loosened his swaddling clothes, and he popped his arm out." She tentatively held out the dragon charm bracelet. "The bracelet was tight around his poor arm and—"

"Did you take it off?" My voice was harsher than normal, but given my dream and Rhaegos's warning, my mind went to the worst-case scenario with Eero. "Did you take his bracelet off?"

The woman winced, and I heard fussing in a nearby basket. She glanced at it and then at me. "I thought the bracelet was hurting him somehow. Look at his arm."

I glanced down at Eero's arm. A light pink line encircled it where the bracelet had been, but it didn't look like when something was binding the skin too hard. It almost looked like a light sunburn. I brushed my finger against the skin, but it didn't seem to bother Eero.

The bracelet warded off magic sent here by Rorik or one of his necromancers. The pinkish skin is where the bracelet pulled the magic away from him and protected Eero.

My heart squeezed as I gingerly put the bracelet back on Eero and tried not to think of what could have happened.

"Did I ever tell you to take the bracelet off?" I kept my voice low and neutral. The wet nursed needed to know I was pissed, but I wanted her to know why, and what needed to happen in the future.

She shook her head, tears streaming down her face. "I'm deeply sorry, my queen. I promise I wasn't trying to harm him."

"Do you know why the dragons gave him this bracelet?"

She shook her head again. "I supposed it was something given to all aethlings by the dragons?"

"You know about the necromancer the High King and I are trying to fight, don't you?" She nodded this time.

"He would hurt not only the High King and myself, but our son. Paavo and Senja gave Eero this bracelet to protect him." I knelt despite my body's protests and laid Eero back on the bedding. He began to fuss.

"Do you see where the bracelet was?" I pointed out the quickly fading pink line around his tiny arm.

"Yes, my queen."

"That is where the dragon charm bracelet protected Eero from the dark magic. If he hadn't had the bracelet on when he was attacked…" I shuddered, fiddling with the bracelet to make sure it wasn't too tight or too loose.

"I'm deeply sorry, my queen." The wet nurse's voice was penitent, and I turned to see her kneeling before me, more tears pouring from her eyes as she bowed, her face to her knees. "I beg your forgiveness and that of the dragons."

I turned back to Eero. He seemed calmer now, but as I undid the swaddling cloths to rebind him, I saw scratches across his arms and the top of his chest. They were too big to be from him scratching himself, and I hadn't seen them on him previously.

"I forgive you. But…" I pointed out the scratches. "Unless this was your doing, this is why he needs to keep the bracelet on at all times."

The wet nurse nodded in my periphery and I continued to wrap Eero up. It wasn't as tight as usual, but I was too awake to give him back to the wet nurse and try to sleep. Slowly, I rose, then gestured for her to give him to me. As I stood up, I felt the birthing cloths shift between my thighs and groaned. I would need to clean myself before going back to bed, anyway. But I could deal with that later.

As the wet nurse handed Eero to me, she apologized once again. "I'm sorry, my queen. This won't happen again, I promise. I understand now why he had the bracelet on." She gripped her hands together as if trying to comfort herself, tears still flowing. "I'll be happy once the awful necromancer is gone for good. Maybe go home once again."

I paused, a thought striking me as I stood there. This woman had just given birth as well. Her own child lay in a small cradle next to where Eero had been sleeping. When she had been given the position of wet nurse, I hadn't thought to ask her about her past. My heart softened, wondering what exactly had brought her here.

"Where is home for you?"

"Etelaranikä, my queen. I fled with some of my family, but my husband and brothers are still there, fighting the thegn-heir." Her mouth pinched shut and trembled for a moment before she looked at me. "I hope you and the High King destroy the thegn-heir soon. Maybe then my husband will have a chance to see his youngest."

I nodded, my heart aching for her. "I understand." Rhaegos's words from my nightmare brought a chill to my heart. Rorik and Ryluth were growing stronger, even as we spoke. The sooner Haldrek and I got rid of Rorik, the better. "I know that the High King and I will do everything we can to get rid of Rorik once and for all." I rubbed Eero's arm through the swaddling cloths. "Not only for our peace, but for the Lohikärra that this little one will someday rule over."

Chapter 8

After feeding Eero and cleaning myself up, I finally fell back asleep, ready for some peaceful dreams. My sleep was quiet, the sense of Rhaegos wrapping around me and Eero in spirit.

It wasn't until one of the servants pulled open the bed curtains and let some light in that I awoke. The light blinded me and Eero squirmed as the young girl looked at me.

"My queen, Thegn Andrattür wishes to take the next meal with you. Do you wish for me to bring her to your quarters?"

Still groggy, I nodded and looked down at Eero. He had returned to sleeping, so I watched his chest rise and fall ever so slightly. Despite last night's adventures, he seemed peaceful.

You are a good mother, and he feels safe in your arms.

I smiled at Rhaegos's comment. The thought, that I was a good mother already, both felt foreign and comforting. It was something I wanted, and I would do anything to protect Eero from the dangers that threatened us.

And I believe you will. For now, though, let him rest. Let the nursemaids tend to him. Sivath tells me Mattie has some pertinent information for you.

I sighed, realizing Rhaegos was right. Scooping Eero up from the bed as gently as I could, I gave him to the wet nurse and let the other servants dress me. I was curious about what Mattie had been researching in the past few days. As bad as I felt about not interacting as much with her, I knew she probably didn't mind and had been exploring the palace's library. I also wanted to figure out what time it was. The sunlight had been bright in the bedroom, but given it was the middle of summer, that meant little.

As soon as I walked out, Mattie looked up at me and grinned. She sat at the large table filled with food. Another smaller table was set up nearby, and there were stacks of books and scrolls on top of it.

"Good morning, sleepyhead. Or maybe I should say good afternoon."

I blinked. "What time is it, anyway? Last night was rough. I know I slept in, but I don't feel like I slept that much. Why didn't anyone wake me up?"

"It's near midday." Mattie waved her hand at the spread in between us. "Hence all the food. I doubt anyone woke you up because you are still recovering from childbirth. You're going to be tired and achy for a while. Even if you're moving around during the day, you're still going to need more rest than normal. Anyway, what was rough about last night? Was Eero fussing more than normal?"

My mind went back to everything that had happened, and a weighty sense of doom settled over me. I grabbed a piece of bread to calm my stomach. "I had another nightmare last night." Glancing around the room, I lowered my voice. "Rorik is growing stronger. I think he tried to lure me back into his realm, because I dreamt of some place here in Lohikärra I'd never been to before and..." I shook my head. "Rhaegos had to rescue me. Right as she grabbed me, a bloodcurdling scream shattered the dream, and she told me that Rorik has been sacrificing people to Ryluth."

Mattie's former mirth disappeared from her expression. "That's why Sivath has been saying what he has." She put her spoon down and reached for one of the scrolls. "And why he wanted me to look for that darn prophecy here when I couldn't find it at Mirratoft."

"What has Sivath been saying? What prophecy?"

Without looking up, she said, "I've been studying ways to fight necromancers, as it's something I'm supposed to be very well versed in as Thegn of Andrattür. And there is plenty of material at Mirratoft on that." She glanced up with a weak smile. "But you know me. I've already gone over most of it and organized the stuff that's most relevant. Sivath, however, has been telling me I need to know more. And I've been a bit irritated by him because how am I supposed to know more if I have studied everything in Mirratoft's library? I keep asking him what else I need to know. He's been maddeningly vague, talking about some prophecy involving a foreigner with the Heart and Strength of Lohikärra. Like I know that the Heart and Strength of Lohikärra were titles given to Bjornulf and Freya. But who is the foreigner he's talking about? What does it have to do with necromancy?"

I tried not to laugh. "He is a dragon. Rhaegos has been vague as well, if that helps."

"You're getting a lot more information from her, though."

"Only because Rorik keeps dragging me into his realm and trying to kill me."

"Which is probably the other reason Sivath has been pestering me to do more research. As soon as Llamryl and I arrived here from Mirratoft, Sivath was telling me where the library was, pushing me to visit it."

I grabbed another piece of food. "Are you and Sivath still getting along?"

Mattie looked up at me in surprise. "Of course. I've just been frustrated, not knowing what exactly I'm looking for. Sivath has been fine, but when he gets worried, I get worried." Her expression fell. "I mean... he's a pretty ancient dragon. He's seen a lot. If he's worried, then I know something is up." She shook her head. "I'm sorry. I didn't want to add to your stress, especially with the dream you had last night." A frown stayed on her face as she started puttering around with the scrolls. For a moment, she reminded me of Skuti when we had first arrived in Svangendom and the sudden nostalgia for easier days hit me hard.

"It's fine. What did you find on fighting necromancers? Is it information Haldrek should know as well?"

"It's likely stuff Haldrek already knows. Like the fact that a necromancer has to have some kind of token to wield the necromantic magic. A staff, a pendant, something like that. When Rorik tossed us back to Fargo, he had gotten his hands on the Staff of Tenelth and that gave him enough power to do everything he was capable of at that point. The staff, with all *its* magic, allowed him to focus and expand his own magic."

"But he doesn't have it anymore. So he must have grabbed something else. Or would reviving Ryluth with sacrifices have done that?"

Mattie shook her head. "He could have sacrificed a million people and not been able to bring back Ryluth. He had to have had something before that." She sighed. "The fact that Ryluth is back is going to make all the fighting more difficult." Both of us were quiet as she chewed her lip thoughtfully. I knew that sign well enough. She was putting pieces together in her mind and was not happy with the picture she was getting. It was something she'd done countless times in high school when someone had done something stupid or unfair.

"What are you thinking?"

"I'm thinking this fight with Rorik is going to be a long and extended one, not the quick battle Haldrek is expecting. Not if Ryluth is channeling his power into Rorik."

I nodded. "We need to get rid of Ryluth before we can get rid of Rorik." The words felt heavy and dry on my tongue. How did you get rid of a zombie dragon in the first place?

"That seems to be the solution. But I don't know if the magic and tools Bjornulf and Freya used would work again. Tenelth sacrificed and bound himself to Bjornulf in order to get rid of Ryluth the first time. Haldrek can't exactly do that, right? He's already a haldraga."

Rhaegos snorted in annoyance, and I got the distinct impression that there was more to the story than either Mattie or I knew.

"Maybe you can research more of what exactly happened when Ryluth was destroyed in the first place? Rhaegos makes it sound like the stories we grew up with weren't entirely accurate."

Mattie widened her eyes. "But my dad..."

"Would have created the games off of the stories he knew. What if he just knew the general story? The library here should have stuff from a long time ago, right? Maybe even stuff from Bjornulf and Freya's time? Or their kids?" A thought popped into my head. "What if that prophecy Sivath has been pestering you about is part of the puzzle? Maybe there's something in it that explains more of the story?"

Mattie smiled, and I sensed Rhaegos was pleased.

"I think you're on to something, Ina." She glanced back and forth between the table of scrolls and the table of food.

"Let's eat." I grabbed another piece of bread and began putting meat and cheese on it. "Then we can go downstairs to the library and see what's there."

Mattie and I spent a few hours in the palace's library, a place I realized I needed to make more use of. I'd spent so much of my time in Drattüjert figuring out how to be a good High Queen that I hadn't thought much of the library. It made Svangendom's library look puny in comparison.

Those hours made my mind spin with all kinds of thoughts about the past and the future, but I felt no closer to the answer we were seeking. After talking to Haldrek and cuddling with Eero, I fell asleep, hoping some rest would help.

Instead, I was tossed into yet another vivid dream. This time, though, I could feel Rhaegos's presence near me. We were in a massive grassy field with a few boulders peeking out from the tall grasses. On one rock in particular, a young woman, dressed in armor, sat with her knees curled up to her chest. Even though she seemed relaxed, I got the sense she was deep in thought. The wind blew strands of her long blond hair across her face, and the only thing keeping it from blinding her was that most of her hair was braided and weighed down with trinkets. She was obviously someone of importance.

You should know who she is, little one. Though perhaps enough time has passed that no one knows what she truly looked like.

Rhaegos's words surprised me. So this person was someone famous, or well known. I racked my brain for which hero of Lohikärra she could be. As I hurried toward her through the grass, she let her legs hang down from either side of the rock she was on, as if riding it. When she pushed her hair away from her face, I saw her clearly. She looked like a more world-weary version of myself.

Rhaegos...

This is a memory of the past, little one. Though this woman shares blood with you, this is not you.

The woman lifted her head and cocked it, as if listening for something.

"Beroan?"

I paused, recognizing that name. If she was calling out for Beroan, that meant this was—

"I'm afraid not, Freya." An ominous-sounding voice popped up behind me, and I spun around to see a familiar-looking man. Even though I'd never seen him before, I knew exactly who he was.

"Ryluth." Freya spat out. The sound of armor rustling told me she had gotten up. The man in front of me, although covered in scars that crisscrossed his face, seemed unfazed by Freya now standing ready to fight.

"In one of my many forms. I bring my congratulations."

"What congratulations? There is nothing that would bring you here to congratulate me."

"Are you sure? You carry my kin's seed within you. Most humans would consider that something worth celebrating. Do you not?" He stepped forward and the heavy weight of doom flooded out from him.

"I doubt Bjornulf would ever call you kin, even if you both descend from the same father. This child will carry on our fight against you and yours, however long it takes."

Ryluth laughed. "You seem so certain of that, little one."

"It has been foretold. By not only Tenelth, Sivath, and Beroan but also by the Vollr."

Ryluth's expression shifted slightly, as if this was a bit of news.

"How certain were the Vollr of this prophecy? Was it one of their visions? The ones that *may* come to pass?"

"It was a vision that will come to pass. There is no *maybe* in that statement."

A huff of derisive laughter came from Ryluth, followed by a powerful gust of wind. Freya screamed and a thud sounded as I ran out from under the rock's ledge. She lay on her back, fury coloring her expression. Without thinking, I went to help her, but my hands couldn't grab on to anything.

This is a memory, little one. There is nothing you can do. Freya and her children will be fine.

I stood back, slightly annoyed with myself. Freya scrambled up and unsheathed her weapons, a long blade and an equally long axe.

"My scales are much thicker than your weapons can endure, little one."

Ryluth turned around the corner. Now he was a massive dragon, stalking Freya as he tossed the stone she'd been sitting on with his right wing. Freya and I flinched at the same time.

"Are you afraid yet, little one?"

Freya stumbled back, keeping her distance while anger swam in her eyes. "Never."

"You should be. Did you think I wouldn't demand payment for taking my heir away from me?"

That changed Freya's reaction. The anger slipped away, fear replacing it. "Thorege was merely a pawn. You never cared that he was your seed. He was just a means to an end."

"As all humans are. But he would have brought me great power at the sake of my brother. I will not forget that you and Bjornulf took that power away from me." Ryluth snapped at Freya and she dodged him by barely an inch. "You and Bjornulf took my heir, so I will take yours."

He swung his left wing at her, the closest claw aimed at her skull. She dropped to the ground and slipped through the grass, invisible except for a slight rustling. I ran after her as Ryluth chased us both.

"You don't get to escape me that easily, Freya!" The grass around Ryluth broke under a powerful gust of air as he lifted to the sky. "You are a fool if you think I can't find you from above!" He zoomed forward, eyes and snout focused on the ground. Freya had disappeared once more, and all was still as Ryluth flew across the grasslands, twisting and spinning to find her. Out of the corner of my eye, movement caught my attention, and I saw a smaller dragon divebomb Ryluth. Even from my vantage point, I could hear the harsh sound of scales being pulled out of place and flinched as Ryluth's howl boomed across the memory.

Rhaegos shuddered in my mind. *Sivath knows how to hurt other dragons very efficiently. As well as direct their attention where he wants it.*

I watched the smaller dragon zoom around Ryluth, as if egging him on.

"Sivath! I will destroy you this day as well." With that, Ryluth turned his back on his hunt and flew after the smaller dragon. A hint of amusement filled my mind, and I wasn't sure if it was me or Rhaegos reacting to the scene.

A head popped up above the grasses and surveyed the area before running off into the horizon.

The dream grew blurry for a moment, When it cleared, I found myself in front of an older style of tent, one I'd only seen in scrolls or books about Lohikärra's history. A woman with vibrant red hair ran out and scooped Freya up into her arms.

Beroan always was—and is—a maternal dragon. More so than many.

"She was your mother, right?"

She is my mother. Yes. In this realm and all other realms where dragons exist. But she cared just as much for the humans, elves, and other sentient peoples who came before her as she did for her own offspring.

"I can see where you get that part of your personality, then." My voice was soft as I continued to watch the scene unfold between Beroan and Freya. An intense feeling of pride overcame me and I was glad my compliment had pleased Rhaegos.

"I told you to be careful, little one." Beroan's voice was gentle as she held Freya. I stepped closer and saw tears streaming down Freya's face. She buried her face into Beroan's braid, which muffled her sobs.

After a few moments, she pulled back and took a deep breath.

"I'm sorry, Beroan. I didn't think... Ryluth hasn't come near the camp in so long. I thought I was safe. And the smells of camp..." She leaned her head back into Beroan's braid.

A small laugh came from Beroan. "Now you see why I told you to go to Drattüjert? It will be safer there. Ryluth knows when the Heart and Strength of this land combine, he will lose."

"And he sees the child I carry as that combination?"

"In his own narrow and literal way, yes. He will hunt you down until he is destroyed, or until he can eliminate any chance that your and Bjornulf's seed takes root in this land."

"He said this was in retaliation for killing Thorege, though."

Beroan laughed. "He will use any excuse to destroy you and Bjornulf, you know that. Thorege was merely a pawn. Even now, Ryluth schemes and plots with others who follow him. He has no love for any of his offspring. You know that."

Freya nodded. She was quiet for a long time before whispering, "I will miss Bjornulf terribly while I am stuck in Drattüjert."

"Do not think he won't miss you as well. I'd bet a scale off my back he will travel back to Drattüjert many times between now and when your offspring are all born." Beroan squeezed Freya once more, and the memory faded away.

"There is much magic in Drattüjert, then and now. The combination of Heart and Strength brought Ryluth low in the past and it will do so again. But how that combination plays out may be different this time."

Before I could open my mouth to ask Rhaegos what she meant, I was back in my bed, the darkness of the night around me. The room was quiet except for the light snoring of a few servants and the nursemaid currently with Eero. As calm as my surroundings were, my heart still thudded heavily, and the memory of Freya felt like it was my own.

Heart and Strength. Freya and Bjornulf. If that combination was what we needed to bring Ryluth down, we'd have to figure out who or what those things were now.

Chapter 9

The next time I woke, it was morning and I could hear Eero fussing. Another voice tried to soothe him and, as I became more cognizant of what was going on, I sat up and pulled open the bed curtains.

"Bring him to me." Tiredness added a sharpness to my voice.

The wet nurse looked up at me wide-eyed. "I'm sorry we woke you. He's just being a bit fussy." She rocked him and patted him on the back, but to no avail.

"Bring him to me." I held my arms out for him, mildly annoyed he wasn't already there. After waking up from the nightmare memory, I'd had difficulty going back to sleep. I hadn't wanted to wake him, but I also missed having him next to me.

The wet nurse reluctantly brought him over. As soon as he was in my arms, I could see pain covering his face. It broke my heart, and I kissed him on the forehead before putting him on the bed in front of me.

"What's going on, sweetheart?" I hoped the wet nurse was right, that this fussing wasn't anything unusual, but something in my gut told me otherwise.

Gently, I unswaddled him, pulling the smooth linen cloth away from his body to reveal more angry red scratches across his chest and arms. I gasped and heard the wet nurse murmur, "By the dragons."

I glanced up at her and then back at Eero. These scratches were fresh, making me sick to my stomach. Yet he still wore his dragon charm bracelet.

My attention returned to the nursemaid. "Did you take this charm off him at all last night?"

She shook her head. "I promise I didn't. Look, it still has the pink mark under it."

I turned back to Eero and saw a hint of pinkness under the bracelet. Magic had been cast on him and it was doing its job. But where were the scratches coming from? For a moment, I wondered if they were from Eero himself or the wet nurse, but they didn't look light enough to have been made by him. The scratches were regular in pattern, but not like what a human hand would make. At least as far as I knew.

Snuggling Eero close to my chest with only my nightshirt between us, I reached out to Rhaegos, hoping she wasn't too exhausted from last night's memory.

I am here, little one. You are right to think that something else made these scratches. I can guess, but only Senja or Paavo can tell you why their magic is only partly protecting your son. Have the servants fetch either of them.

I glanced up to see a small crowd of servants watching me, including the wet nurse.

"Someone go find either Senja or Paavo. I need to speak with them."

A couple of the servants hurried out while the wet nurse grimaced.

"I'm sorry, my queen. I promise—"

Putting my hand up to stop her, I said, "I believe you. Rhaegos thinks something magical created these scratches. Something more powerful than we expected." As I spoke, Eero began sucking on my nightshirt and fussing again. He was hungry. While I hadn't been making much milk, I uncovered my chest and let him latch. "I want to stay with him today. Just until the dragons and I can figure out what is going on."

The woman nodded, and I saw tears brimming in her eyes.

"I'm not mad. I'm just... worried. Tend to your child today and hopefully Senja or Paavo will give me some good news."

I continued to nurse Eero as much as I could while another nursemaid brought me some balm for Eero's cuts. He whimpered a little while I applied it, then focused on sucking as hard as he could. My heart ached for him. It ached for the wet nurse as well, who I could still hear in the little alcove with her child. It ached for everyone who was dealing with this situation.

"Ina?" The door creaked open and I saw Senja poke her head in, concern etched across her face. Above her, Paavo's face also showed worry.

"Come in. I wanted—"

Senja hurried in, Paavo right behind her. She sat down on the bed and Eero whipped his head around, unlatching from me a bit painfully. I grimaced as I covered myself up.

Senja held out a finger and gently stroked Eero's cheek as he stared at her.

"One of the servants told us the charm didn't work last night?" Paavo touched the beaded bracelet with one of his fingers and sighed. "It still has magic in it, but..."

"But what?" Senja and I both looked at him and I saw the wet nurse slip out of the alcove as well.

"Whatever magic has been attacking him is diminishing the magic within the charm."

"What?" I stared at Paavo in horror, then at Eero. I thought the dragon magic would be enough to keep him safe.

"It's a corrupting magic then, isn't it?" Senja kept her focus on Paavo. "Ryluth's magic, you think?"

"I was only on my first lifetime when Freya and Bjornulf destroyed him, but yes. It feels like his magic. He had a powerful presence about him, unique even among dragons." Paavo turned his attention to me. "What has Rhaegos said about this? I doubt she's been silent."

"She could only guess at why yours and Senja's magic only partially protected Eero. I think it's assumed by all that this is Rorik and Ryluth's doing. I had a dream last night. A memory of sorts." The images were faded, but the emotions were there, as intense as when I'd been in it.

"What was the memory of?"

"Ryluth confronting Freya when she was pregnant with Wiglaf and Ottkatla. He tried to attack her, to kill both her and her children, rumbling on about revenge for his heir and…" I paused, trying to remember the rest. "Something about the Heart and Strength of Lohikärra combining? I think?" I shook my head, feeling hungry and exhausted.

Senja gestured toward the door as I returned my focus to Eero. "Would Ryluth try to kill Eero like he tried to kill Freya and her children?"

Paavo and Senja looked at each other for a moment before Senja nodded. "That wouldn't be a surprise. At least from the stories I grew up with. The comment about the Heart and Strength of Lohikärra is interesting. I want to say there was an old prophecy, ancient even in my time, about the Heart and Strength of Lohikärra uniting this land. It was commonly used to refer to Bjornulf and Freya. Most people thought they had fulfilled the prophecy."

Paavo nodded his head. "It was a prophecy given before Bjornulf was even born. To Mursoth. Then Tenelth and the other dragons who arrived here brought it with them. The prophecy of the Heart and Strength uniting Lohikärra was fulfilled with Bjornulf and Freya, but…that doesn't mean they are the only ones who have been deemed the Heart and Strength of Lohikärra." He scrunched his mouth, as if deep in thought, then looked at me. "Haldrek is from Andrattür, and you are from Svartån, correct?"

I nodded. That was something Paavo and Senja should already know.

He turned to Senja. "How many times have the various descent of Bjornulf and Freya ruled over this land of dragons?"

Senja frowned. "Once each, I believe. Haldrek is the first High King from Andrattür since Wiglaf's son."

"So a full circle has been completed since Bjornulf and Freya? Hmm…" He stood silent for a moment, then shook his head. "Regardless, we need to strengthen the charm." He gently took Eero's wrist in his hand and Senja placed hers on top.

Place your hand on Senja's. I have some magic to spare.

I did as Rhaegos bid and Paavo began humming. A charge of energy coursed through me and Eero began to fuss. I stroked his head with my hand to soothe him. After a moment, the energy dissipated as Paavo and Senja pulled back their hands.

"It's only a short-term measure, I'm afraid." Paavo's voice was apologetic. "With the more power Rorik and Ryluth gain, the more magic it will take to protect those they attack."

"So we need to figure out how to defeat them. Permanently."

Paavo nodded. "I'm beginning to think it will take both the current Heart and Strength of Lohikärra to do that."

I spent the rest of the morning and most of the afternoon in the library with Mattie, looking over scrolls and flipping through a few books. When I told the nursemaids I would be keeping Eero with me for the time being, they brought me a large piece of cloth that would allow him to stay bound firmly to my chest. At first I was uncertain, but as they finished binding it, not only did it feel solid, but Eero's weight against my chest made me feel calmer. He slept well, fussing only a few times when he was hungry.

I savored every minute of it, even with our body heat combined making things warmer than normal. Thankfully, Mattie had a spell to keep us cool in the library.

With the dragons' comments about the Heart and Strength of Lohikärra, and Sivath's insistence on a prophecy involving them and a 'Foreigner', Mattie had renewed her search into anything that could possibly reference the three, both in the past and possible futures.

As I finished looking over one scroll, I leaned back and relaxed to the sound of Eero snoring on my chest, something I doubted I'd tire of anytime soon.

"Are you positive the Vollr didn't say anything about the Heart or Strength of Lohikärra in your visions?"

I opened my eyes to see Mattie staring at me. "There was nothing verbal in my dreams except for the voice saying 'you have a choice to make'. Just images. And Haldrek said the vision they gave him was the same."

"Hmm..." Mattie returned her focus to the scroll and began drumming her fingers. "Most of the references here are about Bjornulf and Freya. Which is frustrating. Obviously, they were the original Heart and Strength of Lohikärra, but I don't see anything about a future Heart and Strength of Lohikärra. Or a Foreigner. Maybe a prophecy hasn't been given yet?" She shook her head. "It wouldn't make sense though. If Sivath told me to look for a prophecy, it has to have been given. And it would be from the Vollr."

"Paavo seemed to think there could be another one—or set of people—who could take on those titles. And he made an interesting comment about Haldrek being from Andrattür. Something about a full circle."

Mattie frowned thoughtfully. "Like the fact that this is the first time a ruler of Lohikärra has come from Andrattür in two thousand years?"

I nodded. "Haldrek said something when I arrived about how Bjornulf and Freya set up who would rule after them. How each of their children's descendants would have a chance to rule."

"And with the death of Haldrek's uncle Kalle and his legitimate heirs, that ended the time for Heidrunefoss, which was sired by Bjornulf and Freya's youngest child." Mattie nodded, chewing on her bottom lip, a sure sign she was mulling over the various facts once more. "So all of their children's descent have had a chance to rule and now the cycle starts over again. But with you and Haldrek being married, the houses of both Andrattür and Svartån have joined. So the cycle will be different this time around."

"In a good way or a bad way?"

She shrugged. "Neither. Eero is not only the heir to Haldrek's title, but yours as well. Unless you and Haldrek have more children. Then your second eldest will become heir to Svartån and Eero will continue to be heir to," she gestured to everything around us, "all of this. Regardless of how many children you have, the houses of Andrattür and Svartån are technically both ruling together right now, and for however long your descendants reign."

I sighed and leaned back, pulling my pendant away from Eero's head and placing it on my shoulder. As soon as I did, it warmed up in my hand. Flipping it open, I smiled as soon as I saw Haldrek's face.

"We've arrived here at the thegn hall in Bragidrattür. All in one piece."

"That's good. Did Rorik's men hassle you?" I couldn't remember if Haldrek's journey was going to take him near the border with Etelaranikä yet.

He grimaced. "We never faced them directly, but every town we entered spoke of their presence and recent raids. It's something I'll have to talk to Gunner about. I specifically sent warriors to make sure these raids would cease," he sighed, "or at least lessen. The fact that they are attacking villages farther and farther away from Etelaranikä is not good news. But I will deal with that later. How are you doing? How is Eero?"

I pulled my pendant off and angled it to show both Eero and me relaxing in the chair. Eero made a louder than normal snoring sound and Haldrek grinned widely.

"I already miss you two terribly. But the sooner Rorik is dead—"

"The sooner you can come home." I glanced up at Mattie, who raised an eyebrow. "I'm in the library with Mattie. We're looking over the records for a prophecy about the Heart and Strength of Lohikärra that includes a foreigner. Rhaegos showed me a memory last night involving Freya, and that phrase kept popping up. Then with what happened to Eero last night—"

"What happened to him?" Haldrek's expression darkened with concern. "He looks fine. Is he not well?"

"I woke up to him fussing more than normal. He had more scratches on his arms and chest. Rhaegos confirmed they were from some kind of magic attack Rorik has been sending our way."

"What about the charm Senja and Paavo created? Don't tell me the wet nurse took it off of him again?"

I shook my head. "It was still on. When Senja and Paavo saw it, they told me that whatever magic Rorik is using, it is diminishing the magic within the charm. They and Rhaegos recharged it, but Paavo said that the longer Rorik and Ryluth are alive, the stronger their magic will be and the harder it will be to protect against it."

Haldrek swore under his breath in Lohikärran, and I grimaced.

"I will head out to the border between Bragidrattür and Etelaranikä tomorrow at the latest. I will destroy Rorik if it's the last thing I do."

A heavy sense of doom fell over me, and I shook my head. "Please be careful. I think it's going to take more than just physical attacks to destroy Rorik. You will need magic and..." I glanced over at Mattie. "The dragons keep speaking of this Heart and Strength of Lohikärra as if it will help destroy Ryluth. We can't destroy Rorik without destroying Ryluth." My voice squeaked, making Eero shift in his sleep.

"I know. And I've heard of the Heart and Strength of Lohikärra before. They are one of the many names given to Bjornulf and Freya. When they both joined together with the dragons and became haldragas, that's how they were able to fight and kill Ryluth. But..."

"But what?" Part of me was afraid to ask why Haldrek hesitated.

"I've never heard of anyone being called the Heart or the Strength of Lohikärra since Bjornulf and Freya. If we need that to get rid of Ryluth..." Haldrek shook his head. "You two keep searching. Maybe there is something in the library that you can find. Perhaps some of the more educated servants can help too. If there's some kind of connection between Bjornulf and Freya's titles and destroying Ryluth, we'll figure it out. I promise. In the meantime, I'll keep fighting Rorik and his men. Maybe if they're put on the defensive, it'll keep Rorik's attention on me instead of you and Eero."

My heart sank at the thought. "Please be careful, Haldrek. Promise me."

He nodded. "I have no intention of dying anytime soon." A small smile crossed his face, and I knew he was trying to comfort me. In the background, I heard a door open and someone's muffled voice. Haldrek glanced away from his pendant, then back. "I'm going to speak with Gunner now. Be safe, keep searching, and let me know if anything else happens."

I nodded, unable to speak as the glass in my pendant went dark.

After a moment, Mattie murmured, "We'll figure this out. Don't worry. The Vollr gave you a vision of you and Haldrek growing old together, right?"

I nodded once again.

"Then that future is still in the cards. Especially if they gave Haldrek that same vision with lots of descendants."

"But..." I stopped. Haldrek's vision was set in stone. Or at least that was what he'd been told. Mine was still variable, but the chance of my last vision coming true seemed to fade with every day.

"Let's keep searching. If the dragons are making a fuss about this Heart and Strength stuff, then there must be something. We'll find it and use that knowledge to get rid of Rorik and Ryluth once and for all."

Chapter 10

Over the next week, things got better. There were no more nightmares for me, and Eero's injuries healed quickly. After a few days of peace, I felt more comfortable letting him stay with the wet nurse as I rested or spent time in the library with Mattie, poring over more texts about Freya and Bjornulf. Most of it we already knew, lore Haldrek and Mattie's dad had put into the games or materials both Mirratoft and Svangendom had access to. I'd even asked Skuti to double check what was at Svangendom in case there was something we had overlooked.

But nothing had proved useful thus far. With Haldrek keeping me updated on the futile fighting between Bragidrattür and Etelaranikä, I was impatient to find something.

So when Mattie gasped and dropped the book she was reading, I looked up sharply from my own tome.

"Did you find something, Mattie?"

"I think so. It's about how Bjornulf and Freya slew Ryluth. Like the battle itself. It's referring to them as the Strength and Heart of Lohikärra. Specifically, Bjornulf is the Strength of Lohikärra and Freya is the Heart of Lohikärra. Listen to this: *The Strength, though mighty and bearing dragon might and soul, could never defeat his foe. Until the Heart strengthened by her dragon kin did join to insure their enemy's fall. Only once they fought together could they slew the one who flew.*" Mattie looked up at me. "That has to be it. Bjornulf and Freya had to fight together against Ryluth to defeat him. And only after they had each become haldragas. That makes sense."

"But they fought side by side plenty of times, right? Bjornulf didn't just leave Freya in their camp or here in Drattüjert, right?"

Mattie grimaced. "Yes, and no. Many of the texts I've read state he was very protective of Freya. Not in a creepy way, but he valued her safety and that of their children over his own. They fought together, but especially after Freya began bearing their children, I think it was more sporadic."

In many ways, Haldrek is like Bjornulf.

The comment from Rhaegos surprised me and I sat up straight. She wasn't wrong. Even though Haldrek wasn't half dragon, he had been raised by them. And he had the affinity to them that Bjornulf would have had. He was also very protective of me. Had been ever since we met. I certainly didn't feel like Freya though and that twisted at my heart.

"Huh."

This time, Mattie looked up at me. "What?"

"Rhaegos just said Haldrek is much like Bjornulf. She's not wrong."

Mattie frowned, deep in thought for a moment, and nodded. "I never thought of it that way, but that is an interesting insight." She tapped a page in her book and said, "This writer talks more about Bjornulf's and Freya's attempts to kill Ryluth. Apparently, both of them tried more than once by themselves before becoming haldragas, and Bjornulf attempted it at least once after joining with Tenelth. That incident led to him being seriously injured and Beroan turning Freya into a haldraga herself. Though it sounds as if their ceremony was less dramatic than most haldraga ceremonies."

"How so?"

"Instead of crash landing on the person, Beroan merely joined hands with Freya and bonded with her that way. It still knocked Freya out, but yeah, less dramatic."

I leaned back in my chair, stretching my cramped muscles. "So, to kill Ryluth, Freya and Bjornulf had to become haldragas."

"Correct. From everything I've read, the only way a human can even think of fighting a dragon is if they're a haldraga. Especially a very powerful, full grown dragon."

"So if anyone is going to kill Ryluth now, it's going to be a haldraga. Like Haldrek."

Mattie nodded. "Or you or me or any of the abthanry. There are more haldragas in the world now than there were in Bjornulf and Freya's day."

"And it's not going to be a one-person job. So Haldrek can't do it on his own."

"Correct." Mattie kept tapping her fingers. "To kill Ryluth, we'd need multiple haldragas working together. But I think there are more layers to this story than we're realizing."

"Why do you think that?"

Mattie grimaced. "The only time I see the terms 'Heart and Strength of Lohikärra' is regarding Freya and Bjornulf slaying Ryluth. That's the only time those terms are used."

"What about the prophecy that came before Bjornulf ever existed?"

"Still referred to him destroying Ryluth."

I sighed, frustrated. Maybe I was being dumb, but I felt like this was getting us nowhere. My head ached and my stomach grumbled as I sat there thinking.

Little one, remember this: sometimes descriptions are metaphorical. That way, the true meaning can only be found by those who sincerely search for it. If the skalds of Lohikärra only refer to Freya and Bjornulf by a certain title for a certain time, there is a reason.

"Mattie?"

She popped her head up, one eyebrow raised. "Yes?"

"What if... what if the reference to Bjornulf and Freya being the Heart and Strength of Lohikärra was only supposed to be about them ridding this land of Ryluth? It's symbolic, right? You said that only when Bjornulf and Freya, as haldragas, fought side by side were they able to destroy Ryluth. Do you think Bjornulf kept Freya back because he didn't want her to get hurt? Especially after they started having kids of their own?"

Mattie nodded. "That would make sense. Maybe Bjornulf thought he could handle Ryluth on his own because he was half dragon and technically brothers with Ryluth. Or at least a half-brother."

"But he couldn't do it alone. So he and Freya needed to fight Ryluth together. Using whatever skills they had to work together."

Mattie nodded. "That probably required a lot of trust on Bjornulf's part. Especially if he was used to doing things himself and he was willing to do anything to keep Freya safe. Supposedly, they had a bond from the moment they met." She reclined in her chair and started rubbing her temples.

"You think there could be another Heart and Strength of Lohikärra? Even without a prophecy or vision?"

Mattie shrugged, not opening her eyes. "I mean, yeah. Maybe the prophecy hasn't happened yet. Or it's not needed? Especially if you had two individuals who fit the same description as Bjornulf and Freya?"

Rhaegos churned in the back of my head, making me wonder if Mattie was on to something. Before I could open my mouth, Mattie stood up.

"Are you hungry? I just realized how long it's been since breakfast. That may be why all of this is giving me a headache."

My stomach grumbled, and I nodded. "Let's see if there is still food out in the Great Hall. If not, we can grab something in the kitchens." I got up myself, knowing that even if eating food didn't give us a lightbulb moment, it would at least make this task feel less overwhelming.

That night, I returned to Haldrek's and my quarters, feeling more worn out than usual. I hadn't been very physically active, but trying to wrap my mind around the stuff Mattie and I had discovered in the library was mentally exhausting. As soon as I walked in, I saw Eero with one of the nursemaids and Lady Taimi as they sat in front of a small fire near the far wall. I was glad to see her. It'd been a few days since she'd last visited, even though she was one of the few people who had an open invitation to visit the antechamber.

Taimi turned and faced me with a grin. "How have you been today, Ina?"

"Good." An intense desire to hold Eero overwhelmed me as I walked to where they sat. "I've missed Eero, though. Is he sleeping?"

The nursemaid nodded. "He's been fussy today, but I think it's the normal babe fussing. The others and I have been checking him. He's not had any new scratches or anything."

"That's good to hear." I held out my arms and she handed Eero over. "Thegn Andrattür and I have been searching for anything that can help us with defeating Rorik. She found something today that might be useful."

Taimi's face brightened. "That's wonderful to hear! What did she find?"

"More information about when Bjornulf and Freya fought and defeated Ryluth. She—we—think that is the key to defeating Rorik."

The nursemaid's expression turned pale. "A terrifying thought, that is."

Taimi frowned. "Defeating Rorik or the fact that Ryluth is back?"

"The fact that Ryluth is back, of course. All the stories talk of how terrifying he and his followers were." The nursemaid turned to me. "You know the stories of Freya before she met Bjornulf, don't you?"

I shook my head. "Not really. I mean, I know some about her family. Her mother was connected to Ryluth and there was hostility between Freya and her. But nothing much else."

"Freya's mother was a Priestess of Ryluth." Taimi answered, her voice solemn. "She had cursed Freya to become one of Ryluth's brides because of a promise she made to him. The legends say that is the reason he chased after Freya until she and Bjornulf finally slew him."

The nursemaid continued, "There were women known as Ryluth's brides. Some gave themselves to him in exchange for protection for their kin, and others were promised to him by their kin. Freya was the only one of those promised brides who ever broke his curse." She looked back at Taimi. "I was downstairs earlier today, visiting some of the priestesses in the High Queen's Home. There are new rumors coming from Etelaranikä."

"What kind of rumors?" Eero began to fuss and I started rocking him, holding him firmly against me.

"You know about the kidnappings, right? They're getting worse. Used to be just outlying farms and some of the smaller villages. Now the walled settlements are getting attacked and their young women and men are being taken."

"Both women and men?" I'd known about the women, but why would they kidnap men?

The nursemaid nodded, and Taimi looked at me. "Rorik's probably running low on those willing to fight with him. Even in Etelaranikä, I doubt there are many who would willingly follow a necromancer."

I grimaced, my stomach churning and my anxiety beginning to rise once more. Mattie and I were close to an answer, but the practical application of that answer still felt far off. "That sounds logical. I'll have to mention it to Haldrek next time I speak to him."

"That is wisdom, indeed." The nursemaid curtsied to me. "I don't mean to leave on such a solemn note, but if you have no more need of me, I would ask to leave for the evening meal downstairs." She glanced at the servants, who were currently setting up a meal on the table behind us.

"Of course. Lady Taimi and I will be fine. As will Eero." I smiled down at him while he slept heavily in my arms.

The nursemaid curtsied once more and hurried out of the antechamber. I took a seat next to the table as Taimi followed me.

"Senja mentioned Rorik has been sending more of his accursed magic your way." She smiled gently at Eero and I could see some concern in her expression. "I wish there was something I could do to help. Alas, I don't know what I can do."

I nodded. "There's not much I feel I can do. Until—" My pendant warmed up and I looked at it in surprise. Usually Haldrek called me after the evening meal. I flipped it open with my free hand and gasped.

Haldrek smiled tiredly, but he was still covered in blood and sweat. "Today has been a day. Are you alone?" Taimi gently nudged me and took Eero as I stood up and hurried into the privacy of the bedroom.

As soon as I closed the door, I nodded. "Taimi and I were just sitting down to eat while Eero was sleeping. What happened to you? Are you all right?"

He nodded. "A bit bruised and beat up." He touched his face and grimaced as he looked at the blood. "I promise this isn't mine. Or at least I don't think it is. We were in one of the border towns today when some necromancers attacked. I don't think they expected me or half a sattar of warriors to be in town. They started grabbing anyone they could and casting vile magic at any villagers who retaliated, but as soon as my men and I charged them, they fled."

"So the blood...?"

"The only good necromancer is a dead necromancer, as far as I'm concerned. Even if they didn't grab anyone from Lysafjord today, they would have gone after another village tomorrow."

I nodded. "One of the nursemaids said rumors from Etelaranikä are spreading. Rorik's men are kidnapping not only young women, but young men as well. She thought Rorik's forces might be dwindling, and he's trying to keep that from happening."

Haldrek sighed. "It wouldn't surprise me. Actually," he paused, his brows creasing as if deep in thought, "that makes sense. The gesith of Lysafjord told me today there's been word of a man in Etelaranikä trying to single-handedly fight Rorik. Or at least antagonize him. Guess where he heard that?"

"Where did he hear that from?"

"One of the few warriors from Etelaranikä who had been kept alive from a previous attack. The man swore up and down he had no love for Rorik, but Rorik's men had kidnapped him and forced him to fight on Rorik's behalf."

"How has Rorik been able to enforce that? Wouldn't anyone who hated him at least try to escape, or sabotage his plans?"

Haldrek nodded once more. "He said he was brought before a terrifying dragon and made to swear an oath to it or become its next meal."

Rhaegos made an angry rumbling sound in the back of my mind, and I winced.

So that is Rorik and Ryluth's plan. They are raising up a new army of Priests of Ryluth. Taking those who would not follow Rorik and forcing them to fight for him while training those who would follow Rorik to worship Ryluth and do his bidding.

I shuddered at Rhaegos's words.

Haldrek furrowed his brows in concern. "Did Rhaegos just say something to you?"

I nodded. "She believes Rorik is raising up a new army of something called the Priests of Ryluth. Basically, those who willingly follow Rorik are being trained to worship Ryluth and those who won't willingly follow him are being forced to fight."

Haldrek's frown deepened, and he swore under his breath. "That's not news I wanted to hear, but I'm glad to know it either way. It makes sense, with the attacks and all." Someone handed him a piece of cloth from outside of the pendant's view and he scrubbed his face with it, wiping away most of the blood, sweat, and grime. "Let's talk of something lighter. Tell me how you and Eero have been doing. I need some good news right now."

I smiled and walked back into the antechamber where Taimi continued to rock Eero while nibbling at some of the food that had been brought out.

"We're doing well. The last few days have been peaceful, and Eero hasn't had any more scratches or other unusual injuries." I sat down in my chair next to Taimi and pulled off my pendant to make it easier for Haldrek to see both her and Eero.

Haldrek laughed softly. "It's good to see you, Aunt Taimi. You look very happy."

"It's not often I get to rock babies anymore, and it's a lovely thing to do. I need to nudge Hrimfax once more about that part of his thegnly duties." A teasing smile crossed her face. "Until I can do that with my own grand babes, I will happily hold any aethlings who come along."

Haldrek laughed once more, and I turned the pendant back to see him. He looked happier, more relieved and relaxed than at the beginning of our call.

"So things are going well here. I'm thinking I might keep Eero close though, especially at night, in case Rorik tries something again. Not that I don't trust the nursemaids or the wet nurse. I just…"

"Want to soak in as much time as you can and keep him safe?"

I nodded, tears brimming in my eyes.

Haldrek's smile widened. "And here you thought you wouldn't bond with Eero."

I laughed, the tears streaking down my face.

"I'm going to go bathe and get all this battle grime off me. You continue enjoying this time with Eero and soon it will all be but a memory. I promise."

Chapter 11

That night, I slept with Eero next to me, snuggled in the small basket the wet nurse used as a crib for him. Though I trusted her and the rest of the servants, I wanted to spend as much time with him as possible. A sinking weight in the back of my mind told me these moments would be rare in the future. As much as I tried to brush them away, and even as Rhaegos ignored them, they stuck around. I figured spending time with Eero was better than just leaving him to the nursemaids. The last thing I wanted was for him—or any other children Haldrek and I might have—to feel was neglected.

But I hadn't expected newborns to wake up so often and be so hungry. Even though I had tried to nurse Eero, after the first week or so, my body made little in the way of milk, so I'd reluctantly let the wet nurse take over all of his feedings. Which meant I was waking up every few hours to hand him over to her. That left me more exhausted than I expected.

When I woke up in the morning to him fussing, I felt like I'd barely slept. Taking him out of his swaddle, I gently checked for any more injuries. Even the slightest scratch could mean Rorik and Ryluth had found their way through the charm's barriers.

The magic of the charm is still strong, little one. I sense that Ryluth's attentions, at least, have been diverted elsewhere.

"That's good to hear, but I still want to check." I didn't want to insult Rhaegos, but unwrapping Eero and checking him over would calm my anxieties. Picking him up, I saw no new scratches and no scars from the previous ones. As I snuggled him against my chest, I took in a deep breath, expecting the lovely baby smell that usually emanated from him, only to smell the real reason he was fussing.

Rhaegos began laughing in my head as I crinkled my nose. The bed curtains opened slightly and the wet nurse poked her head in. "Is he hungry again, my queen?"

I grimaced. "Possibly. But I think his previous feedings are bothering him now."

She took a sniff and laughed, holding her hands out for him. "I can take care of both situations, if you'd like."

I nodded, reluctantly giving him to her. As soon as she disappeared, my heart felt heavy again, and I questioned going back to bed.

There will be time to rest later. Sivath tells me Mattie has found something new and is on her way up here as we speak.

"Then I should probably get dressed." I gingerly got out of bed. Even though it'd been nearly a month since Eero's birth, my body still complained when I got up in the morning. I hoped that would go away soon.

A few minutes later, I entered the antechamber fully dressed and found Mattie looking excited, her hands crossed in front of a book.

"I think I found it, Ina. The missing piece we were trying to find."

"About Bjornulf and Freya?"

She nodded as I trudged over to the nearest table and chair and sat down with a thud.

"Long night?"

I nodded. "Eero kept waking up to be fed. I enjoyed having him by my side, but it was tiring to have to hand him over to the wet nurse every hour or so."

Mattie laughed. "Geirny was the same way after she was born. I remember being so tired for those first few months, until Llamryl convinced me to let the wet nurse feed her more often. Then it got better. Now she's an active little kid." Mattie grinned. "She took her first few steps for me last night. Llamryl said she's been doing it for him, but every time I see her, she'll plop on the ground and happily crawl to me."

I smiled at the thought and wondered for a moment where Haldrek and I would be when Eero started walking. That would be next summer, probably. Would Haldrek be here? Or would he still be fighting Rorik and Ryluth? Would worse things happen between now and then?

Ina...

I sighed as Rhaegos gently nudged me out of my gloomy thoughts. I had to think of a bright future. Even if dark times were ahead, there was still a light at the end of the tunnel, right?

"Ina?" Mattie looked concerned as she put the book down and I shook my head.

"I'm fine. My thoughts just... I don't think I got enough sleep last night, and it's affecting my mood."

Mattie nodded and opened the book to where she'd put a small strip of leather. The runes were tiny and there were notations along the edges.

"You remember that super ancient prophecy about Bjornulf and Freya being the Strength and Heart of Lohikärra? I found a copy of it, one that Sivath verified was correct. There are two parts to it."

"What?"

Mattie nodded again and continued, her tone becoming more and more excited. "The first part talks about the Heart and Strength of Lohikärra uniting this land and destroying the dragon who would enslave it. Obviously talking about Bjornulf, Freya, and Ryluth, right?"

"Right. What does the second part of the prophecy talk about?"

"It talks about Bjornulf and Freya's seed keeping Lohikärra safe from the dragons who would destroy it."

"Hasn't that been happening all along?"

Mattie shook her head, grimacing. "No. When was the last time you heard of a dragon trying to destroy Lohikärra? Or any of its people?"

I thought for a moment. "Never, really. If it's a prophecy, wouldn't other people have noticed it?"

"They may have thought it meant the same thing you did. That it's been happening all along. I mean, what's the phrase that someone, dragon or human, always says at pretty much every ceremony?"

I shrugged.

Mattie raised an eyebrow at me. "Some variation of *as long as Tenelth's descent reign over Lohikärra, everything will be fine.*"

"Okay... so is that referring to this prophecy?"

"I don't think so. But I think it's why no one has really looked at the second half closely. The first part came to pass when Bjornulf and Freya killed Ryluth. There hasn't been a reason to assume the second part had to do with anything else."

"So there's a second prophecy, dealing with Bjornulf and Freya's seed keeping Lohikärra safe. Any clues to how? Or who? I mean, most, if not all, of the people of Lohikärra can claim them as their ancestors."

Mattie nodded and pointed at a couple of lines in the book. My knowledge of Lohikärran runes wasn't perfect, but I was able to read the part she pointed to.

The united seed of Strength and Heart shall save Lohikärra from the dire dragon's descent. Together with those foreign to the dragons' lands, shall the dire dragon's descent meet with defeat once more.

"That second line is interesting. Is that referring to the Foreigner Sivath kept pestering you about?"

Mattie grinned. "I thought so too. Which is why I asked Sivath about it."

"What did he say?"

"Very little, except that a woman named Ottkatla gave this entire prophecy."

"Wait. My ancestor?"

Mattie shook her head. "Sivath told me Bjornulf's human mother was a priestess of those who worshiped air dragons, such as Tenelth and his father, Mursoth. Apparently, she was gifted with visions of the future. Much like the Vollr. So, while Sivath wasn't with them at the time of this prophecy…"

"He knew about it. And he knew about Ottkatla. Is that why Bjornulf and Freya gave my ancestor her name?"

Mattie shrugged. "It wouldn't surprise me. But that's why I think these couple of lines are different. They were part of a prophecy. They are connected to the first one, which is wholly about Bjornulf and Freya defeating Ryluth."

"So Bjornulf's mother knew about what is currently going on? Over two thousand years ago?"

"I think so. Which means Bjornulf and Freya aren't the only people in Lohikärra history who will be called the Heart and Strength of Lohikärra. They weren't going to be the only ones to defeat Ryluth. While Bjornulf and Freya may have gotten their extra boost to kill Ryluth from the dragons, the fact that most of their descendants already have that power, means the new Heart and Strength will need allies from outside of Lohikärra." Mattie took a deep breath and grinned. "At least that's my theory. Sivath hasn't told me I'm wrong about any of this yet. I think this is the prophecy Sivath has been hounding me about. The Heart, the Strength, and the Foreigner."

"Then it's probably the best lead we have so far. Do you think you could find anything else on this? Or are you burnt out from research?" A small laugh escaped my lips. "This trip wasn't just supposed to keep you in the library."

Mattie laughed as well. "I may take a break to spend some time with Llamryl and Geirny and enjoy the city, but you know me and libraries."

I nodded. Libraries had always been Mattie's favorite places.

"Take some time to relax, then. I'll ask Rhaegos about her thoughts as well." Before I could say anything else, the door cracked open and a couple of servants brought in plates of food for us. I'd forgotten about breakfast, but now my stomach grumbled. "In the meantime, I'm hungry. Let's eat. Maybe that'll give us more ideas."

Mattie's words stuck with me over the next few days as Haldrek let me know of more reports from Bragidrattür. As peaceful as my time currently was, both Bragidrattür and Etelaranikä were locked in a battle for survival, not only against Rorik, who had yet to show his face, but against rising tensions from the neighboring villages and settlements on either side of the border. With every raid by Rorik's men, willing and unwilling, tensions were rising between the various communities.

The news made me anxious and more impatient. Part of me wanted to be with Haldrek and fight Rorik, worried that the longer he was alive, the worse his attacks would become. Another part of me feared that if I left Drattüjert—and Eero—something bad might happen in my absence. Even during the times I left Haldrek's and my chambers, my heart ached to be back with Eero, and worry about his well-being stuck in my head.

That said, on the advice of the nursemaids, and the midwives who had been helping me with my own recovery, I walked down to the lower levels and took in some fresh air from the interior garden. Whatever magic had created it—and there had to be magic since it stayed pleasant all year long—felt like a relaxing embrace as soon as I made my way to the center and sat on a bench. It felt strange now to think this was the place where Rorik had opened up a vortex. For a moment, I tried to think how long it'd been. How long *had* it been since he'd tossed Haldrek and me back into Fargo? It had almost been two years.

And here we were still dealing with Rorik and his machinations.

"Ina?"

I looked up to see Sibila and Senja enter the interior garden. Immediately, my mood improved, and a grin crossed my face.

"Hi. I was told to get some fresh air, and I figured this was a good enough place to do that."

Both of them sat on the bench with me as Sibila looked up at the view above us. Ever since Haldrek and I had shifted around our inner circle of hersirs and counsellors, Sibila had seemed more at ease in the palace. While she still talked with her dragon frequently, she seemed more aware of what was going around her and I assumed, she felt safer here now.

"I've always loved this garden." Sibila turned to Senja. "Was it here when you were the aethling?"

Senja shook her head. "Under my grandfather, this was one of the meal halls originally. Just for our family and his closest counsellors or any honored guests." She wrinkled her nose at the thought, as if disgusted by some memory. "I hated how dark and gloomy it always was. Plus, there hadn't been many pleasant meals here. When Paavo and I retook the palace, he created this for me, a pleasant space to remind me of our adventures together." She glanced around. "There are plants from every part of Lohikärra here and Paavo's dragon magic keeps it nice, even when it's bitter cold outside."

"I've noticed that." Taking a deep breath, I let myself relax for a moment. It was nice. This garden felt like a place outside of time and space, a moment protected from the surrounding chaos.

"How have you been doing, Ina?" Sibila's voice brought me back from my reverie.

"As well as can be expected. I miss Haldrek and wish there was something more I could do to help. He's fighting Rorik's men, but I don't know how much progress he's making. Part of me wants to go out and fight alongside him, but…"

"But what?" Senja placed her hand on mine and the sense of being comforted came over me.

"But I'm also afraid that if I leave the palace, Rorik will do something to Eero while I'm away." Tears dripped down my face, surprising me. The peace and comfort from a moment ago disappeared as my fears returned.

"Has Eero been wearing the charm Paavo and I gave him?"

I nodded. "He keeps it on, even when being bathed. There haven't been any marks on him since the last time. I'm pretty sure it's working, but I still worry. I know Rorik and Ryluth's power is growing. Even Rhaegos has said as much."

Senja leaned me into her shoulder as I sniffled. I hadn't sniffled in years, but the weight of worry was heavy on my chest.

"Rhaegos isn't wrong." Sibila's voice was soft. "I've sensed him in my dreams. He's tried to pull me in to his realm a few times, only for Tesroan to rescue me. But each time it's been harder for her."

Senja squeezed my hand and looked over at Sibila. "I'm surprised you haven't mentioned that in our conversations, little one."

"I didn't want to worry you. Your duty is to the High King and High Queen, I believe. Not necessarily a hersir whose brother is being a bully."

"My duty is to all those who reside in Drattüjert, and especially within the palace. Your brother is being much more than a bully." Senja turned back to me and I sat up, sensing there was more on her mind.

"Paavo and I have been speaking about this situation concerning Rorik. As loathe as both of us are to say it, perhaps there is some wisdom in you, Ina, going to fight alongside Haldrek."

"What?" Both Sibila and I stared at Senja in surprise.

"Why? Is the High King not able to defeat Rorik by himself, or with his sattars?"

Senja grimaced. "If he and Rorik had fought before Ryluth's return, then yes, the High King would have easily defeated him. But now that Rorik has bonded with Ryluth, he is a much more difficult foe. Even more than many of the dragons expected."

"Wait. Rorik was already a haldraga." Sibila's expression contorted with pain and fear. "What happened to…"

"The dragon who originally bonded with him? She is still alive. I know that much. And she is still in this realm, which means she has either bonded with another member of the abthanry, or she is being held captive by Ryluth."

The weight in my chest shifted to my stomach. I hated the idea of anyone, even a dragon, being trapped by Ryluth. Knowing what Rorik had done to the other dragons, I could just imagine what he'd do to a dragon he'd originally been connected to, now that he had Ryluth's power.

"That said, the fact that she is still in this realm makes me believe she has bonded with another member of the abthanry, which may be a blessing."

"Another ally?" I whispered, wondering who that person could be, or how Haldrek could find them.

"Yes. Rorik's former dragon wouldn't have bonded with just anyone. Even while weak, dragons are still strong in spirit. That brings me back to the other reason why Ina, you may have to fight alongside Haldrek to destroy Rorik and Ryluth."

"Why?"

"Something you and Mattie have been trying to figure out. Why Bjornulf and Freya needed to work side by side to defeat Ryluth. If I may, there is some information I know of their story that I don't believe was ever written down."

"Why not?"

Senja grinned. "Because Paavo told me. His own memories of the battle between Ryluth and our first ancestors, Bjornulf and Freya."

"He was there?" Sibila's jaw dropped as she gaped.

"I don't know if he was fighting other dragons, since he was on his first life cycle when this all happened, but he was at the battle. He fought beside many of Bjornulf's men and caught a glimpse of Ryluth falling from the sky, crushing many of his own warriors beneath him."

"Was that what killed Ryluth?" I frowned, thinking it sounded too easy.

Senja shook her head. "Dragons are tougher than that. No, it merely knocked him to the ground. He had enough energy to transform into his human form. Paavo said he was battered and bloody, but still full of spite. Apparently, he had fed upon a few of his brides beforehand." She grimaced. "Bjornulf attacked first and while he severely injured him, Ryluth knocked him back and began slaughtering whatever warriors came near him, both his own and Bjornulf's. As Bjornulf lay injured, Freya was nowhere to be seen. Many, including Paavo, thought she'd been killed already."

"Obviously she wasn't." Sibila smiled.

"Of course not. As Ryluth staggered up to Bjornulf, she ran up behind him and attacked him with two small, but very pointy, battle axes, a type known to break through dragon scale. As soon as she hit him, he went down and Bjornulf scrambled to his feet. He took the blade Tenelth had given him, which every High King or High Queen has wielded since then, and slew Ryluth then and there."

"So Bjornulf and Freya literally worked together to kill Ryluth. Neither of them could have done it by themselves."

Senja shook her head. "That's from Paavo's own eyes. He told me another thing: that battle was the first Bjornulf and Freya had fought side by side since Freya had born Wiglaf and Ottkatla."

"Huh." Thoughts started rolling around in my head. Thoughts I knew Haldrek wouldn't be happy with if I told him about them. "How long after Freya had a kid did she do this? She didn't pop the baby out and then go out fighting, right?"

Senja laughed. "I don't know, but I doubt it. Paavo would know better, but if the histories are correct, Ryluth's death happened perhaps a couple of years after the birth of her youngest child at that point."

I sighed, knowing that was one of the barriers I had right now. My body was still healing from childbirth. Even if I was a dragon-attacking ninja like Freya, I still would need more time to regain my strength, both physically and magically.

Senja squeezed my knee. "I know that sound. You're frustrated you can't be next to Haldrek like Freya was with Bjornulf, aren't you?"

I nodded. "How can I when it's been only four weeks since Eero's birth? I've gotten better, but I'm nowhere near where I was before I was pregnant."

"Perhaps you aren't as far off as you think. Let me check on a few things. If I can help you heal, I will. Normally, I believe in not rushing things, but time seems to be of the essence." She stood up, and Sibila did as well. I joined them, my butt and legs aching from sitting on the hard wooden bench.

"Thank you, Senja. Given the danger Rorik and Ryluth present, I'll take whatever aid I can."

Chapter 12

I fell asleep more quickly than normal that night. After talking with Haldrek, and hearing more grim news, I dozed off next to the shallow basket with Eero inside of it.

When I opened my eyes, I was back in the valley with the bright-roofed farmhouses. I stood next to a stream and high above me on the other side of the valley was the ledge that I'd almost fallen off.

"Rhaegos?"

I had no idea if this was another illusion from Rorik, so I kept my guard up. There was no sign of Rhaegos's presence. Instead, I felt the intense urge to follow the stream beside me. Turning around, I saw a thick forest in the distance. Even though it was heavily shadowed, I didn't sense any danger from it.

Instead, the breeze nudged me forward, and I dug my heels into the ground.

"Last time you nudged me in a direction, I nearly fell off a cliff. You really think I'm going to follow you?"

There was no response, and I laughed. Whatever was trying to manipulate me needed to try harder.

As soon as the thought passed through my mind, a sharp crack boomed through the valley. I jumped and spun to see what had made that noise. To the left, grayish clouds hovered above a massive hole in the cliff's side. Had that been here this whole time? It had to have been. I glanced back at the cliffs on my right, trying to remember how I'd seen this place before.

Shaking my head, I watched the grayish clouds. They continued to shift and rumble above the hole, growing larger.

A sense of unease fell over me and I knew in an instant I was vulnerable here in the valley. Especially with no weapons. The farmhouses might be safe, but they were farther from me and closer to the ominous clouds. The forest could hold who knows what, but it was closer. If whatever was causing the clouds was up to no good, I'd rather be hidden in the forest.

Without another thought, I ran toward the forest, trying to imagine it being a safe place. Or at least finding Rhaegos to figure out what was going on.

Instead, as soon as I entered the forest, I was met with a large stony path that curved upwards and hugged the ridge above my head.

Something moved in the forest, unseen, and I started moving up the path, sensing that was the safest course for now.

Rhaegos? I hoped she was around. Even though this was a dream—I hoped it was a dream—I felt very alone. I wanted out. I wanted to be back where it was safe.

Yet there was nothing as I went up the path, moving above the trees and the valley below. After a few moments, the cave appeared in front of me, the ominous gray clouds roiling above it, emanating a thick layer of magic over the area. It wrapped around everything, leaving my vision hazy.

Before I could decide anything, footsteps clicked toward me from the cave. I ducked behind a couple of large bushes, hoping I was hidden from whoever was coming. Peering out, I watched as two men in pitch-black costumes walked out. Their garb was cut like most Lohikärran tunics, but they also wore some kind of cape over their clothing that looked familiar. Adorned with black feathers and dragon scales, they almost looked like miniature dragons who had partially shifted into their human forms. One of them waved his hand and the roiling gray clouds faded into nothingness.

"Are you sure there is no one in the valley?" One of the men spoke, and he sounded younger, perhaps my age.

His companion scoffed. "Our lord's scouts have returned. This valley is still fully ours. There is no one down there who isn't loyal to Rorik or Ryluth. Even if there was, Rorik would know. Do you doubt his power?"

"No. Not at all." The younger man's voice didn't sound confident in the least. After a few moments of quiet, he asked, "What decision has Rorik made about the prisoner? I assume he is more valuable alive than dead."

"He is, indeed. Though Rorik's Norycian ally is in Drattüjert as we speak, posing as the emperor's nephew, the true Norycian prince has value still. Once the High King and Queen are thoroughly destroyed and their powers consumed by Ryluth, the prince will be a perfect bartering chip for dealing with his relatives in that land."

My body went stiff as I listened to their conversation. Rorik's Norycian ally? I thought back to when the imposter had been in Drattüjert. That had been the only Blodnar—or Norycian—person I knew of in the city. And he'd been posing as Henry.

Were they talking about Henry?

If they were, that meant Henry did have connections to the Blodnar. And that meant he'd been in Lohikärra. And he was Rorik's prisoner. That meant he still was. My heart sank. He had absolutely adored the Lohikärran video games and if being Rorik's prisoner was his first experience in the real world of Lohikärra, that would suck.

"How long do you think it'll take before Rorik overthrows those two at Drattüjert?"

My attention turned back to the two men.

"Not long, if the Norycian is to be trusted."

"Are Norycians to be trusted?" The younger man retorted, and both of them laughed.

"Either way, the High Queen knew the Norycian prince as a child, so it probably won't be hard for that mage to trick her into believing he's her childhood friend." The older man's voice oozed with smugness. "You know how women are. Once she's out of the picture, it'll be easy to take out the High King. He's so devoted to her, it'll destroy him to think she betrayed him."

My stomach twisted in knots. Obviously, this was a memory of some kind, even if I couldn't sense Rhaegos's presence anywhere. These men had been wrong. But were they still around? Would I have to deal with them if I fought alongside Haldrek? They didn't seem like more than rank-and-file mages, even if their magic was strong. Still...

"Once Rorik is High King, the other two will be dead in short order. We'll be able to take our pick of what lands we want to rule over."

"Even with the other thegns who have aligned with Rorik?"

The older man scoffed again. "You think Rorik is going to let them keep their power? No. He knows they're weak and not loyal to him. Once he's High King, only those who are devoted to him will get power. People like us."

"People who were exiled..." the younger man muttered, casting up a thick magical cloud. "I will take Andrattür, then. Destroy the wench pretending to be in charge right now and her entire family."

I clenched my fist to hold back my anger, knowing this was from the past. Still, if these two men were still alive...

Movement from the corner of my left eye caught my attention. Someone—or something—moved quietly within the shadows of the cave, unbeknownst to the two battle mages. I watched as a man in tattered Lohikärran robes snuck up behind the two men.

A very familiar man.

I gaped as Henry took a blade and quickly slit the older man's throat before going after the younger man. Despite the magic the younger man had been casting, Henry quickly subdued him as well. With another quick attack, both men were dead, lying in a pool of their own blood. Their spirits rose up behind him and, though they tried to attack Henry, he was oblivious.

"Ugh. If these men weren't such awful bastards, I'd feel bad about what I just did."

There was a pause, as if he was waiting for a response, then his shoulders slackened as if he'd been chastised.

"I know. The fewer followers Rorik has at his beck and call, the better, but it's still not pleasant to kill people."

More silence and I frowned. It almost seemed like Henry was speaking to an invisible person, or even a dragon, had he been a haldraga.

He wasn't a haldraga, right?

"Remind me how to get rid of them permanently, again." Pause. "Please?" Another pause. "I know I should be memorizing this."

Henry pulled his shoulders up and raised his hands to the air like he was about to perform one of the death rites.

"*Tenelth, Lohikarras første drage.*" He paused and the ghosts stopped their attacks, instead stepping away from Henry as if afraid. "*Hastighet denne sjelen. Vanære i liv og død. Til Lyrroths ytre bunnfall.*"

I looked over at the spirits of the two men as they twisted around, unwilling to submit to the death rite Henry had just cast over them. But it was too late. Within moments, they had disappeared, taken to Lyrroth for the rest of time.

A grunt interrupted my shock. I turned to see Henry rolling one of the bodies off the side of the cliff. I winced as I heard it thud below.

"Even if they were worthless in life, maybe their bodies can make good fertilizer for this place." He pushed the other body off the edge and wiped his hands on his tunic before glancing back at the cave. "Let's go. I have no intention of ever returning to that place again."

Henry jogged past me down the path, ignorant of my existence. As soon as he passed the spot where I knelt, the dream faded out and I opened my eyes to the inside of my bed. It was still dark, even with the faint lines of light from between the bed curtains. Next to me, Eero continued to sleep. His little snore soothed me.

Rhaegos?

Yes, little one? Her voice was soft, and my body relaxed, knowing I was safe.

What did I just see?

There was a rustling around in the back of my mind, and I got the impression Rhaegos had been unaware of my dream. However, she didn't seem too alarmed. In fact, she seemed amused.

It seems one of my kin wished for you to see a memory of hers. I do not fault her for that. Especially since the knowledge she gave you may very well be instrumental in Rorik's downfall.

I fell back asleep soon after that dream. Though no more visions came to me, my sleep was fitful as my mind raced to figure out everything Rhaegos's kin might have been telling me. When I finally woke up to Eero's hungry fussing, I felt like I hadn't slept at all.

I snuggled him for a moment and then, as I passed him over to the wet nurse for feeding, my pendant grew warm.

Flipping it open, I smiled tiredly at Haldrek. He looked much more awake than I did. Still, I was happy to see him.

"Good morning, *mine drawing*."

"Good morning." I yawned. "One of Rhaegos's kin kept me up last night."

Haldrek frowned in confusion, and I could hear people's voices in the background.

"I had another dream. About Etelaranikä." I hesitated to say more, knowing Haldrek probably wouldn't be happy to hear I'd seen Henry in my dream.

Tell him my kin showed you those who are actively fighting against Rorik in Etelaranikä. And cutting down his followers.

"What kind of dream? If it was one of Rhaegos's kin who was speaking to you, it probably wasn't a nightmare, was it?"

I shook my head. "They showed me a valley in Etelaranikä with steep cliffs on either side and a small settlement of farmhouses with bright red roofs. On one side was a cave where Rorik's men were apparently staying. The dream was more focused on those who were fighting them."

"Who were fighting them?" Haldrek glanced up at someone outside of the pendant's view and gestured for something before turning back to me. "That valley sounds very familiar, but if it's the place that I'm thinking of, it's well within the territory Rorik controls."

I nodded. "The impression I got was the valley was mostly empty except for those who either followed Rorik or had been kidnapped by him. Also, the people fighting him."

"Local Etelaranikans?"

"I think so. No one—" I paused for a moment to choose my words carefully. "No one in identifiable armor, at least. I couldn't tell what land they were loyal to, but I assumed they were local. They seemed familiar with the area in my dream. And they were more than happy to kill any of Rorik's men who crossed them. There was also one person doing death rites for those they killed, sending Rorik's men to Lyrroth." I stopped, not wanting to seem like I was oversharing or hiding anything.

Haldrek nodded, and a smiled crossed his face. "That is good news. If someone was doing death rites, that means some of the abthanry have stayed strong against Rorik."

"I thought most of Etelaranikä was loyal to Ingrid?"

"Most are, but you know how gesiths can be about power and trying to ally themselves with whomever they think is winning."

"Of course. But are all of Etelaranikä's gesiths loyal to Rorik now?"

Haldrek shook his head. "It's an even split between him and Ingrid. Which is why I'm heading into Etelaranikä today. Aallotar and Gunner are with me, and we're going to start pushing Rorik back. I think it will go well." He tried to smile, but it looked half-hearted, as if he was trying to believe his own words. "The more battles we win in Etelaranikä, the easier it will be to persuade the gesiths to follow Ingrid and fight Rorik. Once that's done…"

"You can return home." I whispered, trying not to let my voice crack.

"I can return home. To you and to Eero. I miss you both terribly." Haldrek's voice was more confident in these words, and it hurt. I wanted him back myself. "How is he doing?"

"Good. Eating well, sleeping well. Being a baby. He's nursing now, otherwise I'd show him to you."

Haldrek's expression grew sadder. "Maybe I'll contact you once more before we ride into Etelaranikä. I do want to see him one more time."

"You won't be able to contact us once you're in Etelaranikä?" I frowned, unable to think of a reason why that could be.

"There is strange magic going on in Etelaranikä. Likely due to Rorik. Gunner rode across the border with some of his men yesterday and when he tried to contact me on his pendant, there was nothing."

"What do you mean? Like you didn't see him or…?"

"His pendant stopped doing anything. The magic wasn't gone, but it was suppressed. Once he returned to the Bragidrattür side, his pendant began working again."

That news worried me. Of course, it made sense that Rorik would cast some kind of magic to keep Etelaranikä isolated. Or as isolated as possible. That would be dangerous. Not many thegns and gesiths used their pendants in battle, but still, if something happened…

"Please promise me you won't do anything too heroic in Etelaranikä. I need a husband, not an epic saga, when everything is said and done."

Haldrek's expression lit up as he grinned. "I promise I will protect myself while in Etelaranikä. I have no intention of dying anytime soon."

"You've said that before, Haldrek."

"And am I still alive?"

I had to laugh softly at that, even it was to keep me from crying.

"Please be safe, Haldrek. Eero..." I stopped myself before completing the phrase.

His smile disappeared as he nodded. "Eero needs to know his father. I know. I refuse to let history repeat itself. While my childhood wasn't terrible, I don't want that for Eero. I want him to be raised by more than dragons and servants. As it is, Teminth has promised me I will defeat Rorik and return to Drattüjert alive." He kissed the glass on the pendant. "I love you, Ina. I will be home soon. I promise."

"I love you too." My throat tightened up as I tried not to cry. My mind went blank as I tried to think of something, anything, to keep our conversation going. Even a few more minutes. Just as I opened my mouth to say something, anything, someone pulled the bed curtains open and the wet nurse handed me Eero.

"I overheard the two of you talking, and he finished feeding just a moment ago."

I smiled at her with gratitude and maneuvered my pendant so Haldrek could see Eero as he rested in my lap. The swaddling clothes were loose and Eero kicked at them, sending part of the linen up with every kick. The dragon charm bracelet was still firmly on his arm as he waved his hand around for a moment.

Haldrek chuckled softly. "He's growing so fast. All the more reason to deal with Rorik and return home victorious."

I turned the pendant back to me and whispered, "Come home safe. I know you will, but still... come home safe."

"I will. I promise." He kissed the pendant once more and said, "I need to go now. As soon as this is over and I can use my pendant again, I will contact you. I promise."

I nodded and without another word, my pendant went dark.

Chapter 13

The next few days were dreary, both weather-wise and in my head. Though Rhaegos comforted me from time to time, confirming Haldrek was still well, a heavy weight fell over me and I struggled to stay composed as I returned to my duties as High Queen. It'd been nearly six weeks since Eero's birth and even if my body was still healing, I knew I needed to start doing other tasks and showing my face more often. The fact that I'd stayed mostly on the upper floors, with the exception of a few trips to the library, wasn't lost on me or those who normally interacted with Haldrek and myself.

"Queen Ina?" I looked up from the fabric I'd been stitching, still haphazardly, but better than before, and saw Salla staring at me. She smiled gently, and I looked around to see the other hersirs had already left. I'd been in my head longer than I expected.

"Sorry..."

"It's all right. No one will blame you for being deep in your thoughts. There is a lot on your plate right now." She walked over and sat next to me. "Taimi told me you were worried about Haldrek and Eero?"

I laughed softly. "I'm always worried about them. Haldrek, especially now. I don't like not knowing what's going on when he's away. Rhaegos keeps telling me he's fine, but I still worry."

"Of course. Because you love him. You love both of your boys. Just like I did. Well, I still love them both, even if my husband is now in Mirroth." She rubbed my shoulder as tears streamed down my face.

"I wish there was more I could do. I wish I could be a dragon and just snap up Rorik like a snack so he'd stop bothering everyone."

Salla laughed. "Don't we all? Even though he was a good enough child when he was little, his father's actions did nothing to help him."

"Gustav's machinations?"

Salla nodded. "Rorik always desperately wanted his father's attention and approval." A scowl crossed her face. "And all Gustav cared about was becoming High King when it was never his fate. He rotted the poor boy through and through."

I never thought of Rorik as a 'poor boy', especially after all he'd done to me and my loved ones, but I guessed no one ever started off evil.

"Do you think Eero could end up the same way?" The thought popped into my head, but I tried to push it away. I had enough to worry about.

Salla laughed, as if the idea was ridiculous. "By the dragons, I don't think so. He has two parents who are terribly devoted to him and even…" She paused, shaking her head. "Even if something happened to you and Haldrek, how many more people would be there to love him and teach him? No, if something happened to you and Haldrek, he would likely end up like Haldrek. With a community of family and dragons to watch over him."

"Didn't Rorik have those as well?"

Salla shook her head. "Not as much. I think Gustav's influence was more powerful than any love and devotion Ingrid or the others could give him."

I nodded. While I was grateful Eero likely wouldn't fall into the same trap as Rorik, I could see now why Salla referred to him as a 'poor boy'. Not that I could fully agree with her.

Salla nudged my arm. "Should we get something to eat? I think that may improve your mood. And perhaps some time to cuddle your lovely little boy. I know that always cheered my soul when it was feeling heavy."

I smiled at the thought. She was right. Food and baby snuggles would improve things. If Mattie was around, I could check on any other information she might have found. Even if I wasn't a dragon who could gobble Rorik up, I could still do my part.

That afternoon, I made my way into the library with Eero snuggled up to my chest. With everything going on, I tried to keep him near me when I could. Just as I expected, Mattie was at a table surrounded by enough books and scrolls to nearly hide her. In the corner, I heard giggling and Llamryl's voice softly reciting something in Lohikärran.

"I didn't know we had children's books here in the library."

Mattie looked up at me, then at Llamryl and Geirny.

"I don't think he's actually reading what's written in that book. She grabbed it when we came in here and refused to let go. So he scooped her up and started reading it. I saw the title, and it's something related to economic treaties from a few hundred years ago."

I laughed and glanced over at Llamryl and Geirny again. The image of Haldrek doing that with one of our children crossed my mind. Would that ever happen? I could see

Haldrek doing it if we had some free time, but would we? Would there be a time when we weren't fighting someone?

"Ina?"

I turned back to Mattie. "Sorry. I've been lost in my thoughts a lot today."

"That's understandable. Did you come in here for something or...?"

"I just wanted to see how things were going. If there was any other information you'd found about Bjornulf, Freya, Ryluth, or any of that stuff. Even if I can't directly talk to Haldrek, maybe something worth sending a messenger?"

Eero squirmed a little against my chest, so I began rocking back and forth.

"Nothing specifically about Bjornulf and Freya. At least nothing confirming Paavo's story. Not that I think he's lying. Sivath has said as much, but there aren't any written records of Freya's actions that day. Just that Bjornulf slew Ryluth, and she 'fought beside him'." Mattie leaned back and sighed. "That said, I found something that might be of interest. Though I don't know how it would help you or Haldrek defeat Rorik."

"What is it?"

"A few references to the 'Heir of Ryluth'. Rorik mentioned that as his title now, didn't he?"

I nodded. "What about this Heir of Ryluth? Was it a specific person or just a title?"

"Both. Apparently Freya had a half-brother, whose true father was Ryluth."

"Wait. What?"

Rhaegos's presence shifted around in the back of my mind and I could feel her annoyance. Apparently, she knew who this person was.

Ryluth has always been willing to strike deals with whomever he believes will further his grasps for power. Freya's mother was one such individual. She wanted a child to ensure her power and Ryluth gave it to her in exchange for receiving Freya as one of his so-called brides.

"He was the literal and metaphorical heir of Ryluth. Offspring to subjugate the humans. Just as Ryluth's other offspring did with other sentient races." Mattie's voice faded as she hunched back over, reading something. "Freya's brother was basically the anti-Bjornulf. Sivath told me both Freya and Bjornulf had to fight him as well in order to kill him. It was the first time the two of them fought side by side and it was a blow to Ryluth."

"Wait. Ryluth cared about one of his offspring?"

Rhaegos huffed in derision, and Mattie shook her head. "No. When this Heir of Ryluth was conceived, some of Ryluth's magic became part of him. Sivath said, because of the curse Ryluth put on Freya, he also drained some of his magic. He didn't so much care about his 'heir' or Freya as much as regaining his power and then some. When Freya's curse was broken, and when she and Bjornulf killed her half-brother, some of Ryluth's power was also destroyed."

"That makes more sense." I paused for a moment, thinking about Rorik. "If the original Heir of Ryluth was Freya's half-brother and Rorik is now the new Heir of Ryluth, wouldn't that mean Rorik's half-sister would take on Freya's mantle? Or am I overthinking this?"

Mattie shrugged, but before she could say anything, Rhaegos rumbled in my head.

Freya's title as Heart of Lohikärra had less to do with her blood relations and more with her relationship to Lohikärra. Thorege—Freya's brother—wished to destroy the humans of this land, as does Rorik. Freya and Bjornulf as the Heart and Strength of Lohikärra devoted themselves to protecting those around them. Their titles, as such, are more symbolic.

"Apparently I am overthinking this... at least according to Rhaegos."

"What did she say?"

"The titles of Heart of Lohikärra and Strength of Lohikärra are symbolic. It had more to do with Bjornulf's and Freya's positions within Lohikärra. They were the ones protecting it from Ryluth and his heir."

Mattie's eyes widened. "That would make you and Haldrek the modern versions of Bjornulf and Freya. You two are the Heart and Strength of Lohikärra."

Her words hit me hard enough that I had to sit down. If that was the case... I needed to fight beside Haldrek to defeat Rorik and Ryluth. Eero began to fuss against me as I whispered, "Shit."

Rhaegos didn't confirm my conclusion, but she didn't deny it either. I spent that night and the next day mulling over the new information and how I could use it to help Haldrek. While I did want to fight beside Haldrek, the thought of leaving Eero was terrifying. I knew he'd be safe, whether he was with the nursemaids, Mattie, or the dragons, but part of me didn't want to leave him. He was still so young, still a baby. What happened if both Haldrek and I got killed? The thoughts went round and round in my head. Even if logically, I knew at least one of us would be safe, I still felt anxious about leaving.

So I tried to focus on other things. I tried to focus on the problems of Drattüjert. Tending to the High Queen's Home and arranging for any supplies they might need. Anything that felt easy to fix and kept my mind off Rorik and his machinations.

Apparently, that wasn't in my future today.

As I was talking to one of the Priestesses of Tenelth in the High Queen's Home, a servant came barreling in, eyes wide with panic. He stumbled to the ground, landing on one knee and bowing his head before both of us.

"My queen! Senja demands your presence! It's urgent." He gasped for air, and fear flooded through me. Senja never demanded anything.

"I'll go. Where is she?"

"With the Lady Sibila. In her quarters."

I hurried out, not waiting for the servant. By the time I reached the hall where all the hersirs' quarters were kept, I was met with loud, painful screams. A few servants and other hersirs stood frozen, watching Sibila's door.

What in the name of the dragons was going on?

I ran inside to see Sibila pinned to the bed by Paavo and Senja. Her body twisted back and forth in a way that made me cringe. More unsettling was the voice projecting from her mouth. It wasn't Sibila's voice, but a man's voice. It was furious, speaking in a language I'd never heard before.

Sibila stopped twisting for a moment, her body collapsing on the bed like a rag doll. Paavo still gripped her arms and, though I couldn't see his face, his tone told me he was as angry as whatever was possessing Sibila right now.

"You have no claim on this woman's soul. Leave now."

The masculine voice barked out a laugh. "My heir gave her soul to me, and I shall take it, you pathetic runt. Who are you to fight me?" Sibila's body arched upward as she gasped in pain. The voice continued, "I will take what is mine and rain destruction over all your pathetic humans."

Sibila's body twisted once more and a pop sounded from her shoulder. This time, she shrieked and started whimpering in pain.

"Senja?" I whispered, not knowing how to insert myself into this scene.

Senja turned to me and exhaled with relief. "Please. I need your necklace. Just for a moment."

Sibila's body twisted again, and she choked out another anguished cry. I quickly undid the dragon ring necklace and handed it to Senja.

Immediately, she pressed the ring into Sibila's throat. "Leave now, Ryluth."

The male voice screamed in agony as Sibila's body lurched away from Paavo and swung its legs around to hit Senja. She grimaced and repeated herself. "Leave now, Ryluth."

This time, the male voice grumbled in anger, and Sibila's body flopped onto the bed. We stayed frozen for a moment before Senja leaned down, pressing her ear against Sibila's chest.

"She lives. Both she and her dragon survived, but just barely." Sitting back up, Senja cupped Sibila's face as Paavo popped her arm back into place. Sibila whimpered, her eyes still closed. Senja leaned in until their foreheads were touching and whispered something I didn't understand. Sibila relaxed and I exhaled, sensing the tension in the room evaporate.

After a moment, Senja sat back up and turned to me.

"Thank you, Ina, for coming so quickly. You continue to rise up to your name and title." She handed me the dragon ring necklace. "This ring seems to be of more use than any of us expected."

As I took the necklace back and tied it around my neck, I asked, "What happened here? Did...?" I didn't want to say the words I was thinking. Had Ryluth really possessed Sibila's body? How?

"It is as you believe, Queen Ina." Paavo's voice was gravelly and more tired than I'd ever heard him. "Ryluth was trying to consume Sibila's soul to gain more power." Paavo glanced at Senja's grim expression for a moment before focusing on me. "I believe Rorik offered it to him."

"But how? Has this ever happened before? Didn't Ryluth eat his victims in the past? I thought..."

Paavo nodded. "For him to try to consume a soul that isn't physically within his reach is a new trick I've never seen or heard of. The fact that he was strong enough to try it worries me."

"Are we all in danger now?" My mind immediately went from how many people there were in the palace, to how many people there were in the city, to how many people were in Lohikärra. If Rorik could just offer up someone else's soul, what would keep him from doing that to anyone and everyone?

Paavo shook his head and pointed to my dragon ring necklace. "For those with baubles blessed by the dragons, they should be protected. Otherwise..."

"Didn't Sibila have her bracelet on? I remember Senja blessing it at some point."

Paavo frowned and Senja pulled back the sleeves of Sibila's dress. There was nothing on either wrist.

"Did she forget to put it back on?" Senja moved swiftly to a wardrobe and began searching it as Paavo pulled his attention back to me.

"Baubles blessed by us dragons may provide some defense. However, we all know Rorik is not one to give up."

"So he will go after others?" My throat tightened. I'd be safe, Eero would be safe, possibly Haldrek and any other haldraga, but I doubted most of Lohikärra had anything blessed by the dragons.

Senja hurried back to Sibila and put the bracelet on her arm. Nothing changed, but both dragons relaxed slightly.

"So Rorik will go after others now? Even if he physically can't reach them?" I tried to hide the panic in my voice. My family and loved ones might be safe, but what about others?

Senja looked at Paavo for a few minutes before he nodded. Then she looked at me.

"He will try. And he may succeed. However, if we are lucky, he will only try on those he has a connection to."

"I believe," Paavo ducked his head down and a sense of tiredness emanated from him, "he can only offer up the souls of people he knows. It would be mightily difficult for him to offer up a random person. However, that is my belief. It isn't something I know."

I nodded, my heart heavy. How I wished I could talk to Haldrek right now. Let him know what was going on.

Rhaegos?

No need to ask, little one. Her voice sounded as tired as Paavo's. *We dragons know what tricks Rorik is up to. Haldrek is safe and Teminth has already warned him of this recent development.*

Thank you, Rhaegos. I tried to emphasize my sense of gratitude and she seemed pleased. I looked back at Sibila. She was still resting, and even though she was pale, she looked peaceful.

"Let me know if there is anything else I need to do to help. Otherwise, I'm going to see what I can do to protect, or at least inform, others here in the palace." I thought back to the High Queen's Home. How many people there had interacted with Rorik at some point? They would need dragon-blessed baubles, or at least the priestesses would, if they didn't already have them.

Paavo and Senja nodded and stayed by Sibila's side. Without another word, I hurried out of the room.

Chapter 14

I spent the rest of the day doing what I could to protect those in the palace, even if they didn't know it. Thankfully, the priestesses of Tenelth already had multiple dragon-blessed items between them. They quickly agreed to always have one around, especially with the Etelaranikän refugees, just in case. I was relieved to hear both Mattie and Llamryl had been gifted dragon-blessed rings once they were married.

By the time I went to bed, I was exhausted. Physically, mentally, and emotionally. I curled up next to Eero's basket and passed out, looking forward to a deep, dreamless slumber.

As soon as I closed my eyes, however, I sensed I was somewhere different. Some place more ominous and foreboding. I reached out for Rhaegos, only to feel a stiff barrier wrapping itself around my mind. Panic started to swell and I did my best to tamp down the feeling. If I was back in Rorik's realm, I'd fight him. Even if I didn't have any kind of weapon on me, I could still use magic.

Ominous laughter filled my mind, and it sounded like the voice that had come out of Sibila earlier.

Ryluth. My insides tightened with anger.

The laughter continued until the voice spoke.

You aren't as stupid as Rorik made you out to be. Not so good for him, but wonderful for me.

What the hell?

I don't know what this 'hell' place you speak of is, but I can smell your disbelief and terror. Ryluth made a gleeful laugh. *I can smell Freya's blood running through your body. Which means you belong to me, just as she belonged to me.*

Despite the fact that I couldn't see anything, I sensed something coming toward me and pulled my left shoulder back as something shot past, leaving a cold, rotting smell in its wake.

Rhaegos? I hoped she was near enough to hear me.

That pathetic, back-stabbing wretch cannot save you here. I have more than enough power to lock her out and destroy you, if I wish.

I ducked down as the smell of death and decay rushed over me. Even Ottkatla's Barrow didn't smell as terrible as this realm did. I fought back the urge to vomit and tried to think of what I could do to protect myself. Would magic have any effect on Ryluth here? If it did, what kind of magic could I use? What had Freya used to fight Ryluth?

My hand slipped down my side, and it comforted me to feel my armor. At least I had that. As my hand hit my belt, I felt something different hanging from it. My sword sheath was gone, but in its place was... an axe? I felt my other side and there was another axe on my other hip.

As handy as those were, I hadn't really trained with axes. If and when I got out of this realm, I'd have to remedy that.

Pulling the right one out, I tried to sense Ryluth in the darkness. His smell was still here, permeating everything, so I couldn't tell if he was near or far. Whether this was Rorik's realm or another one, my sense of positioning was off. There was nothing to tell me if I was in a massive hall or a small room.

Something creaked near me and I ducked again, the snap of dragon's teeth echoing above me.

You are quick, little one. All the better. I will relish my victory when I crunch on your bones.

The axe in my hand felt slightly warmer, and a quick jolt of confidence rushed through me.

"Only if you can catch me." I darted forward, praying Ryluth was still behind me, and tossed an orb of light up and away. I imagined it hitting some kind of ceiling and splattering all over it, leaving some kind of lighted residue.

Sure enough, it hit something and cast a dim light over a part of the space. Enough to keep me from colliding with a massive, scaled tail.

You think you are so clever. But if you can see me, then I can definitely see you.

The tail swung around, knocking me to my knees with a painful grunt. The axe smashed into my fingers as I swore in pain.

Ryluth said nothing, but his laughter rang out inside my skull. Irritated, I spun around and stuck the point of the axe into the tip of his tail. A howl echoed throughout the chamber, and I went flying again as he swished his tail. My hand let go of the axe and I rolled to a stop on my back, the dim light of my previous spell casting shadows on a hulking creature. Anger and pain radiated from the dragon and I thought I saw a wing riddled with holes.

Before I could blink, it flashed over me and I flinched, rolling to my side. Something bony scratched against my armor and I shuddered, the image of one of Ryluth's claws searing itself into my mind.

The tinkling of metal on stone made me open my eyes, and I saw the axe I'd swung into Ryluth's tail skitter toward me.

You think you can defeat me with your pathetic human weapons? I will rip you limb from limb and feast on your screams.

As I grabbed for the axe again, a thought popped into my head. *How dramatic.*

You think me dramatic? Ryluth swung his tail around and I jumped, swinging the axe into his tail as it flashed under me. I was rewarded with another howl as I rolled away from Ryluth's tail, trying to imagine where he was in this darkness. *I speak of nothing I haven't done in the past and that I won't do in the future.*

An image seared itself into my mind of Haldrek in battle with Ryluth. Ryluth's mouth gaped open, revealing more rotted flesh and bones sticking out from between his teeth. Haldrek cried out in pain as Ryluth's jaws snapped around him. Fear and agony swept over me as the dragon consumed him, and then looked around. Other loved ones popped into my vision: Mattie, Llamryl, Geirny, Taimi, Salla, Sibila, and finally, a basket with a baby crying in it. Instantly, I knew who was in the basket. *Eero.*

Ryluth opened his mouth and dove to gobble all of them up. I wanted to scream, but instead, I opened my eyes as the smell of death hit my face. I swung one hand axe as hard as I could while pulling the other one out.

Ryluth howled again as I began pelting him with blows from both axes. Much to my surprise, he pulled back. I jumped forward, continuing to swing the axes and feeling a satisfying crack every time they hit a scale.

Enough! A gust of wind smelling like death and decay hit me and I flew back, my helmeted head hitting the ground with a thud. Some unseen force pulled the axes from my grip as it pinned me to the ground.

You think you are so mighty? You think you can defeat a dragon? Then come fight me and my Heir yourself. I welcome the challenge.

I hesitated, trying to gather my breath and my thoughts before responding. Apparently Ryluth took this to be fear.

If you don't, I will kill your loved ones before you. Every single one.

He pulled back his head and lunged for me, mouth wide open as I flinched, unable to defend myself. Just as he was about to bite, everything disappeared and I was back in my bed, arms and legs curled up in a defensive position.

It took me a moment to register the sounds around me. The screaming next to me. But as soon as my mind was clear of the nightmare with Ryluth, I heard everything.

Spinning around, I pulled Eero from his basket. He squirmed back and forth, his entire face red as he howled.

I tried to soothe him as I laid him between my legs and on top of the woolen blanket. Pulling the swaddle cloths away, I saw something staining them red.

"Eero?" My voice pitched with panic as I yanked the remaining fabric from him. Underneath his bindings, something had scratched a large 'X' into his chest.

"By the dragons." The words were soft, but jerked my attention to the nursemaid who had pulled my bed curtains open. The light from outside was dim, so I knew it was early still.

"Go get Thegn Andrattür and the dragons. Now!"

The woman disappeared, and I examined the cuts on Eero's chest. They weren't deep, but they were more than the scratches from before. While the bleeding had stopped, the cuts still looked painful and raw. I gently covered Eero's chest and pulled him up to mine, hoping I could soothe him further. He wriggled his arms against me and I saw the bracelet. That made everything worse. While there was some pink around it, it looked like whatever magic had attacked him had overwhelmed Senja, Paavo, and even Rhaegos's magic.

Rhaegos.

Rhaegos? Even my mind's voice was choked up with fear.

I am here, little one. Ryluth played a dirty trick on us all. If he was able to get through the magic barriers of three dragons, then our time to defeat him and Rorik is quickly fading.

Icy fear slid down my back and tightened within my chest. Of course, the one person I really wanted to talk to, I couldn't right now.

I know you all aren't messengers, but... I hated to ask Rhaegos to check in on Haldrek or let Teminth know what was going on.

Teminth is aware. He refrains from telling Haldrek more than he can bear, though. Even though he grows in wisdom, Haldrek's weakness is yours and Eero's safety. Teminth fears he might do something rash if he knew the extent of Ryluth's attacks.

I didn't know whether to take comfort in that.

Footsteps clattered through the antechamber before the bedroom door squeaked open. Within moments, Mattie's face popped through the bed curtains.

"What's going on? The nursemaid was in a panic, saying something had attacked Eero."

I pulled open the swaddling cloths, revealing the large 'X' on Eero's chest.

"Does he still…" Mattie's voice faded as she spotted the bracelet. "By the dragons. What happened, Ina?"

"Ryluth attacked me, and Eero as well." My voice was low as I tried to keep my composure. "I had a nightmare. Ryluth…he pulled me into some realm and fought me. He told me if I didn't come and fight him myself, he would destroy my loved ones." Those words echoed in my mind, and I shuddered. "I don't know what progress Haldrek has made, but it's not enough. I need to fight Ryluth. And Rorik. The longer I wait, the more powerful they will grow and the more danger they will be to everyone. Not just here in the palace, but across Lohikärra. You remember what he tried with Sibila."

Mattie nodded, but said nothing as more footsteps made their way into the bedroom. Senja and Paavo popped into view, their eyes widening as they stared at the scratches on Eero's chest. One of the nursemaids ducked into the crowd, carrying a basket full of what I hoped were balms and bandages.

"Did he have his charm on?" Senja turned her focus back to me.

I nodded. "This all happened while we were sleeping. Ryluth pulled me into another realm…I don't know if it was his or Rorik's, but he was threatening me, then attacked me. I was just telling Mattie that he said if I didn't come and fight him myself, he would destroy my loved ones."

Paavo's expression darkened as he glanced at Senja. She shook her head, and he turned back to me. "This mark is a warning. The fact that he was able to break through the magic of three dragons and from some distance… He did this to push you into a fight."

"Well, it's fucking working." I snapped, my fear and anger coming to a head. Paavo raised one of his eyebrows in surprise and Senja grabbed his arm. "I can't contact Haldrek because of the magic Rorik cast, making the pendants not work. I can't even sleep without him or Ryluth attacking me or the people I love." Turning to Senja, I pleaded, "You said you might be able to help me heal faster? It's been six weeks since Eero was born. I want to take the fight to Ryluth and Rorik. Put them on the defensive."

"You can't fight a dragon alone, Ina." Paavo hesitated for a moment. "I say this with all due respect to Rhaegos. Even with her strength aiding you, Ryluth and Rorik are powerful foes."

Indignation welled up inside of me as Eero whimpered in pain.

"Then what the hell am I supposed to do, Paavo? Watch helplessly as an undead dragon and necromancer destroy my family and friends? Faint from fear and hope my own death isn't so terrible?"

Paavo's expression darkened further with irritation as the air in the room grew heavy. The nursemaid paused and even Mattie stepped back. But I was done with waiting, with being passive. I stood up, not scared by Paavo's emotions. He was nowhere as scary as Ryluth had been last night.

Relax, little one. Though Paavo's wisdom is limited by his life cycles, he is indeed trying to help.

"I can't relax when I see my loved ones being hurt." Looking over at Eero, I couldn't help but see fear and helplessness in his expression. I knew what that felt like. There was nothing I wouldn't do to protect Eero—or anyone else I loved—from the same. I turned back to Paavo, ignoring his irritation. "Look, I know you are trying to help. Rhaegos has told me as much. But I can't just sit around and wait. And I have no intention of fighting Ryluth or Rorik alone." I stopped as the puzzle pieces from the last few weeks began to come together.

"Ina?" Mattie frowned and I turned to her.

"Bjornulf and Freya. When they fought the Heir of Ryluth and then Ryluth himself. Both times it was together. They had to work together. Neither of them could fight those enemies alone."

"Yeah?"

"What if Haldrek and I have to fight Ryluth and Rorik together? What if the attacks in Bragidrattür weren't just to kidnap fighters for Rorik and 'brides' for Ryluth? What if those attacks are also distractions used to pull Haldrek in the wrong direction and keep him from really doing anything?"

Mattie nodded. "That makes a lot of sense, strategically. If you go out to Etelaranikä, your plan is to meet up with Haldrek?"

"Yeah. I mean..." Another thought popped into my head and I looked back at Senja and Paavo. "What were the weapons Freya used to kill Ryluth? That went through dragon scale?"

"Hand axes." Paavo's irritation had disappeared. "Made specifically for cutting through dragon scale."

Senja looked between me and Paavo. "Are you wanting to fight with something like that?"

I nodded. "Last night, I had some on my body. When I went after Ryluth with them, they actually hurt him. But I'd never seen them before."

A rare smile crossed Paavo's face. "That's because Freya's hand axes were never handed down. She kept them here in Drattüjert until her dying day."

"So they're still here?"

Senja shrugged. "I don't see why they wouldn't be. No one has ever needed to use them, so I don't know if they're still here in the palace armory or elsewhere."

I nodded as my brain began formulating a plan. I couldn't stay here much longer. As much as I was loathe to leave Eero, confronting Rorik and Ryluth was the only way to keep him safe.

"Do you wish to wield those hand axes?"

"If they are still around. I'm going to use anything and everything I can to defeat Ryluth."

Paavo took a deep breath and sighed before looking at Senja. "Then let's go find those hand axes. If Ryluth and Rorik are to be defeated, time is of the essence."

Chapter 15

Later that day, I found myself dressed in my thegn armor and making sure I had everything I needed. Anxiety washed over me and part of me wanted to stay at the palace. Stay close to Eero and pretend Rorik and Ryluth were simple foes Haldrek could defeat alone.

But I also knew we were far past that.

Despite Senja's and Paavo's initial hesitation with my plan, they helped me prepare. Senja used some of her magic to help strengthen and heal my body for the journey ahead. Paavo found Freya's hand axes and brought them to me, along with a brief lesson on how to use them and where they'd be most lethal on a dragon. He also promised to travel with me—in his dragon form—to the edge of Etelaranikä and ensure my safety.

Still, as I patted my hips, feeling both of Freya's axes, as well as my thegn sword on my back, I couldn't help but worry I still wasn't prepared enough. I blinked back tears and turned to check on Eero once more. Mattie held him in her arms as he slept, and I wondered if this was how Haldrek had felt when he left for Bragidrattür.

"I'm going to miss him." My voice squeaked, and I coughed to hide the sound.

"Hopefully, you'll be back soon. I was thinking about the second prophecy, and I think you and Haldrek fulfill it. Between the two of you, you're both the heirs of Bjornulf and Freya, as well as 'outsiders'. At least you fulfill the 'outsider' part."

"Because I'm from a different realm?"

Mattie nodded. "I think it could be translated that way. If that's the case, how many people from outside of Sethys are here in Lohikärra. You? Me?"

"Possibly Henry, if he's still alive."

Mattie nodded. "There hasn't been any information about him? At least recently?"

I shook my head. "Not that I think he was considered a huge lead or someone to worry about. At least not in Haldrek's eyes."

"You two have had much to worry about in the last year or so." Llamryl hoisted Geirny into his arms. "When you killed the man masquerading as your friend Henry, most people thought nothing more of the situation."

"And yet I'm pretty sure he isn't dead. Not if the memories from Rhaegos and her kin are accurate."

"So you think Henry is still alive? In Etelaranikä?"

I shrugged. "I hope so. The memory I saw showed him fighting Rorik's men, so if he is, I think he'll be an ally. Either way, my first job is to find Haldrek and join up with him. Rhaegos has already said she'll help me find my way through the magic Rorik cast over Etelaranikä. If Haldrek and I find Henry after that, or even if I find Henry before I find Haldrek, so be it."

Mattie nodded, looking me over in my armor. "One last thing... Are you sure you want to head out by yourself? I know Paavo has said he will travel with you in his dragon form, but still..." Her grimace told me how concerned she was. To be honest, normally I would have loved to have a group of warriors with me. But I also knew it would make me more of a target than usual.

"People will take notice if I go marching into Etelaranikä with a band of warriors, and I won't know if those people will be loyal to Haldrek and myself or to Rorik. Plus, I want to travel as quickly as possible. The sooner Haldrek and I join up, the better."

"Aren't people going to notice your thegn armor?"

I nodded. "Probably. But I plan to wear a traveling cloak, so hopefully if I'm traveling fast enough, people won't pay attention. They'll think I'm some random warrior coming to fight. I'm also not going to be stopping in any villages or inns. This is all going to be as quiet and quick as possible." I knew it wasn't the greatest excuse, but it was what I had. Time was still of the essence.

Mattie sighed, saying nothing, and I gently took Eero from her arms. He squirmed a bit and settled back down, snoring. My heart broke at the idea of leaving him here.

"Is Haldrek going to be expecting you?" Llamryl's voice was soft, and I looked up.

"Rhaegos said Teminth would let him know when I was near. Until Rorik's magic is gone, none of the pendants will work."

I had checked mine before getting dressed, hoping I could quickly 'level up' and maybe get an extra edge over Rorik and Ryluth. Unfortunately, my pendant wasn't quite full. When—not if—I returned to the palace, it would definitely be full, several times over. Taking a deep breath, I gently kissed Eero's forehead, trying to keep my composure. Tears were already forming in my eyes and I didn't want to wake him with the crying I would inevitably do today.

"I love you, little one." My throat squeezed shut for a moment and I took another breath. "My dear little Eero. I'll be back soon. I promise. I'll come home when we're all safe. You, me, your father. We'll all be home. Together."

Handing Eero back to Mattie, my eyes were already blurry. Part of me was glad I was going alone. I didn't want too many people seeing me like this. Mattie and Llamryl were fine, but the people of Drattüjert needed to see Haldrek and me as tough and strong and... everything I wasn't feeling right now.

"Thank you, Mattie. I appreciate this. All of this." I glanced between her and Llamryl. "Both of you. I'm glad you're here. I... I don't know what I'd do if I was in a different situation. If you all weren't here. Thank you."

Mattie wrapped her free arm around me and tucked Eero into her chest as we embraced. Llamryl placed his hand on my shoulder as well.

"I'm glad we can be here to help. Just promise me you'll come back alive and in one piece. Okay?"

I nodded. "I have no intention of dying by Rorik or Ryluth's hand—or claw. When this is all said and done, Haldrek and I will be back. Lohikärra will finally have peace."

It felt strange traveling by myself as I left Drattüjert. No one bothered me, so either they didn't know who I was, or they knew exactly who I was and didn't dare question me.

I didn't know which was better.

Riding until nightfall and taking the main road east, then south, I soon found a clearing and with Paavo's help, I made a small campfire, ate, and slept.

It was that way for a few days until I was at the edge of Etelaranikä. After letting Mattie know where I was and bidding Paavo farewell, I made my way into the thegn land.

Despite knowing what lay ahead, I was surprised by how beautiful Etelaranikä actually was in the late summer.

There is a reason many people have fought to live and rule over this land.

"Yeah. It's a shame you-know-who is doing you-know-what." I looked around, not seeing anyone, but realizing too late Rorik could have spies waiting here in the forest for me.

There is no one around, little one. And you know you can speak to me in your mind. Rhaegos's light laughter told me she was teasing me. I was glad for that. If she was in a mood to tease, it meant I could relax, at least slightly. Still, staying quiet was probably the best course of action.

What direction should I go to find Haldrek? I sat in front of a fork in the road, having no idea which was the better path.

Either will take you to him at this point. He is near the heart of Etelaranikä.

I thought for a moment, going back to the dreams and memories I'd had of that village in the middle of this thegn land.

Rhaegos? That valley I saw? Which path would take me there?

You wish to fight Rorik yourself?

No. But if the valley is between me and Haldrek... It might be worth the time to scout it out. Unless it's too dangerous?

Rhaegos laughed. *The valley is safe for now. As long as you don't go into the caves, you will be fine.* She paused. *Take the left one if you wish to scout the valley. It will not add much time to your journey.*

I nudged my horse and took the path to the left.

It was nearly dark by the time the trees thinned out and I found myself at the edge of the valley. Though it didn't look exactly like the valley from my dreams, in my gut I knew this was the place.

Unfortunately, it looks like you will have to camp here for the night. But one of those farmhouses may work.

Do you think any of Rorik's men are in them? I feel like those would be the perfect place to take over.

Rhaegos stayed silent for a moment, and as I was about to speak again, her presence rustled in the back of my mind.

I don't sense anyone with a connection to Ryluth in the valley, though I can sense one of my kin in the farmhouses.

Another dragon?

Yes. Specifically, one who has bound themselves to a haldraga. I'm curious. There is no danger for now, but my kin is ailing more than normal.

That was a surprise. I urged my horse through the dim twilight. With Rhaegos's help, I was able to make out the few farmhouses and guide myself to the dragon or haldraga. Much to my surprise, when Rhaegos nudged me to stop, I didn't see the bluish light that would denote a spirit from the Realm of Ghosts.

Here?

Yes. My kin is inside.

I got off my horse and slipped a small blade from my boot, just for defense. There may have been an injured haldraga inside, but I didn't know who else might be hiding.

There is no one else in the farmhouse, but if the haldraga is near death, they may try to fight.

That made me feel slightly better. I gently touched the doorknob, keeping tension on it to stay as quiet as possible. Much to my surprise, there was no lock engaged, and the door was already ajar.

As I opened it further, a deep groan came from the person inside.

Syralgos? Rhaegos's tone was one of deep confusion.

"I'll fight you! I'm stronger than you think!" The familiar voice hit me hard.

I cast an orb of magic at the ceiling, lighting the room up as I stepped inside and shut the door.

"Henry?"

Laying on the floor in front of me, Henry looked like he'd just gotten his butt kicked. Blood and dirt covered his now scruffy face and at least one of his eyes had been freshly injured. The other one was bruised, but healing.

"Ina? What the hell are you doing here?" He stared at me for a moment through his better eye and then at the orb of light. "Are you..." He groaned and slumped back. "Syralgos says you aren't with Rorik. Good."

"Is Syralgos...?"

"My... the dragon who bonded with me. Like in the games." Henry sighed in pain. "Do you have any medicine? Or healing powers?"

I grimaced. Mattie had taught me a couple of spells, but nothing more than could cure a headache. "I can try something Mattie taught me. I don't know how well it'll work."

"Mattie's here too?" His good eye widened.

I nodded as I knelt by his side. "Her dad was the Thegn of Andrattür, and now she is."

A grin lit up Henry's face. "Cool." He closed his eyes as I raised my hands over him and tried to imagine his aches and pain fading away. A power much stronger than my own coursed through me.

Thank you, Rhaegos.

It's best to help allies in their time of need.

After a moment the power ceased, and Henry rolled to his side. Sitting up, he pulled himself to the nearby wall and leaned against it.

"Thank you. You're a sight for sore eyes."

"It's been a while since I've seen you. At least..." The imposter came back to mind, and I sighed. This was going to be awkward. I pull my cloak off my shoulder, revealing the hilt of Freya's Menace. "Before we do anything else, I need to get this over with." Pulling the sword out, I heard a high-pitch squeak come from Henry.

"What the eff are you doing, Ina? I'm not your enemy! I promise!"

"I'm not trying to hurt you, Henry. Do you know what weapon this is?" I stopped walking toward him and tried to be as unaggressive as possible. Something I was already failing at.

"It's a fucking sword, Ina. What are you doing?"

"It's Freya's Menace. The Destroyer of Illusions. I need you to look into it."

"Look into it?" Henry looked between me and the sword. "What am I supposed to see?"

I frowned. "You, of all people, should remember. It was in the games."

Henry stared at me for a moment, his jaw dropping. "You have *the* Freya's Menace? That blade?"

"Are there any others?"

He shook his head. "Not that I know of. How'd you get it?"

"Rhaegos gave it to me. Soon after I arrived in Lohikärra." I knelt next to him and cast another orb of light just above us. Angling the blade in my hands, I saw Henry's reflection. The same Henry I'd known back in Fargo. I exhaled in relief and sheathed the blade.

"Did I pass the test?"

"Almost. One other question. Who are you attracted to? Guys or girls?"

Henry frowned. "Guys, duh. Why would...?" He grimaced. "Cass—Cassius—made it to Drattüjert, didn't he?"

I nodded. Before I could say anything, the sound of boots against gravel hit my ear, and I instantly got rid of the mage light.

"Hey, what's this horse doing here?"

My eyes widened, and I silently swore at myself.

Don't you worry, little one.

My horse neighed, and after a moment there were hoofbeats running off.

"Hey! Where is it going?" Footsteps faded away from the farmhouse. "C'mon! We need that horse!"

The men continued running after the horse, and after a few minutes of silence, I exhaled.

"That was close." Henry looked around me. "I'm guessing Rorik's men decided to come after me this time."

"I didn't see anyone when I was riding into the village, though."

He shrugged. "They might have already been in one of the other houses. Or they found the scum I got rid of and came after me. Don't know and don't care. Just glad they came after you found me."

I nodded. "Have you been staying in these houses while you've been fighting them?"

"Sometimes. I've been fighting Rorik ever since I arrived in Lohikärra. Not long after I arrived in," he gestured in the air around us, "Sethys." He shifted over to the fireplace, where a few embers were still alive. I followed him and gently stoked them with a few wisps of fire from my hand.

As the embers lit up and warmth emanated from the fireplace, Henry laughed. "Tell me, how freaked out were you when you arrived here? Because I was probably more scared than I had ever been in my life."

I laughed myself. "Pretty freaked out. I woke up in a cart, face down in someone's lap, tied up. When I sat up, it looked like the opening scene from the last Lohikärran game."

"Seriously?" Henry chuckled, and I felt a deep sense of calm wash over me. It reminded me of all the time we had spent playing the games. "I wonder how awkward it was for the person whose lap you landed in."

"Probably pretty awkward." I grinned in spite of myself. "Though I don't think he's too mad about it now."

"Why not?"

"Because we're married."

Henry rolled back as laughter boomed from him and he clamped his hands over his mouth. We both sat there silently for a few moments, listening, hoping for continued silence. When no sounds came, he relaxed.

"Sorry. Probably should be less jovial until we're in a safer place. Either way, congratulations. He's good to you?"

I nodded. "He even stood up to my mother at one point, after Rorik tossed us back into Fargo."

Henry grunted, sitting back up. "How did that go?"

"As expected. She tried to run him over with her car. Also, turns out Robert was from Lohikärra all along. Rorik's father sent him to keep tabs on me while I was growing up. I guess to see how much I could be used to manipulate my father."

"Huh." Henry shook his head, and his stomach grumbled. He stood up slowly. "There are still some provisions here. I'll grab them and we can trade more stories while we eat. It's been forever since we've had a chance to hang out. I miss those times."

I smiled as I turned back to the fire, willing it to grow a little more. "Same here."

Chapter 16

Henry and I talked well into the night, nibbling on whatever meat and vegetables he'd been able to scrounge in between fighting Rorik. The conversation was easy; it was as if we were just picking up from the last time we'd hung out. Completely different from when I'd been around the imposter. When I fell asleep that night, and while Henry took his turn watching for more of Rorik's followers, I rested easy.

In the morning, when I woke up, Henry was already up. Morning light peeked through the cracks in the shut-up windows.

"Morning, sleepyhead." Henry grinned impishly at me as he brought over a bowl of something that smelled good. I looked inside to find some broken up, mushy bread concoction.

"It's Etelaranikä bread. Rabbit meat and vegetables cooked inside of a loaf. This loaf was kinda dry and hard, so I added some water and tried to make it more edible." He grabbed a spoon from the fireplace's hearth and I started eating. The mash wasn't terrible, given the ingredients used to make it.

Once I finished, I gave him back the spoon and bowl and asked, "What did you have planned for today?" I knew I needed to find Haldrek, but I wondered if helping Henry wouldn't make things easier overall.

"The same thing I do every day; piss off the necro." Henry grinned, turning his attention away from the window. "I've been going after any fighters or mages I see coming out of the cave. Syralgos taught me the death rites, so I've been sending them to Lyrroth, too. That way Rorik has fewer followers and he can't reanimate any of them."

I grimaced, wondering if he knew about the raids into Bragidrattür. "Rorik is still kidnapping people. Sending fighters and lesser necromancers there to snatch people from their homes."

Henry grumbled. "I've been picking off everyone I've seen coming out of that damn cave, though."

"Caves usually have more than one entrance."

"Yeah, but I thought I got all the other ways in and out."

Remind him not all entrances may be of this realm.

"Rhaegos says Rorik could have other entrances through other realms. Which, given that he has at least one realm he can drag people into and torture..."

Henry groaned. "Duh. I should have thought of that. All the more reason to get rid of him. Are you ready?" He glanced out the window one more time, then held his hand out to me.

I nodded. "I should introduce you to Haldrek and the others who are fighting with him. Aallotar and Gunner. Then we could pool all our knowledge."

Henry nodded as we slipped out of the door and into the morning sunlight. "Haldrek is your husband, right? The guy whose lap you woke up in?" I gently jabbed Henry in the arm, and he chuckled. "That'll be a heck of a story to tell your kids one day. Still can't believe you and Mattie each have a kid. I guess things are different here."

I nodded. "Finding myself in Lohikärra and becoming its High Queen certainly wasn't something I expected in high school."

"I don't think any of our lives ended up the way we expected. For better or for worse." Henry's tone softened. As we'd talked the previous evening, he'd told me about everything that had happened after Mattie and I disappeared. Including how he and Alex had broken up. They'd stopped talking after Alex had gotten into his dream schools and Henry had barely gotten into the local community college. Not that his grades had been terrible, but Alex had gotten into a bunch of private schools where not even being the high school quarterback was impressive enough.

He'd told me about how his stepdad had been pissed off at him for not applying to other schools and how everything had fallen apart right before a big storm hit Fargo and his mother had decided it was the best time for the two of them to leave. At that point, their car had gottten destroyed by another car tumbling into them. When he'd woken up, he'd been chained up inside a Roman-style dungeon.

Needless to say, the last couple of years didn't sound exactly like fun for Henry.

"You're right about meeting up with Haldrek and his buddies. After those two fighters almost found us, I had a sinking suspicion they may have alerted others to people still living in the farmhouses down here. I don't want that. "

"Why not?" We'd slipped over to the bottom edge of the cliff, into a space where it was difficult to see the cave opening. However, that meant anyone coming out wouldn't see us either.

"For some reason, Rorik doesn't like his men squatting in those farmhouses. Still haven't figured out why. Maybe he doesn't trust them and wants to keep his cronies close?" Henry shrugged. "Either way, if he gets word that someone is down in the valley, he might start sending more of his thugs to investigate, and I don't want that. It's been nice having a spot to rest in when I finish for the day."

"Or when you're badly injured and need to hide?"

He laughed. "Or when I'm badly injured and need to hide." As we made our way up the path, he asked, "If you just had a kid, are you sure you're able to fight? I mean, I'm sure you're great and all, but..."

"It doesn't matter. I'm out here because if I don't do anything, Rorik and Ryluth will eventually kill the people I love. Including my son. I have to go after them. Even if it kills me."

Henry stopped and turned around. "If anyone should die from this ordeal, you're the last one who should." He winced. "You know what I mean. The only people, creatures, whatever, are Rorik and Ryluth. And maybe me. But I don't want to think about that." He continued climbing, and I followed him.

"What do you mean?"

"Lohikärra is in shambles because my parents decided to hook up and their parents took issue with that. If Lohikärra wasn't in shambles, do you think Rorik would have been able to do what he's done?"

"Yes. Even if there wasn't a war going on, Rorik's dad Gustav would have been plotting to take over the throne. So would plenty of other thegns. Plus, you're not responsible for your parents' actions. I doubt they got together with the idea of causing a war."

They didn't. The opposite, actually.

"Rhaegos said they were trying to create peace."

Henry grunted and kept walking into the cave. As I followed him, I grabbed for my sword, then thought better of it. Instead, I pulled out Freya's hand axes. If I was walking into a dragon's lair, might as well arm myself with the weapons to fight it.

"What is the plan anyway, Henry?"

"Find Rorik's thugs, kill them, wash and repeat."

"Do you plan on fighting Rorik at some point?"

"If I find him, yes. He's a sneaky bastard."

I opened my mouth, but stayed silent as footsteps echoed toward us. Henry pulled out his blade and stepped in front of me.

"Game time."

As the two men came around the corner, they stopped. Much to my surprise, Henry didn't immediately attack.

Instead, he laughed and said, "We meet again." Then, with a lunge, he went after them, swinging his sword back and forth while laughing. The men dodged his blows and began swinging at him. He spun around and started sparring with one man, leaving his back open.

It took me a moment to realize Henry wasn't that skilled of a fighter; he was just bigger and stronger than most people.

The other man's hand began to form an eerie green orb of light. I jumped out of the shadows and swung one of the hand axes at him, slicing clean through his arm above the wrist, and he howled. A quick swing of the other axe to his neck and he went silent, his ghost rising almost immediately before me.

"I thought you knew how to fight!"

"I do!" Henry shouted as he cut down his fighter with another blow. "Now we need—" Shouts coming toward us cut him off.

"Crap!" Even though we might be able to take them, I didn't want to spend the whole day fighting. If we were going to find Rorik or at least get information for Haldrek, we needed to do this more stealthily.

"We'll be fine! For Lohikärra!" Henry ran full speed into the group, swinging his sword and shield around like a maniac. This is how he kept getting hurt. I sighed and ran after him.

After a few minutes, the bodies were dead, but the spirits were still trying to fight us.

"What was that? Another half dozen of Rorik's thugs down?"

I nodded. Between this group and the other two, we'd killed about eight of Rorik's cronies in a matter of minutes, but we'd both taken a beating for it.

Henry sat down. "We need to send them to Lyrroth. Do you know how to do that?"

I nodded. "Of course." Taking a deep breath, I felt Rhaegos strengthen me as I began chanting. Even with her help, I was exhausted after only three.

"My turn?"

I nodded and sat down as Henry took my place and started chanting himself. Once he finished, he turned around. "We should probably do the other two so they don't turn into zombies." Taking my hand, he pulled me up.

"Promise me one thing."

"What?"

"After we send these last two to Lyrroth, we'll head back down to the village. If you're going to keep taking out Rorik's thugs, I need to show you a few things I've learned since being here." It was weird being the teacher for once, but if Henry was going to help, he needed more practice. I didn't want him to get killed.

Henry laughed, but it faded away in the dim light. "All right. Probably wouldn't hurt. Let's go then."

With that, I followed him back to the other two bodies.

It was midday by the time we got back down to the farmhouse. I rekindled the hearth embers as Henry rummaged for more foodstuffs. Once we were eating, he looked over at me.

"Sorry about this morning."

"What?" I'd been thinking about what I could teach Henry and how long it would take us to find Haldrek.

"I'm sorry. About this morning. I was being more stupid than normal." He ducked his head down between his arms. "I was trying to impress you. Again."

"Me?" I bit the inside of my lip to keep from laughing. This was serious to him and I didn't want to make light of that. But why try to impress me? Ever?

Henry nodded. "When we were kids, I wanted my friends to think I was a fantastic video game player, not just some newbie. Especially after Mattie arrived. I mean, her dad had created the video game series, so of course she'd know how to play. But I wanted to be really good at something I enjoyed. Now that I'm in the real Lohikärra, I want to be a badass, too. But I'm not. I just swing my sword around like I know what I'm doing and... stuff."

I tried not to laugh, but a grin forced its way to my face. "You want to know something, Henry? I was a terrible fighter when I got tossed here for the first time. Like, I got my butt kicked a lot. I've nearly died, more times than I can count, and I'm still not that great of a fighter. Haldrek and the other thegns? They're ten times better than me, but that's because they've been doing this their entire lives."

"Because of the war my parents started."

"You need to explain that to me more, Henry. I know the imposter came around saying your dad or grandpa was the Blodnar or Norycian Emperor, but even though his story kept changing, I'm guessing there's more to it than that?"

"Cass—Cassius picked up who I was long before I did. But yeah, my grandfather, my mom's father, was the Norycian emperor. My mom was his eldest daughter. Her twin brother is the current Norycian emperor. He got tired of waiting for his old man to die, so he sent assassins to kill him. He did the same thing to me, but between my mom and Cass—back when I thought he liked me—got me out of the palace. Cass brought me here, telling me we'd be safe from my uncle in Lohikärra, and handed me over to Rorik."

"So Cassius and Rorik were working together?"

Henry nodded. "Cassius wants to do to Norycium what Rorik wants to do to Lohikär-ra."

"So that's why he came to Drattüjert pretending to be you. He thought if he could get me to think he was you, then he'd be able to deliver Haldrek and I to Rorik. And Rorik would do the same for him."

"Kinda. Yeah. But I don't think either of them trusted each other. Which is probably for the best." Henry turned to me. "Please tell me Cassius is stuck in some kind of dungeon in Drattüjert right now. When this is all over, I'd love to stab him in the back like he did me."

I grimaced and laughed softly. "He's actually dead. Well, deader than dead. I put him in the dungeons three different times while he was in Drattüjert, and each time he escaped. The last time, he got out, amassed an army of Blodnar—Norycians, sorry—and attacked Haldrek and me." I paused for a moment. "Haldrek almost died."

"Shit. I'm sorry."

"It's all right. He's better now. Which is why he's in Etelaranikä now and I'm trying to join him. But I ended up confronting Cassius and killing him myself. When I tried to send him to Lyrroth, it wouldn't accept him."

"What?" Henry frowned.

"Apparently, there is another place that souls go to if the universe deems them too evil to exist. Rhaegos told me it's a place even dragons fear to speak of. So when I did the death rite for Cassius, his spirit was sent there instead."

Henry shuddered. "Man, I dodged a bullet." After a moment, he continued, "He tricked me into thinking he was my friend. Possibly something more. I still feel stupid about it."

I shook my head. "You shouldn't. The imposter, Cassius, if that was even his real name, was a master at tricking people. He nearly tricked me into thinking he was you. Except he kept getting little things wrong."

"Like what?"

"He kept trying to hit on me, and referred to Alex as a girl. At that point, I was pretty sure he wasn't you, unless Alex changed drastically after high school."

Henry snorted. "No. I mean, I'm still pissed we broke up, and I may have called him a little bitch that night in my anger. But last I remember, Alex still identified as male."

I nodded, and we were quiet as we finished our meal. Once the food was gone, I poked at the fire, letting the embers consume more fuel.

"So your mom is Norycian royalty? What about your dad? You keep saying the big war between the Norycian Empire and Lohikärra was because of them. Was your dad

Lohikärran?" The thought felt familiar, but I couldn't remember from where, whether it had been something Rhaegos had told me or if it had been something else.

"He was. Before my uncle tried to kill me, I got to talk to my mom, and she revealed his name was Jaari. He was a Lohikärran spy and the son of—"

"Kalle." I turned to Henry in surprise. "I remember that name. Jaari was Kalle's middle son."

Henry nodded. "I guess he and my mother fell in love, things got spicy, and they thought that if they could convince their fathers to not hate each other, then Norycium and Lohikärra could be allies, but…"

"It didn't turn out that way."

Henry nodded. "I think that's why my grandfather helped me escape the prison I woke up in. He kept saying something about fixing a mistake he'd made in the past. I guess he thought Jaari had kidnapped my mom or something like that?"

I nodded. "Haldrek told me that story. Your grandfather thought Jaari had kidnapped your mom and sent her to Lohikärra. He demanded Kalle return her or he'd claim Lohikärra as part of the Norycian Empire as recompense. When Kalle said your mom wasn't in Lohikärra, that's what started the war."

Henry sighed. "So thousands of people died because I exist."

Rhaegos rumbled in the back of my head, and I sensed her annoyance.

"You didn't start the war, Henry. All of that happened because of your grandfathers. They chose to lock horns instead of coming together to find peace." A memory came to mind, and I gasped.

"What?"

"Rhaegos. Months ago, when Cassius was in Drattüjert. She showed me a memory of hers. Your mom worshipped her as one of the Norycian goddesses, and Rhaegos answered her plea. I guess your mom knew she was pregnant with you and didn't think she'd be safe in either Norycium or Lohikärra, so she begged for Rhaegos's aid."

"Rhaegos sent her to Fargo?" Henry raised an eyebrow.

I sent Victoria to a place where she and her child would be safe. Though I knew not the child, I knew he would be important in the future. I see it now more clearly. Your friend, now of three worlds, will play an important part in Rorik's downfall. In Ryluth's downfall.

"Ina?"

I looked back at Henry. "Rhaegos just told me why she sent you to Earth, our realm, so to speak."

"Why? I'm assuming Rhaegos is the dragon who has bonded to you?"

I nodded. "The same one who was allies with Bjornulf in the first game."

Henry's eyes went wide. "What did she tell you then?"

"She knew you would be important in the future. Not why, but that you would be. So she sent you and your mother to Fargo to be safe. She just told me you're going to play an important part in both Rorik's downfall and Ryluth's downfall. That's why you needed to be safe."

Henry stared at me for a few moments, and I wondered if he believed me. Then a grin crossed his face. "If that's the case, then maybe... maybe my existence wasn't just a mistake." He brushed the tears from his eyes and nodded. "I believe you, Ina. Help me learn how to fight better and we'll kick Rorik's butt like nobody's business."

Chapter 17

That night after training, Henry and I ate once more, and then I passed out from exhaustion. I knew I was still recovering from Eero's birth and Senja's magic wasn't a cure-all, but I hadn't expected to feel so beat up after everything.

As soon as I closed my eyes, I knew I was somewhere different, but familiar. No longer in the farmhouse, I opened my eyes and tried to figure out where I was based on the shadows.

Rhaegos?

No answer. I couldn't even sense her presence. As I patted my armor and I found my weapons still attached, a sense of relief washed over me. I was in some realm where I still had my weapons, even if Rhaegos might not be near.

Ina. Rhaegos's voice was different. Not like someone was mimicking it, but like she was far away and calling out to me.

That was strange.

Rhaegos?

I waited a few more minutes before realizing she wasn't going to answer. Getting up, I began walking forward, my eyesight adjusting to the darkness of this place. It was like the cave Henry and I had been in earlier, but something was off. More foreboding.

Still, I kept walking forward as if drawn through the twisting and turning halls of this place. I reached out on one side, feeling the rock and doing my best to remember any odd scratches or bumps. Just in case I need to make my way out again.

Rhaegos? I called out again, hoping I was going in the right direction.

Silence. But the atmosphere changed, and I felt the urge to move forward intensify. Following it, I soon heard voices. Or at least murmurs. I couldn't make out the words, but there were people near.

Slowing my pace, I listened for the direction they were coming from and tried to make out the tone of the murmurs. Were they tired? Bored? Angry? As I listened, I stopped, taking in what little light was around me.

I was in a much larger room now. It felt massive. Large enough for a dragon to roost in. Rocks easily twice my size were scattered across the room. It was lighter here as well, but I had no idea where the light could be coming from. As I stepped forward, Rhaegos's voice spoke clearly in my mind.

Hide, little one. This place is not safe.

I ducked behind a massive rock just as the sound of claws clacking across stone began echoing through the chamber. Quickly, I tried to figure out whether I was safe. No one else seemed to be nearby.

The clacking stopped, and I peeked out to see Rhaegos half-shifted into—or out of—her dragon form. She still wore garb that looked like Lohikärran clothing, but larger and more form fitting.

"You still enjoy playing dress up with those human fashions? Your scales look so drab, my trickster niece."

Rhaegos scowled, and I could feel her annoyance, even at this distance. She stared into the darkness on the other side.

"Still sulking in the shadows, uncle? Only cowards do that."

There was a hiss and more clacking of claws against stones. A pale, gaunt-looking man, about the same height as Rhaegos, walked out of the shadows. His walk was a little off kilter, and I wondered if he'd forgotten how to be in a humanoid form during the past two thousand years. His clothing also seemed more tattered, even hanging off in some spots. He glared at Rhaegos and while her expression stayed the same, her voice took on a light tone.

"Is a necromantic revival not everything you expected, Ryluth?"

"Hush your mouth, traitor."

"I was never a traitor. I was never on your side."

Ryluth took a swipe at Rhaegos with a handful of claws, but before he could touch her, the bottom of her long braid wrapped around his wrist and wrenched it away from her.

"I've also had a few more life cycles to hone my self-defense, whereas you seem to have some difficulty walking. Or shifting."

He yanked his wrist away, the claws turning back into fingers. "While you have certainly grown much since I last saw you, you waste your incredible powers on these pathetic humans. You always have. Even the whelp who brought me back and thinks he can control me is pathetic." Ryluth pulled his arms away from his body and I noticed they seemed atrophied. "He thinks himself a great necromancer, when in reality he is nothing of the sort."

"Why did you drag me here, Ryluth? To moan and complain like a bitter old man?"

Ryluth hissed again. "I want you to know you will fail. Even if I am not in the same glory as I was millennia ago, I am still far more powerful than these humans can imagine. Like I said before, you waste your powers on these maggots."

"This world's power isn't wasted on growing a towering forest."

I frowned, confused by her words, but Ryluth merely rolled his eyes and sighed.

"My brother would constantly say that. You are nothing if not your father, Rhaegos. I have yet to see a towering forest. At most, a few straggly bushes fighting over arid soil."

"It seems your necromantic revival has left you blind then."

Ryluth scowled, and the room seemed to darken ever so slightly. If Rhaegos noticed, she didn't show it. Her expression remained neutral as Ryluth continued.

"Even with the pathetic necromancer, I have plans in motion. Plans even you cannot stop. Once your haldraga is dead, there will be nothing to stop me. Sivath has bound himself to some wretch and none of the other dragons, not even your offspring, are powerful enough to stop me." The room shuddered and I felt Rhaegos's alarm course through me, even as she straightened up.

"Have you anything to say for yourself, brat?"

Rhaegos remained silent and movement caught my eye behind her. She was focused on Ryluth, but I watched in horror as a shadowy creature snuck up to her. My own panic flushed out Rhaegos's alarm as I tried to move toward her and the shadow. To my horror, my body refused to move, as if this really was a dream.

Rhae—

The shadow lunged forward, striking Rhaegos in the back as Ryluth jumped forward, attacking her. Shrieks of pain flowed through me as I crumbled to the ground, gasping for air as I closed my eyes, trying to shut out the image of what was to come.

Awaken, Ina! Awaken!

Without any warning, darkness plunged around me, and I screamed.

"Ina! Wake up!"

Henry's voice made me jump. As soon as I opened my eyes, I saw a handful of men barge through the door, throwing Henry across the room onto his hands and knees. I scrambled to my feet, grabbing the closest weapons to me—Freya's hand axes.

"Hey!"

A couple of the men turned toward me as I swung the axes and cut down one immediately. The other one attempted to block the hand axe I'd swung at him, only for my axe to go through the wooden shaft of his weapon. The rest of the shaft released, whacking me in the nose, much to my irritation. I kicked him with my foot, sending him into Henry right as another man stabbed down, plunging his dagger into my attacker's chest. Henry jumped to his feet as I swung around and ducked. A blade narrowly missed me as I stumbled forward on my knee, tackling the man down and stabbing him in the side with the points on my axe.

Henry shouted, and I watched as he charged another man with his shield, knocking him down and stabbing him in the chest.

A flash from the door caught my eye. Another fighter began charging up a spell in his hand. I lunged for him, jumping over Henry. The ball of bluish light hit my right-hand axe instead of Henry. That axe flew out of my hand as I slammed the other into his neck. He went down with a thud as I looked outside to see a half dozen torches disappearing into the darkness with footsteps to accompany them.

"Bastards!" Henry pushed past me through the door, only stopping when I grabbed the shoulder of his shirt.

"Wait." I felt around in the back of my mind, trying to sense Rhaegos. The dream was still fresh in my mind, and I was terrified what it meant in connection with this attack.

"Why?" Henry's voice boomed. For some reason, I wasn't afraid. "We can't let them get away."

That's when the fear hit me. "I can't sense Rhaegos." A flood of panic washed over me and I used Henry to pull myself to my feet. "Rhaegos... something is wrong. Usually I can feel her presence after something like this. After a dream like this. It can't be real."

"Ina..." Henry's voice was softer now, and I didn't realize I was shaking until he sat me down outside the farmhouse. "What are you talking about?"

"My dream. When I fell asleep, I got sent to another realm. Like here, but not. I was in the cave." Gesturing to where we had been earlier, I tried not to choke on my words. "I thought I heard Rhaegos and felt something pulling me forward, so I followed it and came to a giant room. Massive. Rhaegos was there. Talking like they had forced her there. She was mad and Ryluth was arguing with her."

"About what?"

"He called her a traitor, and she told him she wasn't, because she'd never been loyal to him. He wasn't happy about that."

"I bet. Anything else?"

"He..." I paused. "He has other plans. Rorik thinks Ryluth is under his command, but Ryluth said he had other plans that would come to pass once Rhaegos and I were dead."

I shuddered. Had that been the reason we'd woken up to an attack? "Ryluth attacked Rhaegos in my dream. Right as she told me to wake up." That was the only thing that made sense. Ryluth had pulled Rhaegos and me into some realm to make sure he could kill both of us. "Henry..." My voice squeaked as I thought about why Rhaegos wasn't present like she normally was.

"I'm sure she's fine. She's a dragon, after all. It's really hard to kill dragons, right?"

"Not if you're another dragon. Or you have certain weapons." I looked at the one axe still in my hand. Freya's axes had been made to kill dragons. There had to be other weapons like them.

"Then let's go find out." Henry stood up and held his hand out to me. I shook my head, ignoring the spirits watching us. They didn't seem aggressive right now, and I wondered if they expected to be reconnected with their bodies.

"If Rorik and Ryluth are trying to kill us, why not lure us back into the cave? I'm sure there are plenty more fighters and mages waiting for us there. They already know how eager you are to kill them."

Henry dropped his hand. "You aren't?" The hint of anger and surprise in his voice hurt.

"I'm very eager to fight and kill them. But two against how many? Even if we're haldragas. They'll slaughter us. And with Rhaegos already dead..." The words grew tight in my throat.

"Rhaegos isn't dead. Syralgos said she's seriously injured, though." Henry sighed. "You're right. Two against however many Rorik has in there isn't the brightest idea. We need more people."

"We need Haldrek. And his warriors. And the other thegns."

"Do you know where they are?"

I sighed and shook my head. "Rhaegos was my guide. Unless Syralgos can sense where Haldrek's dragon, Teminth is, I don't know much other than he's in Etelaranikä." I groaned. This wasn't going how I'd planned. With every passing hour, both Rorik and Ryluth were growing stronger. Now that I was out of contact with Mattie and the others in Drattüjert, the fear that something bad had already happened overwhelmed me.

"I have an idea, then. I know some people who could help. They would be willing, too. I just hate bringing innocents into the fight, but I guess it's too late for that now. Everyone here in Etelaranikä is either fighting for or against Rorik now."

"Agreed." I reached out, letting Henry help me up. "Plus, someone has to have heard about the High King's whereabouts. Even if I'm trying to keep a low profile, I know for a fact he won't."

"Why not?"

"Etelaranikä needs to see Haldrek as their king. Someone who is willing to fight for them against a terrifying monster. So him being here…"

"Shows that. I get it. Knowing who I know, I think we'll find out where he is." Henry grimaced as we dragged the dead bodies into the farmhouse. "Though I'll admit, I'm not exactly eager to go and say hi."

I looked up at Henry in surprise. "Why? Haldrek is…" Then it hit me. "Oh. Because of what Cassius did?"

Henry nodded. "*You* know who I am. And that Cassius was pretending to be me. But Haldrek doesn't. So if I go marching into his war camp, I'm pretty sure I'm going to get killed. Probably faster than walking into Rorik's cave."

"If we go to Haldrek's war camp, I would vouch for you. Tell him I checked you out in Freya's Menace. He would believe me."

"I'm sure he would. Still… I'm pretty sure it would be awkward to see the dude who tried to kill you walk into your war camp and be like, 'can we be friends?' I know if someone looking like Rorik did that, I'd punch them in the face without a second thought."

"We still need to connect with Haldrek. Even with your friends who are willing to fight. I promise I will vouch for you. Haldrek knew the man who attacked him wasn't the real you. If you knew the person who looked like Rorik was someone you needed to help fight Rorik, would you take their aid?"

Henry frowned and stayed silent for a very long time. Even the spirits seemed to watch us, though they were probably more concerned about the rites we needed to do.

"Maybe." Henry sighed. "That's a bridge for another day, though. C'mon, let's send these bastards to Lyrroth, then head out. As soon as Rorik knows we didn't fall for his trap, I have a feeling his thugs will be back."

Chapter 18

We left well before the sun rose over the eastern mountains and made our way to the nearest village. It was still early in the morning when we arrived and my stomach grumbled as we reached the wooden walls surrounding the settlement.

Henry laughed. "Let's get some food and I can talk to a few of my friends."

I nodded and, much to my surprise, as we walked through the open gate, a few of the guards called out to Henry in greeting. He waved in return.

"This was one of the first villages I came upon when I escaped from Rorik. The people here are good. They've been fighting Rorik ever since... well, I don't think they were ever fans of him or his dad."

"So they'll be more than happy to support Ingrid, and possibly Sibila when all this is said and done."

Henry cleared his throat and stopped. "Maybe. I've heard a few people talk about Ingrid. That's Rorik's mother, right?"

"Stepmother. And aunt. But she's been fighting him since the beginning. Her daughter Sibila has been at Drattüjert since I've been there." I lowered the volume of my voice. "Rorik tried to sacrifice her to Ryluth."

"Hmm." Henry refused to look at me, instead watching the people around us. A few people averted their eyes as he glanced at them, but most seemed comfortable with his presence. "Even if that's true, and I'm not saying it isn't, there are a lot of people here who think Ingrid hasn't done as much as she could. She's been more interested in protecting her daughter than her people."

The comment rankled me, and I retorted, "I forgot mothers aren't supposed to protect their children. Stupid me."

Henry's attention snapped back to me. "Shit. That's not what I meant. I'm not saying I agree. I just..." He groaned. "Once Rorik is destroyed, Ingrid is going to have a lot on her hands. The people probably won't be quick to trust her because of everything that has happened so far."

I nodded, still frustrated, but knowing I'd have to understand. And knowing that this wasn't something I needed to worry about yet. "Fine. So tell me how you gained the goodwill of this place. And I'm assuming others like it."

"Do you remember what my favorite part of the video games were?" He started walking again.

"Fighting anything and everything?" A small grin crossed my face at the memory.

"Well, that, but what else? What were my favorite things to do?"

"Quests?" I laughed as I remembered. "Side quests in particular. Did you ever finish the main quest in any of the games?"

Henry shook his head. "Never. The side quests were more fun, and I didn't have to deal with any world-breaking drama. You know me—I'd rather be doing that kind of stuff than ruling any day of the week."

I stopped, thinking about Henry's mom. "You said your mom's dad was the emperor, right? And now your uncle is? Does he have any children?"

Henry laughed. "None that are legitimate. Not that I'm all that legitimate, either. But there was pressure on him to name me his heir when I was in Norycium. Something I think neither of us were too pleased about."

"Was that why your uncle tried to kill you?"

Henry shrugged. "Possibly. I think there might have been some jealousy between him and my mom. I wasn't in Norycium for too long, but people seemed to like her more than him, even before she disappeared."

I nodded. "Your mom has always been a nice person. At least as long as I've known her."

"Agreed. I miss her." Henry stopped once more, this time in front of a set of stairs. "When I escaped the palace, I got the impression that my uncle... I don't know if my mom is still alive. Right now, I need to focus my attention on defeating Rorik. Once he's deader than dead, then I can turn my attention back to my Norycian family members and deal with them." He gripped one of the stair posts and forced a smile to his face. "But yeah, that's why people here trust me. I've spent the last while doing side quests for them and killing any of the thugs Rorik sends this way."

Without another word, Henry made his way up the steps and opened the door. I followed him inside, taking in the sweet, ubiquitous smell of mead, and listening to whatever song was being sung to entertain those in the main room.

"Hail, young one!"

I looked up to see Henry making his way toward an older man with a huge grin on his face. Keeping my cloak around me, I followed him.

"Hail, Uric. How are things today?"

Uric shrugged and placed two mugs in front of us. "As they always are. You look like you've been fighting Rorik's bastards again."

Henry grinned. "As always." He took a sip from his mug as Uric turned to me.

"Will you be having some mead as well? I am assuming you are with Henry here?"

I shook my head. "Just some kavasir. I can pay for it." As I grabbed for my coin bag, my cloak opened, revealing my armor—and the Svartån insignia on it.

"It'll be no charge, my queen."

I looked back up to see Uric's eyes wide. He quickly filled my mug, averting his gaze.

"Then I'll just leave a few coins here for my gratitude, and some silence." I placed the coins on the counter. Uric nodded without a word.

"You're making this sound like a secret mission of some kind." Henry laughed, and I nudged him.

"No, but I know people will talk, and I want to find Haldrek as soon as possible. Like I said before, you can't take down Rorik by yourself."

Uric kept his gaze on one particular spot of the counter. "The High King doesn't know you're here?"

I shook my head and tapped my armor above my pendant. "Rorik has cast some kind of magic over Etelaranikä that makes it impossible to use the pendants we have. That is why I'm trying to find out where the High King is."

"And him?" Uric gestured to Henry and then looked at him. "No offense. It's not every day you come walking in with the High Queen."

Henry took another sip, but I could tell he was a little annoyed.

"We were friends growing up. As children."

"Back in that Fargo place?"

I nodded. "We both grew up in Fargo before coming to Lohikärra."

Uric cleared his throat. "That is good to know. I have, in fact, heard word of the High King's whereabouts. He's with Thegns Heidrunefoss and Bragidrattür, yes?"

"Last I heard, yes."

"A few of Heidrunefoss's warriors were here not too long ago. Asking for supplies and to see who was willing to help them."

"How did that go?" Henry finished his mead and wiped the rest from his newfound facial hair. I tried not to think about how much he and Haldrek did look like each other.

Uric looked around the inn, then gestured for us to follow him into a smaller room. Once we were inside, he closed the door and looked at me.

"What I'm about to say...it's not that people here in Etelaranikä don't support the High King. We just...we've been dealing with Rorik for a long time. Even while his father was still alive. So many people are tired. We don't know if the High King is going to succeed or not."

I tried to hold my temper. I could understand their frustration. It was mine as well, and not because of Haldrek. Rorik was a bastard, a sneaky one at that. Plus, he had Ryluth backing him...for however long Ryluth chose to. At the same time, I wanted to defend Haldrek and chew this man out.

"The High King will defeat Rorik. I guarantee it." Henry's confidence surprised me, especially after our conversation earlier.

"Why do you say that?" Uric frowned at Henry. "Have you seen the High King?"

Henry shook his head. "No. But I know who he married, and Ina here knows how to fight. Between the two of them, Rorik doesn't have a chance."

I tried to hide my smile and gratitude. Good to know Henry had confidence in me. Uric didn't seem to share his sentiment, though.

"Not saying the High Queen doesn't know how to fight." He nodded to me. "I've certainly heard the stories about you. But Rorik..."

"Rorik has his weaknesses. We've seen them. Ina and I have fought against his necromancers, and they aren't as tough as Rorik would have people believe. The fact that he's trying to force people to fight for him? He's on the defensive. Once Ina and Haldrek have him cornered, they'll be unstoppable."

"If you're so confident, then are you going to fight alongside them?"

Henry glanced at me and nodded. "There was never a doubt. But if the thegns are sending their warriors in asking for reinforcements, then—"

Before Henry could finish, a loud boom made the room shudder, and I grabbed onto Henry to stay upright.

"What in the name of the dragons was that?" Uric pulled the door open, and we ran out with him. People were pouring into the inn as we made our way through the crowd.

As soon as we made it outside, Henry growled.

"Shit."

Outside, chaos reigned as people screamed and I saw a dozen very familiar-looking necromancers. Dressed up in some kind of feathery and scaly regalia, they marched into the village in a semi-circle with a dozen or more undead Blodnar soldiers around them.

Already, the creatures were grabbing people and acting like an informal barrier between the village's warriors and the necromancers.

"Shit is right." Uric glanced at us. "You two ready to fight?"

"Hell yeah!" Henry ran out into the street, pulling his sword and shield out, and started swinging at the zombies who were going after people. As he went after arms and legs, I looked for a space to sneak in and go after the necromancers.

"You gonna fight, my queen?" Uric's tone was a little too sarcastic for me.

"Of course." I pulled out Freya's Menace and ducked through an opening in the fighting, cutting down the first necromancer to get in my way. As soon as he went down, another took his spot as one of the zombies stumbled into me. I slammed my blade across its chest, slicing through the rotted flesh with ease. A frigid blast of air from my left pushed me to the ground, and I looked up to see the necromancer staring at me with an equally cold smile.

"Too-Salpama!"

A bolt of lightning shot out of my left hand, sending him flying, but searing pain recoiled up my arm and I flinched before rolling to my knees. That spell hadn't ever been that painful before. As I got up, something rotten-smelling latched onto my armor. Pulling away, I spun around and shoved my hand into the zombie's face.

"Too-Welli!"

Flames from my palm leapt onto the zombie's face, making it stagger back into a villager's waiting blade.

"Ina! They're retreating!"

I turned to see Henry chasing some of the necromancers out of the village and followed suit. As we ran with several other fighters, we found more undead and necromancers fighting on the path and in the clearing outside.

"For Lohikärra!" Henry shouted as he charged once more into the crowd.

I followed, ignoring the pain in my left arm and shoulder. As a zombie tried to claw my helmet off, I lopped its head into the ditch below us and stabbed it in the chest until it stopped moving. A unsettled feeling came over me. In the distance, I saw one particular necromancer who seemed to be orchestrating everything. While it definitely wasn't Rorik, I could tell it was a skilled necromancer. I charged him, running as fast as I could and cutting down the zombies between us.

As soon as I was within a few feet, he spun around and cast a spell at me, hitting me in the chest. I stumbled back, trying to hold on to Freya's Menace as I landed on my butt.

"Is this what Rorik has to face?" The necromancer's skin was pockmarked with strange scars, and I wondered if he wasn't half-dead himself. "You don't know what reward he has on your head. A reward I will happily take."

An orb of greenish light materialized in his hand. Whatever it was, panic flooded through my body as I stumbled to get up, my legs suddenly not working, the heavy weight of exhaustion pulling me down.

"Too-Welli-Ballo!" I tried to cast a fireball, only to see it disappear as soon as it left my hand.

The necromancer laughed as his orb grew larger. "I look forward to bringing your head and soul back to Rorik."

He flung the magic at me and I flinched, trying to dodge, despite my body refusing to move.

"Over my dead body!" A shadow passed over me. Instead of a green haze enveloping me, I heard a grunt as Henry hit the ground.

"Henry!"

"I'm fine!" He staggered to his feet and slammed his shield into the necromancer's head, knocking him to the ground. I watched as Henry plunged his blade into the man. Another jab and the man groaned.

"Finally. Of course it's just you and me."

I turned to see the other fighters had retreated to the village. Sure enough, it was just Henry, myself, and a handful of ghosts emanating anger all around us.

"They are probably making sure everyone is safe."

Henry grunted and turned back to the necromancer who had nearly killed me. Raising his hands, he began chanting the death rite for Lyrroth. The spirit tried to lash out at him as he finished, but before he could, he disappeared into a swirl of blue haze.

"There are a few more." I laid down in the dirt, terrified of the fact that my muscles had all of a sudden gone weak.

"I'll deal with them in a bit. Are you okay?"

I shook my head, tears now streaming down my face. "I was fine fighting, and then it was like all my energy disappeared. My legs...I can barely move them. And my magic. I'm not that good at magic, but it's never hurt before, or gone out."

"Probably has something to do with the necromantic magic. And the fact that we've been fighting and traveling all day." He looked between me and the dead bodies behind me.

"Go do the rites. Send them to Lyrroth. As long as they're around, it'll bother me. Maybe if I rest, I'll feel better."

Henry watched me reluctantly, and I waved him away.

"Go. I'll be here when you're done."

Not like I could do anything except limply freak out. What kind of necromantic magic had completely knocked me out like this? I felt around for Rhaegos, and while she gently nudged me, reassurance that she was still alive, I got the impression she was too weak to do much more.

Was that part of why I had been so weak? Had most of my strength been because I was now a haldraga? Or was Rorik's increased strength making his fighters stronger?

"Ina?"

I looked over as Henry walked back from the bodies. There was no blue haze within my limited vision.

"I'm still here. Trying to figure out why my body has betrayed me."

Henry laughed, leaping down from the path to where I lay in the field. "Can you move your feet?"

I wiggled a foot, then stretched my right leg. My arms still felt weak, but at least my legs were better. The memory of killing Seirye flashed through my mind and I had to admit this wasn't the worst situation I'd found myself in.

"Maybe now the necromancers are dead, your body will be able to regain its strength. Especially if they were siphoning your energy while they were attacking."

"Ugh. I hadn't thought of that."

"They're bastards. I know."

Henry reached out to help me up, but before I could grab his hand, a dagger nicked it and he recoiled.

"Don't you dare touch her, or I will skin you alive myself."

I twisted around as much as I could, surprised to hear a voice I hadn't heard in months.

"Aallotar?"

Chapter 19

"D o you know her?" Henry looked between me and Aallotar. She gestured and a few of her warriors surrounded Henry as he put his hands up.

"Yeah. That's Aallotar. Thegn Heidrunefoss." I turned to her as much as I could. "Aallotar. He's an ally. I promise. He just kept one of Rorik's necromancers from killing me and he's been sending their ghosts to Lyrroth."

"Then what was he doing to you just now?" She scowled at him.

"He was helping me up. Look, we've been fighting Rorik's thugs all day and I'm weak because of some kind of spell. He was helping me get up." I took a deep breath and slowly rolled into a sitting position.

"Isn't this the same man who tried to kill Haldrek last year?"

I shook my head. "The imposter tried to kill Haldrek. This is the real Henry. First thing I did when I saw him was look at his reflection in Freya's Menace."

"And...?"

"I saw Henry. No illusion, no disguise."

"Cassius tricked me as well. The imposter. That was his name. He tricked me when I first got here, then attempted to kill me."

"Oh? It's a shame he didn't succeed."

"Aallotar! Seriously? Who shit in your cereal this morning?" I barely had the energy to keep myself upright, much less deal with Aallotar's attitude. She hadn't been this way before, and I wondered if the fighting in Etelaranikä had made her more sour.

"Look, my warriors and I were chasing a group of necromancers who got away, and then we find some Blodnar-looking bastard trying to have his way with you. Why aren't you more angry? Haldrek's been searching for you ever since his dragon told him you were in Etelaranikä! What have you been doing?"

"Fighting necromancers!" I snapped, rolling to my knees and using my sword to help me stand up. "I have been fighting necromancers and trying to find Haldrek. Whatever magic Rorik put over Etelaranikä made it so we can't communicate through our pendants. Otherwise, I would have contacted Haldrek the moment I left Drattüjert. I thought Haldrek told you and Bragidrattür about that?"

"He did, but I... I didn't believe it. There is no way that Rorik is powerful enough to meddle with dragon magic. Not at that scale." Aallotar looked scared for a moment, then shook her head.

"You don't trust your High King?" Henry shouted, and one of Aallotar's warriors put their blade up to his neck.

Aallotar turned to him with a wrathful stare. "I trust Haldrek. More than you could ever know. But no haldraga is strong enough to—"

"No haldraga, but Rorik has bound himself to Ryluth. And Ryluth has that power." I snapped. The thought clicked in my head and Rhaegos nudged me softly. "Ryluth knows if he can keep Haldrek—or anyone else—from killing Rorik, his own plans will come to fruition." I took a deep breath. "Ryluth tried to kill Rhaegos last night around the same time Henry and I were attacked. So it wouldn't surprise me if..." I stopped. "It wasn't Rorik who messed with the dragon magic in our pendants, but—"

"Ryluth?" Aallotar shuddered and glanced over at Henry. "What have you been doing while you've been in Etelaranikä, Blodnar scum?"

"More than your warriors." Henry winced as the blade at his throat was pushed further in.

"Stop it! Both of you!" Now I was cranky. "Honestly, who ruined your morning, Aallotar? I don't remember you ever being this hostile." I turned back to Henry. "I'd prefer you to stay alive, so you, me, and Haldrek can finally kill Rorik and Ryluth. None of us can do it by ourselves. The longer we stay bickering, the more innocent people are going to get hurt."

I leaned on the hilt of my sword and focused on my breath. Whatever magic had hit me was making my life miserable right now.

You need to rest as much as I do, little one. Rhaegos sounded as exhausted as I felt. She was right. We both needed to rest. And I needed food. My stomach growled as I looked up at Aallotar.

"How close is Haldrek? Is the war camp nearby?"

She nodded. "If you can walk, I can take you there." Her voice was softer now, and I wondered if my outburst had cooled her temper.

"I don't know at this point. Neither Henry nor I have eaten in hours, and I haven't really slept well, either."

Aallotar scrunched up her nose. "Don't worry about the Blodnar scum. My warriors will handle him."

"That's exactly what I'm afraid of. Henry and Haldrek need to meet. No offense, but I think you'd be more than happy to stab him in the back right now."

Aallotar shrugged, obviously agreeing with me but saying nothing. I turned back to Henry.

"How far did we go from the village?"

"Not far." He glanced over his shoulder, trying not to move. "Uric will probably have some food and drink out."

"Who is Uric?" Aallotar asked, her voice cold again.

"The innkeeper in the village, Aallotar," I replied tiredly. "Some of your warriors have been there recently." Turning back to her, I continued, "I think I can make it back to the village. If you don't trust Henry to help me, come with me and send one of your warriors to get Haldrek. I want to see him, but I don't have the strength to walk much farther." I tried to pull my blade out of the dirt and failed.

"I'll help you with that." Aallotar glanced at Henry as she helped me clean and sheath my blade. "I supposed one or two warriors can guard the Blodnar scum." She gestured to a couple of warriors. "You two come with me as well. The rest return to the war camp and let the High King know we've found Ina."

The warriors nodded. The one holding her blade to Henry's neck released him as Aallotar wrapped my left arm around her shoulders, letting me lean on her as we began walking.

"As much as I don't trust the Blodnar you've decided to travel with, I really do hope you're right about him." Aallotar sighed, keeping us away from Henry. "I'm afraid we do need something to change."

Aallotar and her warriors brought Henry and me back to the village, where people were still picking up the pieces from the attack. To say people stared at us while Aallotar helped me walk and Henry had guards behind him—one with a dagger at his spine—was an understatement.

When we arrived at Uric's inn, the innkeeper's eyes widened. Without a word, he opened the door to the room where we'd spoken privately before.

"Man seems to have some sense about him," Aallotar murmured as our group entered the private space. She helped me to a bed in the corner where I laid down. I was feeling better, but I knew food and drink would help.

Uric closed the door slightly behind him and spoke softly. "Do I need to fetch a healer?"

Aallotar shook her head. "Food and drink are probably best for now. The High King will be arriving soon."

Uric nodded without a word and slipped out.

"Can I sit down?"

Both Aallotar and I looked over to where Henry was standing, the warriors behind him still alert. Aallotar grimaced.

"Let him sit down, Aallotar. He's our ally, not our enemy."

"He's *your* ally. Possibly the High King's. I would never trust a Blodnar."

"Aallotar, just let him sit down. He's not going to hurt anyone."

She looked at where I was laying and then back at Henry. "Fine." She gestured to her warriors. "Let him sit. If he makes any sudden moves, you know what to do."

I grumbled, wanting to argue more on behalf of Henry, but my exhaustion kept me silent. Instead, my mind wandered to thoughts of Haldrek, of Eero, and what was going on in Drattüjert. For a moment, I wondered if I'd made a mistake in leaving. Had I been too hasty?

"Are you okay, Ina?" Henry's voice was soft with worry as he sat at the table next to the fireplace.

I realized my face was already wet as I tried to brush away my tears. "No. I'm just missing Haldrek and Eero so badly right now. I came here because things were getting worse at the palace. Everything seemed to be pointing toward me needing to fight Rorik alongside Haldrek and...I'm just worried. I finally have a family I love and who loves me. I'm terrified of losing them."

"I can understand that." Henry glanced at the small fire for a little while. "You said Mattie is here too? Is she...?"

"She's at Drattüjert with her family and Eero. I know he's safe with her, that she'd protect him like he was her own son, but... I still miss everyone."

"If I could, I'd give you a hug and tell you everything is going to be okay." He glanced at Aallotar, who merely scowled at him. "But you've always been the 'mom friend', concerned about others and trying to take care of them. Even when we were younger."

"That's because I was raised to believe I had to take care of everyone. Mattie was more of the 'mom friend', I think. It felt like I had to rely on her for so much. Outside of the chores my mother and Robert required, I don't know if I was that helpful of a person."

"You were. Mattie is a kind of a 'mom friend', but you still care about people, even when you aren't required to. Which is good. You have a big heart. You always have." He glanced up at Aallotar, then at the others in the room as Uric and another person slipped in, bringing a platter of food and drinks. Once Uric had left, Henry continued,

"I know Aallotar doesn't trust me, but I'm making this promise to you, Ina. I'm going to do everything I can to make sure you and Haldrek return to Drattüjert safely to have a happy life together. Especially if he treats you well and makes you happy."

Aallotar scoffed. "What is the promise of a Blodnar? Nothing."

Henry scowled, keeping his focus on me. "I swear by the dragons I will do everything in my power to make sure you and your loved ones are safe."

Rhaegos rustled in my mind and I wondered if Henry knew what it meant to swear by the dragons in Lohikärra.

"Are you sure you want to make a promise you might not be able to keep, Blodnar? When you swear by the dragons, they keep you accountable."

"I know. Syralgos explained that to me right after she bonded with me."

Aallotar's expression changed to surprise, but before she could say anything, the door to the inn boomed.

"Where is she?" Haldrek's voice both made me jump and brought me relief. I twisted up, leaning on my right elbow, both eager to see him and worried about how freaked out he sounded.

"He sounds pissed," Henry murmured as footsteps made their way toward the room.

"He's been worried half to death ever since he found out Ina was in Etelaranikä," Aallotar replied, a hint of annoyance in her voice. I didn't know whether it was directed at me or at Henry.

The door burst open, and Haldrek ran over to me, wrapping me up in his arms. It felt amazing and I started bawling.

"Are you all right? Who hurt you?" He pulled away to look me over.

"Some of Rorik's thugs attacked this village while Henry and I were here. We helped fight them off, but I think I got hit with some magic. Or I'm still weak from no food and little sleep. But otherwise I'm fine."

Haldrek looked at Aallotar, then Henry. Henry waved sheepishly and Haldrek's expression hardened.

"You look familiar. You're supposed to be dead."

"I was not the one who arrived in Drattüjert last year. That was a person who betrayed me as well."

"You really expect me to believe that?" The amount of anger in his voice surprised me. I expected distrust, like Aallotar, but not outright rage.

"I had him look in Freya's Menace, Haldrek. This is the real Henry. He's also been fighting Rorik. He's not the enemy."

Haldrek took a deep breath and turned back to me, his tone still full of anger. "Why in the name of the dragons did you leave Drattüjert? You're still healing, and if anything had happened to you..."

"She was trying to protect you and everyone she loves. Apparently, whatever magic was supposed to be protecting people there wasn't working."

Haldrek spun around and stood up. "Did I ask you to speak? How do I know you aren't in league with Rorik, using illusion magic like the other Blodnar bastard who came looking for my wife and tried to kill me? How do I know you aren't trying to worm your way into her good graces and trying to manipulate her? How do I know you aren't trying to seduce her in some way?"

Henry stood up, taking a step toward Haldrek, and my heart lurched, wondering if they were about to do something stupid.

"Because if I was going to seduce *anyone*, it would be *you*. But I've sworn off men and their drama for the time being. As it is, I see Ina as a friend and a sister, and I've already sworn by the dragons I will do anything to keep her safe and make sure she has a happy future. I am not *her* enemy and I'd rather not be yours."

Haldrek stared at him for a few long tense moments, flexing his fists as if he was toying with the idea of punching Henry. Then he looked over at me and asked, "Are you hungry, Ina?"

I nodded. "Starving. There's been too much fighting going on. I haven't had a chance to eat."

His expression softened and he walked over to the table, quickly preparing me a plate of whatever Uric had made for us. As he brought it over, he sighed and said, "Then let's eat. And then we can figure things out."

Chapter 20

After our meal, I felt better, albeit sleepy and a little lightheaded. Everyone's tempers seemed to have cooled, and I was able to explain in more detail what had brought me to Etelaranikä and what had happened since then. Haldrek still wasn't happy, but he seemed more resigned to the fact that I was here.

"If Rorik and Ryluth hadn't started attacking people in the palace, I promise I would still be there. Having to leave Eero, even with people and dragons I trusted, broke my heart."

Haldrek nodded and took another bite of his bread. "I know. I felt the same way when I had to leave."

"The sooner we get rid of both Rorik and Ryluth, the sooner we can go home."

"Agreed." Aallotar pulled herself from where she'd been leaning and walked over to the near-empty platter of food. With a glance at Henry, she stabbed more meat, then resumed her position. "I miss Vilde and the thegn hall. If Rorik's power is as truly strong as you say it is, we need to go on the offensive."

"It would be good for Etelaranikä as well." Henry put his plate on the table. "They've been suffering for far too long. Both because of Rorik and because of the Norycian war. They need peace. We all need peace."

Haldrek nodded, and Aallotar scowled as Henry ignored her.

"The Heart and the Strength of Lohikärra." I muttered. "And the outsiders." Focusing on Haldrek, I laughed softly. "Rhaegos told me you're a lot like Bjornulf."

"Bjornulf the Brave or Thegn Bragidrattür's nephew?"

"Bjornulf the Brave. I thought that was an interesting comment, seeing as she knew him."

"It's a compliment for sure. I hope one day to be a tenth of the man he was. Don't know if I will be, though."

"You're still young, cousin." Aallotar gestured with her meat-laden knife. "We all are. And Bjornulf didn't become the man of legend overnight. If any dragon is comparing you to him, don't question it."

"I appreciate your confidence, Aallotar. And Rhaegos's confidence as well." Haldrek looked out the window, where the shadows had been telling the time. "We should head out if we're to make it to camp before dark. As much as I trust the warriors here, Rorik's men know where we are."

Aallotar gestured to her warriors and they began preparing to leave.

"How are you feeling now, Ina?" Haldrek's voice was softer. Between him, my exhaustion, and the bed I was lying on, I just wanted to sleep with him curled up around me.

"Better. Tired, but better. If there was some kind of magic affecting me earlier, it's gone now."

Haldrek's expression lit up. "Then let's head back. It'll be safer." He glanced over at Henry. "You are also welcome to come. If we are to work together, it'll be better for you to be in the war camp."

"It'll also be better to keep an eye on him and make sure he can't betray us." Aallotar walked between the two of them as she put her plate on the table and helped her warriors.

"As much as I would like to accept your offer, Haldrek, I think I might be safer here. Somehow, I think I'll get the same reception from the rest of your warriors as I did from Aallotar. At least here in the village, the people know me. I won't have to sleep with one eye open."

Haldrek grimaced, and I nudged him. I agreed that having all of us together would be easier, especially if we couldn't use our pendants. But I also understood Henry's fears. Most of the warriors in the war camp probably wouldn't look too fondly on him.

"As High King, I will ensure your safety in camp. It is that important that we be able to work together without traveling back and forth. That said, you need to understand that many people will see you, not as Ina or Mattie see you, but as a Blodnar who they have warred with these past twenty or so years. You will have my protection, but I expect that you will not engage in any fights."

"So be a doormat because people don't trust me? Sounds perfect." The sarcasm in Henry's voice wasn't lost on any of us.

"Henry...please—"

"You could always force him to come with us. As a prisoner of war. He is Blodnar, after all."

Henry stood up, spinning to face Aallotar. Before he could say anything, Haldrek grabbed his shoulder, and I cleared my throat.

"Henry, please. Haldrek's not asking you to be a doormat. You already know people are going to be on edge, but that's their problem, not yours. We need to focus on the task at hand. Not petty squabbles." I glanced at Aallotar, who ignored me.

"Fine." Henry shrugged off Haldrek's grip. "I'll do it. For you, Ina. And for Haldrek. As long as he treats you well."

Haldrek opened his mouth to say something, and I stood up grabbing his arm.

"Let's go. Henry will be fine. I want to get somewhere where I can rest for more than a few hours." Even though it had been less than a day, it felt like ages since I'd dreamt of Rhaegos and Ryluth's attack on her. I wondered if her injuries affected me as well.

Haldrek wrapped his arm around me and nodded. "Very well. Let's go."

The journey back was relatively quiet, and I tried to relax enough to enjoy Haldrek's presence. Still, something felt off as we walked along the path. Aallotar and her warriors were on high alert, but the road we traveled and the trees surrounding us felt darker than normal, more ominous. My head swam as I tried to stay alert to any noises or movement.

"Are you all right, Ina?" Haldrek's grip on my arm grew firmer.

"I think so. Something feels strange though...like the trees are watching us." I laughed at how insane I sounded.

"Probably not the trees, but—" The whizzing of arrows cut off Aallotar's comment as we ducked to the ground. One of her warriors cried out in pain.

"Fuck!"

I looked back to see Henry charge at something to our left, a group of people covered in dark mist.

"Ambush!" Aallotar charged to our right as Haldrek released me and began fighting alongside her.

I pulled out Freya's axes and began swinging at anyone who came near me. I hit a few men, but my arms grew weaker with each swing and I struggled to keep myself upright with each blow. When our attackers were finally dead, I bent over shaking, using the axes to steady me.

"Ina, are you injured?" Henry's voice calmed me as I shook my head. Someone put their hand on my back and I felt an energy course through me. I looked up to see Haldrek standing next to me. He wore a grim frown, but I could see relief in his eyes.

"You should save some energy for yourself, Haldrek. I'm fine, just tired."

"You're not fine, and I'm going to take care of you."

I stood up and put my axes back in their holders. Guilt began to seep through my veins again. At this point, I was more of a liability to Haldrek and the others. "Maybe I should have waited a few more days. But Senja said she'd healed me before I left."

"It takes women a long time to recover from childbirth and return to their previous fighting prowess." Aallotar walked past me and took her spot in front. "Not that I know from personal experience, but plenty of my warriors have. It's not something to take lightly."

Despite my guilt, part of me wanted to smack her. I hadn't taken any of this lightly. If Ryluth hadn't attacked Eero, I would have happily stayed in Drattüjert and continued to heal.

"C'mon, Ina. We're not far from the war camp." Haldrek wrapped his arm around me and leaned me into him. His tone told me he was trying to hold back frustration. "When we get there, you can rest, and then we can figure out a way to finish this fight sooner rather than later."

It was dusk by the time we reached the camp. I let Haldrek lead me to the main tent as I tried to ignore the whispers around our small band. There was plenty of gossip going around, but that could be dealt with later.

As we entered the tent, I was surprised to see Ingrid waiting for us. She stood next to Gunner, mouth open in mid-conversation. From the way her eyes widened, I could tell she was surprised to see me as well.

"Are you well, my queen?" She glanced in a panic from me to Haldrek and back.

"I'm fine. Just exhausted. I've been fighting Rorik's fighters all day and all night."

She nodded, but I could tell both she and Gunner had plenty of questions they left unspoken. I leaned over to sit on a nearby stool, but Haldrek caught me before my butt hit the seat.

"No. You need to rest."

"I can rest by sitting." As Aallotar entered with Henry and the guards she still had assigned to him, I knew if I laid down, Henry would have to deal with a whole bunch of people interrogating him alone.

"You need to rest by laying down, Ina."

I tried to wriggle out of his grip, but he merely pulled me to my feet again. I loved Haldrek and I knew he was trying to help me. But there was no way I was going to let him, Aallotar, Gunner, and possibly Ingrid grill Henry on his intentions here in Etelaranikä. Henry had helped me and protected me when I needed it. I wasn't about to ditch my friend.

"Ina... I agree with Haldrek." I turned to see Henry watching us. "You look exhausted and if we—all three of us—are going to fight Ryluth," Henry glanced at Ingrid before turning his attention back to me, "all of us need to be at full strength. I'll be fine."

I grimaced and nodded, letting Haldrek lead me into the back half of the tent. As soon as my butt hit the cot, another wave of exhaustion crashed over me. I didn't fight it as Haldrek helped me take my armor and chainmail off.

"I promise I'll be fair to him." Haldrek's voice was softer, more tender now, and tears flooded down my cheeks.

"Please. He's my friend and I know the imposter made him seem like an awful person, but I promise you Henry is a good person. He'll be able to help us fight Rorik."

"I trust you." Haldrek's hand brushed my thigh and I wanted his body wrapped around me, comforting and protecting me. "If he was working with Rorik, or even if he had no loyalty to any of us, he could have used that ambush to escape. The fact that he stayed and helped tells me a lot. Also, Teminth trusts Syralgos, and he's curious to hear her account of what happened when Rorik cast her out and bound himself to Ryluth. Usually, that kind of event will kill a dragon as well as the haldraga."

"Really?"

Haldrek nodded. "That Syralgos survived and bonded with Henry is important. Both Teminth and I want to know how important that is." He pulled his helmet off and leaned his forehead against mine. Our sweat mingled, and I savored every moment we were connected.

"Promise me you will rest while we talk to him. Don't worry about his safety. I have every intention of keeping my promise. The thing I'm most concerned about right now is your well-being."

I nodded. "I'll rest as much as I can then." Haldrek's lips touched mine, and I enjoyed his touch once more, embracing something I knew could disappear soon enough. When he pulled back, I laid down on the cot and let him pile a few blankets on me. The weight made me relax, and I watched as Haldrek slipped into the other side of the tent.

As I lay there, I listened to their hushed whispers. Obviously, I wasn't the only person they didn't want overhearing their conversation. I could hear Aallotar's sharp punctuations interrupting Henry's low tones, then Haldrek cutting her off. Every once in a while, either Gunner or Ingrid's voice interrupted, asking one question or another before letting Henry answer. A few times, Aallotar said something mocking Henry and I could hear him snip back at her. I tried to not laugh too loud.

You need to rest, little one. As do I. Rhaegos's voice was soft, less tired than before, but still weak.

I'm sorry. Today has been horrible for you, hasn't it?

Rhaegos didn't answer, but I felt a sense of confirmation rise from her. *We are connected now. While most dragons are safe from harm while with their haldraga, Ryluth has created mayhem. As usual. So now I must rest and heal alongside you.*

I'm assuming Syralgos is aiding Henry?

She is. My kin, her kin, are all very curious about how she survived. They keep their haldragas in check. Well... only Aallotar's need try.

Why is she so angry now? I know she hates Blodnar, but—

The Blodnar took away nearly everything she loved. Worse of all, they made her feel powerless. So she channels that anger toward Henry.

I closed my eyes as understanding hit me. *Which means she'll probably be hostile to him forever?* As much as I understood why she felt that way, I hoped it wouldn't get in the way of us defeating Rorik and Ryluth.

Aallotar's emotions are her own, not something you need to worry about. She will handle them. If she cannot, her loyalty to Lohikärra with keep her from acting rashly.

I nodded, my body feeling heavier with every moment. Aallotar wasn't someone I needed to worry about right now. Haldrek and Henry and everyone could handle themselves. Rhaegos's presence wrapped around me and I realized just how much I'd pushed myself. More than I should have. Tomorrow would not be fun.

But for now, I needed rest. As I fell asleep, I let the hum of the others' voices fade away into a peaceful bliss.

Chapter 21

The next time I woke up, I felt more energy than I had in weeks. Haldrek's breath on my neck was a pleasant sensation, as was his body against mine. If it hadn't been for my intense need to use the bathroom, I would have happily stayed snuggled up next to him.

But, as it was, I needed to pee. Slowly, I pulled his arm from around my waist, missing the weight and heat of it against my skin. As I rolled out of bed, his arm tightened around me.

"You need to rest, Ina."

"I need to pee. Unless you want me to pee on you."

His arm quickly pulled back and I got up, sighing with relief as I squatted above the pot. Once finished and clean again, I slipped back onto the cot, letting Haldrek wrap one of his arms around me as the other one gently explored my body. I relaxed into his embrace, savoring the moment as I woke up more fully.

"What happened last night after I fell asleep? Is Henry still alive?"

Haldrek laughed, his eyes still closed. "Last I hear, yes. Much to Aallotar's chagrin, I made sure he had a tent to sleep in and not a cage. I still have many questions for him, but he was very open to everything we asked. Teminth also wasn't leery of him, which I take to be a good thing." Haldrek gently stroked my still squishy belly before continuing. "Ingrid apparently had heard of the prophecy you mentioned."

"Which one?"

"She called it the Prophecy of the Heart, the Strength, and the Foreigner. She mentioned Salla instilled a love of lore into her and her sister while they were young. She had picked up on that prophecy about Bjornulf and Freya being incomplete, but all her tutors brushed her thoughts aside."

"It sounds like Ingrid is a lot smarter than people give her credit for. Is she still in camp?" Part of me wanted to talk to her and hear what other insights she might have.

"She is. A lot smarter than people give her credit for. Which is probably why she and Sibila are still alive and safe. But she left last night for her thegn hall. Her visit here was supposed to be brief, anyway." He pulled me closer, kissing me gently on the lips before making his way down my neck and giving me shivers. "Either way, she thinks we are the Heart and Strength of Lohikärra and Henry is the Foreigner spoken of. Ingrid also thinks we won't be able to defeat Ryluth and Rorik without him." Haldrek's kisses stopped as he shifted on top of me and flexed out his left hand, as if trying to wake it up.

"What do you think?"

"I think I was smart to put guards in front of Henry's tent. Aallotar wasn't pleased when she heard Ingrid's prediction, and Henry looked very surprised."

"Probably because he wasn't expecting to be part of any prophecy." I laughed, and then moaned as Haldrek nibbled at the collar of my undershirt. Apparently, he'd been missing me a little too much since we'd been apart.

"Well, if we need him to complete this prophecy, then Aallotar needs to stop taking shots at him. As much as I understand why she feels the way she does, she can't let that interfere with us getting Rorik."

"Agreed. Rhaegos told me Aallotar sees Henry as the reason for everything she's lost."

Haldrek nodded. "She watched the Blodnar kill her beloved uncle Akku in the same battle where they slew my uncle Kalle, his father, and Aallotar's grandfather. When she returned to the thegn hall in Heidrunefoss, she found out they had killed his partner, Saami, and many of the servants who had raised her. Most of her loved ones are dead because of the Blodnar."

My heart grew heavier as Haldrek gently kissed me on the neck. As much as I wanted her to play nice with Henry, I knew I'd have a difficult time reacting any differently than Aallotar.

"Still... we can't let bad blood divide us," Haldrek continued, his mouth moving down to my collarbone. "Aallotar can fight Henry if they choose after we defeat Rorik. And he is kin of some kind, if Syralgos was able to bind herself to him."

His kisses along my collarbone grew more intense. I savored the pressure of his body against mine, even as my mind debated whether to tell him Henry's father was Kalle's son and... technically Haldrek's cousin.

As I opened my mouth to speak, a bloodcurdling scream rent through the camp. In mere seconds, Haldrek and I were both out of bed, hands on the weapons stashed nearest us.

We ran out of the tent to find a group of women running into the camp with a horde of undead fighters and necromancers close behind them. The necromancers began casting spells at any warriors who attempted to attack them head on.

"What the hell?"

"Ina, get back in the tent!" Haldrek shouted as he ran forward.

"No!" I chased after him, hand axes in tow, feeling stronger than I had yesterday. I might have been in my undertunic, but so were Haldrek and a few other warriors.

As I caught up to him and got between the undead fighters and the village women, I started swinging at anything rotten-smelling and corpse-like. A few painful grunts were my reward as Freya's hand axes sliced through the zombies like butter.

A war cry erupted behind me as I blocked one necromancer's attack, crossing the hand axes to keep his blade from cutting into me. Before I had the chance to attack, he dropped to his knees, blade falling to the ground as someone to my right pulled their blade out of the necromancer's side.

"I hate these fucking bastards." Henry's voice made me smile as he darted off to help fight more zombies entering the camp.

I looked around, attacking the nearest undead fighters as I made my way over to Haldrek. The necromancer he was fighting was giving him a difficult time, and I ran over, axe raised, and slammed it into the necromancer's shoulder as Aallotar shoved her dagger into his neck. He collapsed immediately.

"Ina, I told you to—"

Aallotar darted out of my periphery and I turned around as a blast of green light erupted in front of me. I ducked down, letting the magic pass. Aallotar stabbed the man in the gut before dropping him to the ground and stabbing him in the neck. Once she was satisfied he was dead, she stood up, her focus locked on Henry. He ignored her, walking over to Haldrek and me.

"I absolutely hate these necromancers. They're bastards."

Aallotar lunged at him and he stumbled over a dead body, blocking her with a shield he'd picked up.

"What the hell?"

"Aallotar, stop!" Haldrek's voice boomed from behind me and she froze, her sword still mid-swing.

"How do we know he didn't send for those necromancers? It's awfully convenient that they arrived this morning."

I glanced over at the group of women huddled just outside of the fighting carnage. Gunner and a few of Aallotar's warriors knelt nearby, talking to the women.

"Because they didn't attack us. They attacked one of the nearby villages, Aallotar. Those people knew they'd be safe here." I gestured to the women. She looked up, watching them for a moment, then relaxed.

"Fine."

Haldrek walked past me and held his hand out to Henry. Henry hesitated before taking it and letting Haldrek pull him up.

"You fought well, Henry. How often have you faced necromancers before?"

"Every single day since Cassius dragged me here and betrayed me."

"The imposter?"

Henry nodded, glancing warily at Aallotar. "I got my butt kicked the first few times, but after Syralgos bonded with me, she taught me some tricks. Also how to send these bastards to Lyrroth."

Haldrek stiffened as Henry put his sword into its sheath and raised his hands. I knew what was going to happen, and I watched as the spirits of the necromancers started paying attention to Henry.

As he started the first death rite for Lyrroth, the ghosts began to writhe, and a few attempted to attack him. Not that it bothered him. With each completed rite, another spirit disappeared, headed to Lyrroth, if not somewhere worse. After doing it a few times, Henry lowered his hands and shook out his shoulders.

"I know there are more, but I can only do a handful at a time before I need a break."

Haldrek looked back at me, and I nodded. "The spirits disappeared as he said their rites. There are still a few around, but he got rid of some."

He turned to Aallotar. "I need you and some of your warriors to help the villagers." She nodded, and he focused his attention on Henry with a grimace. "Let's finish doing the rites so these bodies can't rise again. Then you need to come back to the main tent with me and Ina. I have more questions for you."

Once we finished sending the spirits to Lyrroth, I was exhausted. The sun was high in the sky and while I had only done a couple of rites, the fact that I was hungry and hadn't fully recovered from yesterday wore on me.

As we walked back, Haldrek wrapped an arm around my shoulders, pulling me in line with him.

"I told you to stay back at the tent."

"The fighting isn't what exhausted me. It was the rites, and that has always happened. You know I can't just stand by when innocent people are being threatened."

He squeezed me, and I knew his words were out of concern.

"I don't want to lose you." His voice was soft, so only he and I could hear his words, even though Henry wasn't far from us. "I don't know what I'd do if something happened to you."

"I'll be fine. Rorik and his thugs will keep coming after me—all of us—until they're dead. We just have to keep pushing forward."

Haldrek pulled the tent flap away so we could enter and grumbled. "Ina..."

I turned to look him in the eye. "I'll be fine. You think Rhaegos wouldn't protect me too?"

"Isn't she injured?"

"She's doing a lot better this morning."

Haldrek sighed and glanced at the small spread of food set out for us. My stomach growled. Whoever was in charge of meals was my hero right now.

"Let's eat, then." He looked over at Henry, who stood in the tent's entrance as if he didn't know whether to stay or go. Haldrek gestured with a grunt, and Henry quickly made his way in.

As we sat down with wooden plates full of food, Haldrek stared at Henry.

"So tell me about Syralgos. Why did she bind with you?"

Henry shrugged, taking time to chew a piece of bread. "Right after Cassius betrayed me, Rorik put me in a cage. He didn't seem to care about what happened to me or what I was doing, so I ended up watching him as he did some kind of ritual to raise Ryluth with a bone he had. As soon as he did, there was a flash and Ryluth was in the room. Big, massive dragon. But there was a body next to Rorik, too. It looked like one of the bodies of his, um..." Henry glanced at us, not sure what to say next.

"His what?" Haldrek's expression stayed hard.

"His sacrifices." Henry grimaced. "He's been sacrificing a lot of people, male and female."

"I know." Haldrek looked away, and I got the impression not every fight against Rorik's thugs had been successful.

"So I didn't pay too much attention to the body. I just tried to figure out how to escape. As I got out of the cage, some of Rorik's thugs found me and beat the crap out of me. They threw me in a pile of dead bodies, because that was what I was going to be anyway. But one of the bodies was Syralgos in her human form. She freaked me out at first. Asked me why a dragon hadn't bonded with me yet. Something about knowing I was the descent of kings."

"The descent of kings?"

Henry nodded. "I found out from my mother after we were reunited in Norycium that... my father was a man named Jaari. A spy from Lohikärra who—"

"Who was the son of the High King Kalle." Haldrek's face darkened as he interrupted Henry. I touched his arm, and he glanced at me. "Did you know this?"

"I only found out a few days ago. Did that not come up at all last night?"

Both men shook their heads. After a moment, Haldrek's expression grew lighter, and he laughed. "Aallotar is going to be furious. You two are cousins. Technically, we all are cousins of one sort or another." His mirth disappeared, and he focused on Henry. "Jaari and your mother, did they...was there any kind of ceremony binding them in Norycium?"

Henry shrugged. "I don't know, but it sounds like everything was pretty hush-hush. Why?"

Haldrek glanced at me, and I instantly knew what thought had crossed his mind. "If Henry is a legitimate child of Jaari and Victoria, he could..." I looked over at Henry. "The only reason Haldrek is the High King now is because Kalle and all of his legitimate heirs—all the aethlings—were killed right before Mattie and I arrived here."

Henry's eyes widened. "Shit. So if I'm not a bastard..."

"You could claim the title of High King for yourself." Haldrek's expression darkened once more.

Immediately, Henry shook his head with a furor I'd never seen from him. "Nope. Nope. I am a bastard. Eff that. I *am* a bastard. No interest, no thank you."

Haldrek frowned and looked at me.

"Henry's never been fond of being in leadership. Even in the games, he'd avoid those quests like the plague."

Henry looked up at both of us. "I prefer to fight and be an adventurer. As much as I would love for my mother to still be alive, if she is, and if my uncle doesn't have any legitimate heirs, people will look at me as the next in line. I don't want that. So, no offense, but I have no interest in claiming any title based on my father's ancestry. As far as I am concerned, I am a bastard."

Haldrek nodded. "Good. I'd hate to have to kill you."

"Haldrek!"

He looked at me, completely serious. "If Henry were to try to claim the title of High King for himself, it would cause just as much chaos as Hardbein or Rorik. I'm tired of that."

I tried to think of something to say, but before I could, Henry shook his head.

"I have no intention of taking anything from you and Ina. You two can rule Lohikärra for all I care. If I need to sign something to that effect, fine."

Haldrek nodded. "Let's kill Rorik first and then I'll take you up on that, Henry. But for now, you're telling me that Syralgos survived and bonded with you?"

Henry nodded. "She still has a grudge against Rorik. She's told me numerous times she's not leaving this realm without making sure he is punished for his crimes. Against humans and dragons."

Haldrek's eyes widened. "Rorik made a foolish mistake when he crossed Syralgos. But we can use that to our benefit. What happened between Syralgos and Rorik is rare. Very rare. I've only heard of haldragas parting ways with their dragons twice since Bjornulf's time, and both times the haldraga died and the dragon returned to the dragons' realm. They never joined with another haldraga."

The tent was quiet for a few minutes as we mulled over all that had been said.

Given Rorik's necromancy, he may already be half dead from his falling out with Syralgos. If that is the case, Ryluth is sustaining him until he deems Rorik worthless.

Rhaegos's words made me shudder. "That makes sense." I whispered, mostly to myself.

"What makes sense?" Henry looked at me in surprise.

"Rhaegos just told me Rorik is more than likely already half-dead from separating with Syralgos. His connection to Ryluth is the only thing keeping him alive or with any semblance of power."

Haldrek grumbled. "He truly has turned himself into the Heir of Ryluth then." Dragging his fingers through his hair, he sighed. "If Syralgos has bonded with you, then the dragons have certainly accepted you, Henry. And they seem to trust you. Or at least Syralgos does. Teminth trusts her."

"Teminth?"

"Haldrek's dragon kin." I clarified. "Just like Rhaegos is for me and Syralgos is for you."

Henry nodded. After a moment, he laughed. "I never expected this to be my introduction to Sethys and Lohikärra. A lot more intense than any of the games ever made it out to be." He took another bite of food. "That said, I made a promise yesterday, and I have every intention of keeping it. I don't know the full extent of what Cassius did when he was pretending to be me, but I know it was bad. I can't go back in the past, but I can make amends. I will fight Rorik alongside you and do everything I can to make sure he is dead. Permanently. If I'm still alive after that, well, I'll do what I can to continue making amends and maybe..." He shrugged. "We'll see what the situation with Norycium is and if my mother is still alive. If she is and my uncle is actually dead, I think she would want peace with you all."

Haldrek glanced at me, then at Henry. "I accept your promise, and your offer to help us defeat Rorik. Norycium can wait. The most important thing we need to do is create a plan. We need to figure out how to fight Rorik once and for all."

Chapter 22

The next morning, Haldrek, Henry, and I stood at the entrance of the war camp in our armor, our weapons sheathed. Most of the camp was awake, and Gunner and Aallotar stood with some of their guard at the ready. Aallotar bowed as Haldrek faced her.

"I thank you for being willing to stay with the war camp, Aallotar. There is wisdom in having an experienced leader here." He glanced at Gunner. "Not that you aren't as well, my friend."

Gunner waved his hand, brushing off the comment. "I have never been a fighter unless forced to. Aallotar is by far the better choice for this situation. I will support her."

"Thank you."

Aallotar still looked annoyed as she cleared her throat. "How long should I wait before I send people to find you all after the Blodnar bastard betrays you?"

Henry scowled as Haldrek crossed his arms. This wasn't the first time Aallotar had complained about Henry coming with Haldrek and me. First, she had been adamant that we bring other warriors to insure Henry kept his promises. When Haldrek had told her that would just alert Rorik to our presence, she had questioned Henry's value. After hours of her and Haldrek going back and forth, she had finally conceded, but not without a dirty look at Henry when she left the tent, and a threat to kill him if he tried anything remotely stupid.

"If Rorik doesn't have any other secrets up his sleeve, I expect us to be back in less than a week's time. If we aren't back by then, bring some of your best warriors into the cavern Henry and Ina described. In the meantime, wait a day, then start making your way toward the valley we discussed."

Still scowling, Aallotar turned her focus to me. "What are you bringing to this, Ina? Last I checked, you were still healing from childbirth. Do you really think you are capable of fighting alongside Haldrek and the Blodnar bastard?"

"Aallotar..." Haldrek growled, and I raised my hand to stop him. If Aallotar wanted to have a pissing contest with me, I could handle her.

"Not all fighting is physical, Aallotar. You know the gifts I have, being a Svanunge. Like Rorik, I have a connection to the realm of the living and the realm of ghosts. As much as I'd love to have this be just physical, we all know Rorik isn't going to play by those rules. Plus, the prophecy talks about the Strength, the Heart, and the Foreigner. Haldrek is obviously the Strength, Henry is obviously the Foreigner, so whom do you think is the Heart?"

Aallotar huffed and shifted her attention to Haldrek. "Fine. Be safe, cousin." She glanced back at me, her expression a bit more contrite. "You as well, Ina. I hope you both come back safely."

Without another word, she bowed and stepped back to her warriors.

Haldrek and I bowed as Henry reluctantly bobbed his head. As Aallotar and the others headed back into the camp, I took a deep breath to settle myself. This was our last stand. When we got to the cave, it would either be us or Rorik triumphant. A small part of me feared it wouldn't be us.

Don't fear tomorrow, little one. It will be a happy day. All is well.

Rhaegos's words comforted me, as well as confused me, while we headed out. The whole time she had sounded worried, but now she sounded confident. Like she knew something I didn't. On the one hand, I was glad, but on the other, why was she so confident now? Had something happened overnight?

She said nothing, only nudging me in response. I took it to mean 'just trust me'. Which, at this point, was all I could really do.

"How long do you think it will take to arrive at the valley?"

Haldrek's voice broke up my reverie, but he wasn't talking to me. He and Henry walked in front of me, their voices soft.

"A few hours. I doubt Rorik's men will be in the valley, though. For some reason, they refuse to stay in the buildings, even though they ran out all the farmers living there."

Haldrek shrugged. "Dragon magic, most likely. I know some people, especially those in more remote locations, will sometimes keep relics or dragon scales in their homes for good luck."

"How do they get them?"

"If a dragon decides to bestow one of its scales upon a person, or if the person is incredibly stupid, but lucky."

Henry started laughing. "Do people really try to steal dragon scales? I know there are stories of people trying, but they don't end well."

"I haven't heard of anyone recently, but doesn't mean people haven't tried. If any of the farmers in that valley had an ancestor who had obtained a dragon scale, chances are the family would have held on to it for protection."

Henry's mirth faded. "It didn't protect them from being run out."

"Dragon magic isn't used to keep physical attacks at bay. But it will keep curses and other types of evil magic from staying in a place. At least that is what I've always been taught. If Rorik and his fighters have truly embraced Ryluth and his dark magic, then a home with a dragon scale probably wouldn't be a pleasant place to stay."

Henry nodded, making a soft murmuring sound I knew meant he wasn't fully convinced. Still, he said nothing as we walked through the forest. As the hours passed and we finally made it into the valley, I was struck once more by how pretty this place was. As much as I loved Svartån, it didn't really have much of a fall season. Etelaranikä, on the other hand, seemed to have more time before heavy snows blanketed it.

The only thing marring the scene before us was the ominous haze of clouds sticking to the cliffs on the other side of the valley. How Rorik or his thugs thought that hid them was beyond me. If anything, it just made their lair entrance more prominent.

Rorik is no longer trying to hide. I don't know if he ever was. The magic you see is not to keep people from knowing he's there, but rather to warn them of their doom should they enter.

"Huh." That made more sense.

"What?" Henry and Haldrek looked back at the same time.

"Rhaegos said Rorik isn't trying to hide himself anymore. That blotch of clouds on the cliff face is a threat."

Haldrek looked back to where the clouds hovered. "He's being more cocky than usual. We should use that to our advantage."

Henry's eyes widened in surprise. "You're ready to go into the cave?"

Haldrek nodded. "Every moment we waste means Rorik grows stronger."

"And the more time he has to hurt others. Our loved ones." My thoughts returned to Eero, and I wondered how he, Mattie, Llamryl, and everyone else at the palace were doing. Had Senja and Paavo been able to keep everyone safe so far?

All are well. Ryluth's and Rorik's attention has been turned back to Etelaranikä now that you and Haldrek are here.

Of course it had. Their attacks on those at the palace had been a way to agitate me into coming to them. At least the attacks on me and Eero.

"Let's go, then." I began walking, trying to keep my legs from getting too tired. "The path to the cave entrance isn't too far from here. The sooner we get rid of Rorik, the sooner we can go home."

Haldrek laughed behind me and soon I heard both men hurrying to keep up as I made a beeline for the path. After a short time, we were in front of the cave, albeit in a thick haze of magical fog.

Someone grabbed my shoulder, and I looked up to see Haldrek by my side. His blade had already been unsheathed, ready for anything that might jump out at us.

"Let's be careful. The clouds may not have hidden this place from the valley, but it's thick enough to hide fighters and necromancers until they decide to fight."

I nodded, slowly making my way around the bushes I had hidden behind before. Haldrek was right. Even if I still had a vague sense of where we were and where the cavern opened up, there could be fighters out already and we wouldn't know it.

Pulling out one of my axes, I stepped forward cautiously, watching for any sudden movement.

"Something about this feels off." Henry whispered. "More off than normal."

"You think Rorik knows we're here?" My eyes darted to what looked like movement, but as I focused on it, it disappeared, blending in with the fog.

"Of course he does. Let's keep moving." Haldrek squeezed my shoulder gently.

As soon as the fog cleared away from the cave entrance, the sound of gravel moving to our right made me jump. I swung around, blocking an orb of green magic with my axe blade.

"Attack!" Henry lunged into the fog, rewarded with a few grunts and shouts. Haldrek and I chased after him, a half dozen necromancers and fighters revealing themselves. As the group surrounded us, I pressed my back against Haldrek's as Henry pulled a couple of fighters away.

One of the necromancers lunged at me and I swung my axe. He pulled back, but not before I had left a gash across his neck. Grabbing my other axe, I swung once more, knocking him to the ground. Haldrek shifted, and I spun around to meet another fighter's blow, blocking him as Henry came out of the fog, stabbing the man in the back.

After a few minutes, the fog lessened, but a blue haze replaced it.

"Did we kill them all?" Henry's face and scruffy beard were already splattered with blood.

I counted the spirits and nodded. "Should we do their rites?" Part of me wondered whether that would pull too much energy from our future fight with Rorik.

Henry glanced down at the bodies. "If we push them off the cliff, even if Rorik made them into zombies, they really couldn't do much."

I grimaced at the thought, but Haldrek moved from behind me. "Let's do it. As much as I want to do the rites, we need to conserve our energy until Rorik is completely dead."

As they pushed the bodies off the cliff, I watched the spirits mull around in disgust, trying not to let it bother me too much. After all was said and done, we could do the rites. Or bring in some local priests to send the spirits away.

I jumped as a hand touched my shoulder. Looking up, I saw Haldrek's grim expression.

"Let's go. The sooner this is over, the sooner we can go home."

The journey through the cave wasn't much easier. Even though we didn't meet up with more fighters, I still had the sense we were being watched. Henry led us, with Syralgos guiding him. Initially Haldrek had hesitated, but eventually he relented, making a comment about Teminth trusting Syralgos.

After what seemed like hours, the path we took expanded into a much larger opening. Though I didn't remember this particular place, it felt uncomfortably familiar. The far edge of the room was lit, even though I couldn't see any kind of light source. Shadows danced across the wall, showing piles of refuse.

Henry groaned as he looked around.

"What?" Haldrek's voice echoed and I looked up. Even though I knew there was a ceiling, I couldn't see it.

"This looks like one of the charnel rooms. Syralgos says it was where she was cast out of Rorik's body and where he raised Ryluth. But..."

"But what?" I asked, looking a little more closely, fearing what I'd find.

"If it is the sacrificial room where Rorik cast her out, it wasn't covered in nearly as many bodies. We need to be careful. Ina...if we need to move on...we can. I know you never liked the barrows in the games."

I nodded. Things had changed a little since I'd arrived in Lohikärra, but I still hated that we were surrounded by human remains. This felt very different from Ottkatla's Barrow. The dead bodies in there had been treated more reverently. This place, though... I could feel a heaviness in the air from the way the bodies had been treated. I couldn't really explain it.

"It looks like there's something on that stone over there." Haldrek's voice was barely audible. "If this was a sacrificial room, there might be something helpful there in finding or fighting Rorik. Or Ryluth." He looked at me. "If you want to stay back, that's fine."

I shook my head, pulling together a grim smile. "This isn't any worse than Svangendom after the Isillas attacked." I took Haldrek's hand so he could lead me across the room, doing my best to walk gingerly and not look at the bodies. Still, I'd see bones, skulls, and chunks of half-eaten flesh that made my stomach churn and the anger inside of me grow.

None of these people had deserved this. Most of the bodies I could identify looked female and young. Probably my age, maybe a little older. How many of these women had dreams of the future that were cut short because of Rorik's bid for power?

"These bodies..." The words slipped from my mouth before I could think of how to end the sentence.

"Brides of Ryluth." Henry and Haldrek answered at the same time, then looked at each other.

"Brides of Ryluth." I whispered. "Women kidnapped and killed to satisfy an evil dragon's thirst for power. I don't even see their ghosts."

"They might be in another room." Henry's answer was half-hearted.

Haldrek shook his head. "Ryluth consumed their souls when he killed them. And consumed parts of their bodies."

"So they'll never get to Mirroth or any other place?"

Haldrek and Henry remained silent, but a sense of being wrong came from Rhaegos.

Once Ryluth is dead again, all the spirits of his victims will be released. There will be much work to be done in the weeks and months after Rorik and Ryluth are destroyed.

My chest squeezed tight with more anger and sorrow. "I swear I will destroy both Rorik and Ryluth if it's the last thing I do. Even if it kills me. None of these people deserved this."

Haldrek pulled me in close to him. "We all will destroy Rorik and Ryluth together." Leaning down, he whispered, "I know what you're thinking, and I refuse to let you sacrifice yourself."

I pulled away to look at him. "And what if a sacrifice is needed again? When Bjornulf and Freya killed Ryluth for the first time, they had to sacrifice something. The dragons sacrificed themselves to make Bjornulf and Freya stronger. How do you know a sacrifice won't be needed again?" The thought of sacrificing myself made my gut churn. I didn't want to do it, but I couldn't live with myself if it meant Rorik and Ryluth kept terrorizing Lohikärra.

"If any sacrifice is needed, it should be me." Henry's voice was quiet and low. "Bjornulf and Freya didn't need to die to defeat Ryluth. And neither should you have to sacrifice yourselves. If a sacrifice is needed, I'll offer myself. I'm the bastard whose existence caused a freaking war. It's the least I can do."

"Henry..." I hated that he thought he needed to sacrifice himself to atone for other people's mistakes.

"We'll figure out when we need to." Haldrek's attention was on something behind Henry's shoulder, and I looked at the stone altar at the edge of the room. "Right now, I think we need to figure out what's on that shrine. Or who. Teminth thinks that the body is of the person who was sacrificed to bring Ryluth back to life."

We all turned our attention to the remains on the altar. I let Henry and Haldrek take the lead again, silently swearing vile oaths against Rorik.

"By Tenelth's mercy himself," Haldrek whispered as they stopped. I'd never heard him use that oath, but the intention was clear. Whatever was on the altar wasn't good news.

"Do you know who this is? Or was?" Henry's voice was nearly as soft as Haldrek's.

"Unfortunately, yes. This is not information her family will want to hear, though."

I ducked around Henry, my curiosity outweighing my fear, only to stop as I saw the body.

Bile immediately pushed up my throat, and I turned away in case I couldn't stop it. What was left of the body was Kamira's. Most of the flesh and organs had been stripped away, leaving a jumble of bones in the rough shape of a figure. The only thing identifying her was her head. For some strange, vile reason, the necromancer had kept her head intact, and through some strange magic, it had not yet begun to decay. Instead, an expression of horror was permanently etched on her face.

I dry heaved away from her remains, remembering how awful she had been to me in Drattüjert. No one deserved this kind of fate.

"I'm assuming you knew her, Ina?" Henry kept his voice quiet as Haldrek came over to comfort me.

I nodded. "She hated me. Aligned herself with the imposter, and I cast her out of Drattüjert right before I killed him. I didn't think she would come here. And...no one deserves this kind of fate. Not even her."

As my stomach clenched once more, Haldrek steadied me. "Rorik and Ryluth will pay for this. All of this. If either of them were redeemable before, this would seal their fate."

I nodded once more, trying to calm myself and slow my racing heartbeat.

"Hey guys... we have company."

Haldrek spun around, and I looked up, my grip on Freya's axes tightening. A small group of people had stopped on the other side of the bone piles. Inside my head, Rhaegos seethed with a rage I had never felt before.

One of the people pulled his hood back, revealing a terrible, familiar smile.

Rorik.

Chapter 23

"Just the three people we wanted to see." Rorik's smug glee made me want to run over and cut him down without a moment's hesitation. Even if Kamira had been a bitch, she didn't deserve this fate. None of the people Rorik had sacrificed to Ryluth deserved their fates.

"We? You and your cronies?" Henry took a few steps forward, brandishing his sword. The necromancers behind Rorik began to chuckle.

"No. Ryluth and myself." A shadow shifted on our right, oozing from a sizeable gap in the wall where I assumed Rorik and his thugs had come in. The shadow was much larger than any of the humans in the room. As it moved forward, it took me a moment to realize the shadow was solid. It was Ryluth, but not in the same form I remembered from my dreams.

"Fight me, you coward!" Henry lunged forward toward Rorik, only to be knocked away by a length of shadow snapping across his armor. He went flying into a pile of bones, his sword dropping as Haldrek pushed me to my knees. The shadowy whip flew over us and a low, gravelly sound echoed through the chamber as I watched Rorik hurry away with his men.

"What the hell?" I whispered.

"Ryluth commanded them to leave. He wants to destroy us himself," Haldrek muttered. "I hope you still have Freya's axes ready."

"Of course."

The crashing of bones on rock took Ryluth's attention away from us for a moment as Henry grabbed his sword and swung around to shout at the last of Rorik's necromancers.

"Stupid cowards! I'll fight you all myself!"

Ryluth's tail whipped around to strike Henry once more and I shouted, "Duck!"

He dropped to his knees, rolling down the pile of body parts he'd been standing on, as Ryluth's tail sailed over him. I took the opportunity to swing one of my axes at the shadowy part in front of me. It made contact and Ryluth hissed, swinging his tail at me. I jumped, just high enough to dodge his blow, then ducked when it came back around.

Staring at Ryluth, a cold slimy feeling came over me as we locked eyes. Even though his features were mostly obscured, I sensed a smugness from him.

Yes, I'm still alive, uncle. This isn't the first time you've tried to kill me, and this isn't the first time you've failed. Rhaegos's voice dripped with mockery and condescension.

Ryluth lunged for me and I sliced at his snout with my left-hand axe as I ducked away. He howled as I tumbled into his tail once more, my other axe sinking into it.

"Ina!" Haldrek attempted to make his way to me, only to dodge the very tip of Ryluth's tail.

"Fight me, you overgrown lizard!" Henry lunged again, swinging at Ryluth's face. His blade slipped across the scales covering Ryluth's mouth and sank into one of his teeth. Much to my surprise, the blade stayed there. Ryluth shook his head, sending Henry flying once again.

Ryluth surged forward, mouth wide open in attack. Henry rolled away from where he'd dropped and I yanked my axe out of Ryluth's tail, swinging both at Ryluth's mouth. I had no idea if my attack would do anything, but the distraction seemed to be keeping Ryluth from injuring any of us seriously.

Much to my surprise, as soon as my axe connected with Ryluth's tooth it shattered, dropping Henry's sword to the ground and spraying bits of dragon bone. Ryluth howled, swinging his head toward me as he made another low, gravelly sound. I stepped backwards, trying my best to stay out of his range.

"Ina!"

I turned my attention to Haldrek just in time to see a clawed wing headed straight for my head. I ducked, glancing up to see the decayed holes in the wing as it fluttered above me. It swung back and Ryluth's body shuddered, making some of the rocks and bones around us scatter.

He howled once more, but this time I got a sense of frustration from the sound.

Rhaegos laughed. *My uncle isn't as powerful as he thinks. This room is too small for him to maneuver well in his dragon form. He tried to shift, but he can't. Use that to your advantage, little one.*

I scrambled to my feet, climbing over Ryluth's tail back toward Haldrek. As well as we seemed to be doing, we needed an actual plan if we were going to win.

Haldrek grabbed my arm as I reached for him, pulling me close, then behind him.

"Are you injured?"

"Not yet. A few—"

A whoop caught our attention, and I saw Henry swinging his blade around and dancing some kind of victory dance.

"What in the name of the dragons?" Haldrek's eyes were wide with surprise as Henry continued dancing, dodging Ryluth's biting attacks.

"He's distracting him. C'mon!" Ryluth's tail lay limp and bleeding. For a brief moment, I wondered if undead dragons healed at all? Or at a slower rate? If that was the case, we might have a chance at defeating Ryluth today. Then Rorik would be easier to defeat.

"What are you doing?"

"Taking the opportunity Henry is giving us. Where is a dragon's weakest point?"

"Base of the skull, top of the head. Ina, are you sure you can reach that spot?"

"If you and Henry can keep Ryluth distracted." I started climbing up Ryluth's spine, not waiting for Haldrek's response as a surge of energy coursed through me.

"Ina—"

I ignored Haldrek over Ryluth's howls, jumping between the spikes along his spine. Yes, this was crazy, but Ryluth seemed to be getting tired, as did Henry. If we could end this—

Ryluth snapped once more at Henry, grabbing his sword and tossing it aside as I hung onto a spike.

"Hey Ryluth! If Bjornulf can kill you, so can I!" Haldrek's shout took Ryluth's attention from Henry briefly, but as Ryluth shifted toward him, my grip loosened. The next thing I knew, I was falling down Ryluth's extended wing, directly toward one of his claws. I tumbled in freefall, knowing it was going to hurt.

As soon as I hit the ground, the air was knocked out of me and my grip on Freya's axes disappeared.

"Ina!"

Ryluth's main claw sliced between my arm and my torso. I flinched, pulling away from it, but the claw hooked into the chainmail on my arm and ripped through it, sinking into my arm. I screamed. As Ryluth pulled his wing back up, my arm exploded in pain.

Haldrek grabbed me as I tried to keep hold of the axes. My blade might come back to me, but I had no idea if the axes would. I definitely didn't want to lose them to Ryluth.

"We gotta go. Ryluth is getting frustrated, and he's going to screech soon if we don't get out of here."

"What about Henry?"

Haldrek glanced back as he pushed me forward. "He'll know to plug his ears. We need to go."

I looked back to see Henry still dodging Ryluth, keeping his attention off us. What would happen once we left?

"Haldrek, we can't just leave him."

"He'll be fine. If we all stay in here, eventually Ryluth will kill all three of us."

"So he's going to be the sacrifice?" My voice went high as we ducked out of the room and into a nearby alcove. Before Haldrek had a chance to speak, there was a bloodcurdling screech. Haldrek grabbed my ears as I grabbed his. My stomach revolted and the fresh wound in my arm burned like fire.

When the shriek ended, everything was silent. Rhaegos shuddered as if the shriek had hurt her as well.

Haldrek stayed on top of me until the sound of plodding feet faded opposite of us. It was clear whose feet made the sound. Ryluth. As soon as his footsteps disappeared, a tight knot swelled in my chest, and I struggled to breathe as tears poured down my cheeks.

Haldrek squeezed me tight before releasing me and sitting up. Even in the dim light, I could see the sorrow etched across his face.

"I'm so sorry, Ina."

Despite being out of the room, the alcove was still not a good place to hide—or rest. As soon as we were certain Ryluth—or Rorik—wasn't coming back, Haldrek helped me out. I wanted to go back into the room to get Henry, or at least to do the rites for his body. Haldrek refused, not because he didn't want to either, but because it was too dangerous. As much as I hated it, he was right.

Instead, we walked farther into the cave system, looking for somewhere to hide until we could figure out what to do next.

When we finally found a spot, Haldrek eased me down onto the ground and pulled out a small leather bag. Rummaging inside, he grabbed a loaf of bread. At that moment, I remembered what his bag was and began to bawl. It was the enchanted bag Haldrek always kept on him, but I'd first seen it in Svartån. It reminded me of the nearly limitless carrying capacity players had in the Lohikärran video games. The same games I'd played with Henry when we were younger. The same games where you never really died, you just respawned. But here, Henry couldn't respawn. This was real. Not a video game.

"Ina?"

"I'm sorry." I took the bread and started chewing on it, trying to stop my tears. It was the common travel bread with meat and vegetables baked into it, but I couldn't figure out what kind of meat or vegetables were in the bread. In fact, it didn't really taste like much more than bread.

"Don't be sorry." Haldrek gently took my injured arm and pulled at the damaged chainmail. I tried not to flinch as he pulled a couple pieces of broken mail from the gash. "It's all right to grieve fallen warriors. Henry was brave, and he kept us safe."

"We should have kept him safe too!" My whole body twitched as Haldrek put something in the gash. It burned, and I fought the urge to scream. Instead, I bit harder into the loaf of bread. When the pain released, I took a deep breath and put the rest of the bread on my lap. "This was the real Henry. Not some imposter. My friend, who kept me safe when other kids would be mean. Who would cheer me up at school when my mother and Robert had been terrible. He didn't deserve to die. It isn't fair."

Haldrek finished cleaning my wound and bandaged it. Then he wrapped his arms around me, pulling me tight into his chest. His armor was hard against my forehead, but the pressure was comforting. "It's never fair when the people we care about die. Never." He continued holding me as I wept, not caring who heard me. After a few moments, Haldrek whispered, "There is a tiny chance Henry may have survived."

"What?" I pulled back from Haldrek, wanting to see his expression. It was still serious and somber.

"Teminth thinks that because Ryluth is not at his full strength, his shriek may not have killed Henry. It may have just knocked him out."

"Are you sure?"

"Not fully. But Teminth can still sense Syralgos nearby."

"She would still be attached to Henry if he was dead, though." I sank back, a wave of weariness hitting me like a wall.

"She could be. That is true, but I know the dragons can sense if another is in a different realm."

Rhaegos? Is Syralgos still in this realm?

A few moments of tense quiet passed in my mind before Rhaegos groaned.

She is near. I cannot tell if she is in this realm with your friend Henry or not, though. Ryluth's screech was meant to kill humans and injure dragons.

Despite Rhaegos's weariness, I tried to fight my own exhaustion. The mere idea that Henry could still be alive made me want to go find him. That's what friends did. They took care of each other. As I got up, Haldrek grabbed my good arm to stop me.

"Ina, I know what you're trying to do. Don't."

"Would you leave an injured warrior to die after a fight?" I snapped. As I tried to pull out of his grip, he held firm.

"Ina, we're too exhausted to go back there." There was no judgement or anger in Haldrek's tone. "You, me, our dragons. If Henry is alive, but people and dragons think he's dead, no one is going to go after him. If he is dead, there isn't much we can do right now. As much as I hate to say it, neither of us are in a position to do any death rites." Haldrek stopped for a moment. "If he were dead, don't you think his spirit would come looking for us? You would be able to see that."

Haldrek was right. As I looked around, there was no sign of any spirits. Not even Henry. I sat back down tiredly, tears pouring down my face. Today had been a long day already. Physically, emotionally, just in general.

"Come rest." Haldrek scooted against the side of our little hidden spot and leaned back. He pulled something else from his enchanted bag and put it on his lap. As he helped me lay down on the soft fur skin, he whispered, "I'm not going to let you get yourself killed either. If I'm Bjornulf, then you're my Freya. Just like they needed to work together, so do we. I need my Freya, my Heart of Lohikärra."

"So what do we do now?" I wiped the remaining tears from my face. Already I was feeling the headache that always followed.

"We rest and plan. Let Rorik and Ryluth think we are dead or injured. And then tomorrow, we kill them."

Chapter 24

I t didn't take long before I was asleep. I had a feeling this time, Rhaegos had helped me fall asleep as much as Haldrek did. I remembered her exhaustion as I fell asleep and wondered if she needed rest just as much as I did.

Before long, I was conscious of my surroundings again. Not that I was awake. I was in another realm, that much was clear. As I tried to get my bearings, I heard a familiar shout:

"Bow before me! I am your master now!" Rorik's voice echoed through the rocky halls.

"Never! I'll never bow before some pasty-faced zombie fucker!" Henry's voice boomed in response. My heart tightened. Were we in the Realm of Ghosts? Without thinking, I ran toward the voices. Even if my physical body was weak and exhausted, I knew I had decent strength here. If Rorik tried to start shit with Henry, he'd have to fight me too.

As soon as I entered the room, I knew it was the altar room. Despite being clear of bodies, the shape was the same, and I saw the same carved out altar on the opposite side of the room.

In the center of the room, Henry and Rorik were squared off, fists at the ready. Even though Henry had always been tall, it surprised me how much he towered over Rorik.

"I said bow before me, peasant!" Rorik's hands glowed both green and blue, as if he was charging up some kind of magical curse.

"He is no peasant!" Another man strode over from behind Henry. I hadn't seen him before, and that surprised me. Slipping into the room for a better look, I noticed he looked like he could be Henry's older brother. There wasn't much of an age gap between the two. That said, he didn't have Henry's nose. Between the clothing he wore and the trinkets styled in his hair, I knew he was Lohikärran.

Rorik's attention turned to him. "And who were you, ghost? You act as if you own this realm."

The man laughed. "No one owns this realm, even the dragons. But I have lived here since you were a squalling babe. You may think you have mastery over the Realm of Ghosts, but you don't."

"Tell me your name, peasant, and I will destroy your soul swiftly."

The man laughed. "You are terrible at negotiations. Or threats. Whatever it is you just tried to do. As it is, I am no peasant. My father was the High King. Your father groveled before me many a time in our youth."

Rorik scowled and launched an orb of magic at the man. He was tossed back against the cavern wall and grunted as he hit it. Even though the man looked worse for the wear, he sat up quickly, shaking out his limbs.

"You stupid—" Henry lunged for Rorik, slugging him in the face and knocking him to the ground. Before he could land another swing, however, he was in the air, flying back toward the altar. As soon as Henry crashed into it, Rorik stumbled to his feet.

"I'm done with you two. For now." He ran out of the room, much to my surprise. For someone who was trying to overthrow Haldrek and me and rule Lohikärra, Rorik didn't like to fight. At least not physically.

As Henry and the other man stumbled to their feet, I moved from my vantage point, hoping to interact with them. I didn't want to freak out Henry too much if we were really in the Realm of Ghosts.

As I stepped out from where I'd been, the room disappeared. Instead, a large yellow eye opened in front of me.

"Where do you think you're going?"

I stumbled back, only to stiffen as I felt a sharp claw poke ever so slightly into my back.

"I haven't even begun what I'm going to do to you," Ryluth's voice rumbled as the eye closed and the space around me began to shake. I flinched, closing my eyes until the shaking stopped.

When I opened them again, I saw a sour-looking man staring at me. He was familiar, with ash-gray skin and deep, rotted scars. His clothing was both pitch black and shimmered with some kind of iridescence as he walked toward me. A cape hung around him and, despite looking well made, it had holes in it, as if something had ripped through it.

"I still don't know why I can shift here, but not in the Realm of the Living." Ryluth scowled, making him look more sour. "Rorik must have messed up the spell somehow. He thinks he is an amazing necromancer, but he's really quite mediocre. I had priests who could raise legions of perfectly restored corpses with a finger snap."

I doubted that was true, but at the same time, I wasn't about to say anything. I might have some skills here in the Realm of Ghosts, but I wasn't sure I could go toe to toe with a reanimated dragon who was probably still pissed about the fact that I'd nearly killed him a few hours prior.

"You weren't anywhere near close to killing me, you insignificant gnat." Ryluth stopped only a few feet from me with a look, as if he was trying to assess me. It was the same expression I'd seen Seirye wear years ago, and even my mother in what seemed like another lifetime. "I hear the other dragons speak of you as if you were like Freya." He took a deep whiff and scoffed. "You may be Freya's descent, but I can already see you have nowhere near her skill or her intellect." He grimaced. "As loath as I am to admit that." He shuddered as he began to walk around me and I shuffled away, keeping my eyes on him at all times. I let my hands hang loose, feeling Freya's axes at my hips.

"Even if I'm not Freya, I can still protect the land she fought so hard for."

Ryluth laughed louder and examined one of his hands, now transformed into a set of claws. "You can barely protect your own offspring. No, soon I will feast on your soul, as well as those of your loved ones. Your mate, your offspring, and the rest of your allies and kin. Rorik may be a terrible necromancer, but he is good at killing people. Very good. I will not fight you. You aren't worthy of my time. I will have him kill you and your loved ones, then bring them to me to consume as I regain my full power."

Rage and powerlessness flooded through my body. Without thinking, I grabbed the axes at my side and pulled them out, swinging them at Ryluth. Even if I couldn't kill him, I could still injure him.

Before I could blink, however, the axes were out of my hands and I was on the ground several feet away. Ryluth slowly walked toward me until he stood at my feet with the axes in his hands.

"You dare think you can fight me, human?"

I froze as he started to swing the axes around, knowing I'd made a terrible mistake. Right as he raised the axes above my head and swung down, I flinched, expecting to feel the blow of those axes against my skull. Instead, there was a scream of indignation and a shout:

"Ina! Wake up!"

"Ina! Wake up!" Haldrek's voice cut through the fog of my sleep, his voice tinged with worry.

"I'm awake." My throat was dry and raspy, the words hurting as I spoke. "What's going on?"

Haldrek exhaled deeply and his head sunk into my shoulder. "I thought... I thought something had happened. Maybe Ryluth's claw was poisoned or something. Some of Rorik's fighters almost found us. You weren't waking up like normal."

"I was in the Realm of Ghosts. I saw Henry. And someone else. They were arguing with Rorik and trying to fight him." Tears bubbled up and poured down my cheeks as Henry's death hit me once more. I couldn't even say goodbye to him in the Realm of Ghosts without Ryluth interfering.

"Who was the other person?" Haldrek whispered as he handed me his water skin. I drank, letting the liquid soothe my throat.

When I finished, I leaned against the rough-hewn rocks. "A son of Kalle. That's what he said. Now that I think of it, he looked like he could have been Henry's older brother."

"Jaari, then. He would be the only one of Kalle's children who hadn't had their rites done. At least as far as I know."

I frowned. "Why? You can do the rites for someone even if their body isn't around."

Haldrek shrugged. "His parents forbade it. I was a small child when everything happened, so I only remember what others have told me. Kalle refused to do his son's rites until the Blodnar emperor returned Jaari's body. The Blodnar emperor refused to do that until his daughter was returned to him."

"And Henry's mother was in Fargo all this time." I leaned forward, stretching my back and brushing the rest of my tears off my cheeks. "When this is done, we need to find her and take Henry's body back to her. Wherever she is. If she's still alive."

"Is there a chance she isn't?"

I nodded. "Remember? Henry mentioned something about his uncle trying to kill him and his mother protecting him. He seemed to think she might be dead."

Haldrek was quiet for a long while, his expression downcast as if trying to find the right words. When he looked up at me, he sighed. "Even if she's alive, she'll be in the Blodnar empire somewhere. As dear of a friend as Henry was to you, neither of us are searching for her."

I opened my mouth to argue, but Haldrek shook his head. "No. I understand why you'd want to send his body back to her—"

"As a mother, I'd want to bury my child." The words squeaked out as my thoughts shifted to Eero. If Henry's mother loved him as much as I loved Eero, she'd be heartbroken to not say goodbye one last time.

"I understand, Ina. But things are still fragile between our two lands. You know this. My information gatherers tell me the Blodnar emperor's son is just as bloodthirsty as his father was. If Henry's mother is still alive, she can come here. To Lohikärra." Haldrek exhaled deeply. "As loathe as I am to grant any protection to a Blodnar royal, I would do that much. But not until we deal with Rorik and Ryluth."

My heart twisted at the thought of Haldrek barely tolerating Henry's mom just because she was Norycian, but I knew I wasn't going to get much more from him. At least not now.

"We should still find his body and put it somewhere safe. So none of Rorik's thugs can take off with it."

"If they haven't already." Haldrek muttered the words off-handedly, then turned to me wide-eyed as I stared at him in horror.

I stumbled to my feet. "We need to find his body. What if Rorik raises him from the dead and uses him to fight us?" The more I thought about it, the more confident I was that Rorik would avoid a physical fight if he could. But use a reanimated fighter? Or force Henry to fight for him? Of course he'd do that.

"Ina, hold up—"

I ignored Haldrek's words as I looked for my weapons and anything else we would need. Freya's Menace lay sheathed against the stone, but her axes were nowhere to be seen. I turned around to see Haldrek holding the partially eaten loaf of travel bread in my face.

"Before we go, we should probably eat something quick."

I grabbed the bread, scanning the area for the axes. They were nowhere to be seen. Where were they? They had to be here.

"Where are my axes? Freya's axes?"

Haldrek looked at where my sword still leaned against the wall. "They should be next to your blade."

I turned and felt around in the dark until something heavy and tapered hit my right glove. Not risking any magic light, I continued to feel around the object. It was one of Freya's axes, but it was cracked. Someone had broken the axe head off from the staff. The memory of Ryluth grabbing them from me sent a wave of icy fear through my body.

"Ina?"

"My... Freya's hand axes, the ones that could cut through dragon scale. They're shattered."

"What do you mean?" Haldrek shuffled next to me, creating a small orb of light with his hand. It lit up the small space and, sure enough, both axes were shattered into dozens of pieces.

"How...?"

"Ryluth. It has to be." Grief and anger over losing the weapons washed through me. "He came after me while I was in the Realms of Ghosts. Told me how he was going to destroy all of us and how I wasn't anything like Freya. I attacked him, but he grabbed the axes and retaliated with them. I only woke up because you called out to me."

The magic light disappeared, and Haldrek wrapped his arm around my shoulders. "I'm sorry, Ina. Perhaps the axes were destroyed to prevent him from using them against you."

"Or maybe he destroyed them when he couldn't use them against me." I took a deep breath and wiped my tears away, trying to compose myself. I wanted to bawl, but feared anyone else finding us.

"We'll still be able to fight him and Rorik. You have Freya's Menace and we know that is just as powerful as the axes."

"I know. But still... first Henry and now my axes. Ryluth is really trying to break us."

"Of course he is. We'll still defeat him. I promise." Haldrek squeezed me tight. When he released me, he tapped the bread still in my hand. "First, we need to eat. And...then we should probably find Henry. At the very least to make sure Rorik doesn't turn him into one of his undead."

Chapter 25

Haldrek and I ate in silence, listening for anyone who might be nearby. But the cave was still deathly silent. Once we finished, we packed up our gear and slipped out of the alcove. Haldrek guided me back in the direction we had fled and I tried not to imagine what we'd find when we returned to the cavern where Henry had fallen.

Much to my surprise, as we got closer, the sound of muffled voices met us. I didn't understand the words, but they sounded like they were chanting.

Haldrek unsheathed his sword. "They're sacrificing someone. We need to get in there. Now."

I pulled Freya's Menace out and followed him into the space. It was much brighter now and a half dozen necromancers stood around the altar at the far end of the room where someone was shouting. One priest leaned over the altar as if he was struggling to hold the person down.

"Hey!" Haldrek shouted, gaining the attention of a few of the necromancers. As they left the altar, I saw the victim. A large, burly man swinging his bound arms and legs, kicking and hitting whoever he could. Despite the gag in his mouth, I could hear him swearing at the remaining priests.

Henry was alive?

My attention turned to movement on my left and I swung at the necromancer who had decided to fight me. I hit him in the wrists with Freya's Menace and he immediately shrieked, dropping and releasing his magic onto the ground. It hit a nearby pile of bones, scattering them, as Haldrek stabbed the necromancer through the back.

More came at us, leaving just the one priest at the altar. Henry kept swinging at him and it surprised me the man hadn't gotten clobbered yet.

"Too-Welli-Ballo!" A large orb of fire sailed toward the remaining necromancers, taking most of them to the ground, where Haldrek and I made quick work of them.

Henry's loud scream brought my attention back to him and the last priest. The necromancer had raised his dagger above Henry's prone body. I lunged, swinging my blade under his outstretched arm. As my sword sank through his robes and into his ribs, he dropped the dagger and crumpled to the ground with a grunt. Haldrek stabbed him in the neck, killing him and releasing the necromancer's spirit, who immediately glared at me.

"That's what you get for trying to kill my friend," I snapped, watching the spirit keep his distance from me, before turning back to Henry.

Haldrek had ignored my outburst and was quickly untying Henry's bound wrists and ankles. "You have a story to tell, my friend."

As I undid Henry's gag, he grinned. "We're friends now?"

Haldrek grimaced and nodded. "I suppose so. If we weren't, I would have let them sacrifice you."

"What?" Henry's eyes widened as Haldrek tried to suppress his laughter. I nudged him in the ribs.

"No, I wouldn't have let them sacrifice you. I fear Ina's wrath more than I do Rorik's or Ryluth's. Still, I'm curious why you aren't already dead. Or a reanimated corpse."

"Yeah. I saw you last night. In the Realm of Ghosts. With—"

"With my dad, Jaari. It was good to see him again. Kinda. Not that being in the Realm of Ghosts was great. But I always wished I could have known him better. After all the stories my mom told me about him." Henry's face fell, and he looked at me. "If you're able to go into the Realm of Ghosts, are you able to see everyone who has died?"

"Theoretically. It's easier if their body is nearby, but that's not a requirement."

Henry nodded. "I asked Jaari if my mom was in the realm with him, but he didn't say anything. Rorik showed up before I could push more."

I shrugged. "During the short time I was there last night, I didn't see her. If she was in the Realm of Ghosts, I would think she'd find a way to be with you and Jaari. I know how much she loved you, and I assume she still loves your dad."

Henry nodded once more. "Yeah. That would make sense."

"How are you still alive? What happened after we, um, escaped?" Haldrek scrunched up the chainmail on the back of his neck and I knew he was feeling somewhat embarrassed.

"I honestly don't know. Maybe I was knocked unconscious? I just remember everything going black after the dragon scream. I woke up to my dad poking me with something, maybe his shoe? He said I didn't belong here. That I needed to go home." Henry's jaw tightened like he was trying to control himself.

"He was probably talking about being in the Realm of Ghosts." I said softly, reaching out for Henry's shoulder. "I saw you confront Rorik. When Rorik called you a peasant..."

Henry laughed quietly. "Yeah, Jaari called him out on that. After Rorik ran away, Jaari, my dad, told me I needed to leave and kick Rorik's butt for him. That I couldn't do it there." He paused for a moment. "You know, maybe you're right. Maybe that's what he was talking about. Either way, he told me to follow Rorik, but as soon as I left the room, everything was black again. I fumbled around for a bit and then a bunch of the necromancers grabbed me and dragged me to the altar." He jabbed his finger at the stone where he'd be fighting to get off.

Haldrek frowned. "Wait, when did they tie you up?"

"When they found me in the dark, I think. They tackled me and I hit my head. One of them muttered something about keeping me alive until they could kill me. Apparently Rorik or Ryluth wanted me not just dead, destroyed."

Haldrek nodded. "Well, I'm glad we were able to help you not die. Again." He glanced at me and I squeezed his glove. All I felt right now was relief. As long as all of us—Haldrek, Henry, and I—were alive and safe, we could fight Rorik. We could win.

Henry glanced in the direction we'd come from and grimaced. "We should probably head out. It won't be long before Rorik knows something is up. Or Ryluth. I doubt we have the element of surprise anymore."

Haldrek and I both nodded.

"Do we know which direction we need to go, when we leave this room?"

Henry nodded. "Syralgos said she'd lead me."

Haldrek glanced once more at me and I squeezed his hand.

"Let's go then. We should confront Rorik and Ryluth sooner rather than later."

As we made our way through the tunnels, my mind mulled over what we would do once we got to wherever Rorik and Ryluth were hiding. It hadn't been lost on me that Rorik tended to flee from every direct confrontation and let others fight on his behalf. I wondered if he would do that again once we found him. Would he let Ryluth fight instead of him again? Probably. Whether or not he did, we'd still have to destroy Ryluth. How were we going to take down a dragon?

Apparently I wasn't the only one thinking about what would happen.

"We need a plan." Henry looked back at the two of us. "I'm guessing we didn't really have one when we arrived yesterday. If we did, it went out the window pretty quickly."

Haldrek grumbled. "We have a plan—kill Rorik and Ryluth. But there wasn't much we could plan for until we saw what was going on in here. We still don't know how many fighters or necromancers Rorik is holding back."

"Syralgos says Rorik's forces are dwindling. He's been sending too many followers out to attack the various villages and he's running low on people, even the undead. His best necromancers he's been keeping here, and we've been slowly taking them out. According to Syralgos, raising the dead takes about as much energy as sending them to the afterlife."

"Huh." That was good news. Even the most resilient Priest of Tenelth or haldraga could only do a handful of rites before needing rest or food. If we'd been taking out Rorik's necromancers, chances were we wouldn't be holding our own against a large army of undead.

Haldrek laughed softly, his voice sounding hopeful. "Rorik might be a capable necromancer, but it looks like he doesn't know how to manage a large amount of warriors or mages for a long time. We'll have to use that in our favor."

"Agreed. That said, Syralgos mentioned we're going to have to fight Rorik and Ryluth at the same time. We can't fully kill either as long as they are connected, even if Rorik is a weak fighter and Ryluth is still half dead."

Rhaegos shifted in the back of my mind, but said nothing. Instead, a sense of unease crept over me, as if she was keeping something hidden.

Is there something I should know, Rhaegos?

She didn't respond, but the unease shifted into a bittersweet sadness, the same feeling I'd had when I left Eero back in Drattüjert. I'd known I needed to leave him in order to protect him, but that didn't mean I wanted to. As the feeling washed over me, I stopped, trying to control my breathing so I wouldn't start sobbing.

"Ina?" Haldrek stopped and put his hand on my shoulder. "Are you all right?"

I took a deep breath and shook my head. "How are we going to fight a necromancer and an undead dragon at the same time? Especially if Rorik keeps fleeing any kind of physical fight?"

Haldrek didn't respond immediately, and I looked up at him. I noticed Henry had stopped as well. Haldrek's expression had turned somber, as if he was trying to comprehend some kind of new information.

"How are we going to fight Rorik and Ryluth together?" Henry's voice was much quieter. "Syralgos said we need to, but she never said how we would do it. Only that we needed to figure that part out."

"We three humans can't fight them together. At least in this realm." Haldrek grumbled in annoyance. "This is why I hate necromancers. They can do this stupid realm shit." He took a deep breath and continued, "Rhaegos, Teminth, and Syralgos will have to fight Ryluth in the Realm of Dragons while we fight here against Rorik. Teminth says Rorik has a talisman that's acting as a connection between the two. He's not certain, but he thinks we'll have to destroy whatever that is to win against both of them."

Henry nodded, and I stood up, Rhaegos's bittersweet sadness suddenly making sense. She was feeling that because… because she was going to have to fight Ryluth while I was fighting Rorik. I wouldn't necessarily have her to rely on. At the same time, another thought flashed through my mind—Rhaegos wouldn't be feeling that bittersweet sadness unless she perceived me as one of her children. The thought felt uncomfortable. Why would a mighty dragon like Rhaegos consider someone like me their child?

Do not underestimate yourself, little one. I wouldn't have bonded with you if I didn't see you as my kin. Though I would never force you to see me as a mother, you are very much like any offspring I have ever had, and I would protect you with every breath I have. In this realm and in any other.

More tears poured down my face, and I turned away from where Haldrek and Henry were still softly talking, going over how we would ultimately fight Rorik and Ryluth.

Thank you, Rhaegos. And I do see you as a mother. Here in Lohikärra, at least. An intense feeling of love filled me and I let myself embrace the emotion, tears and all. Even though I couldn't see, I pretended to watch the hallway behind us. *Please be safe, Rhaegos. I don't want to lose you.*

You won't lose me, little one. Ryluth has never bested me yet, even with his trickery. He won't best me now with Teminth and Syralgos at my side.

I closed my eyes, brushing the tears away, and pushing out a sense of gratitude to Rhaegos.

"Ina?"

I turned around to see Henry and Haldrek staring at me.

"Sorry. I was—I was talking to Rhaegos."

"Any more information on how to fight Rorik and Ryluth?" Henry looked hopeful before I shook my head.

"Nothing more than what Teminth and Syralgos already said. The dragons will fight Ryluth and we'll fight Rorik."

Henry nodded and Haldrek wrapped his arm around me, pulling me toward him and squeezing me close.

"Henry and I think the talisman will be an important part of fighting Rorik and Ryluth. If we can destroy that, it will sever their connection."

"But we're not quite sure what the talisman is." Henry pulled out his pendant. "Your husband thinks it is this, but Rorik's. I think it's something else connected to Ryluth. Syralgos said these pendants usually disappear when the connection between a haldraga and their dragon disappears."

"Rorik is still connected to a dragon, which means he has to have a pendant."

"He could have used whatever relic he had when he raised Ryluth from the dead."

"Maybe both?" I looked at Haldrek and Henry, then glanced back to make sure we were still alone. "Could he have created a new pendant from the relic?"

Both of them shrugged. "It's a possibility." Haldrek took a deep breath and exhaled. "Only way to find out is if we can corner Rorik. Then we can see if he has a pendant or something else."

"So maybe we focus on finding just him instead? Force him into a physical fight?" Henry's tone lifted, and he sounded excited once more.

Haldrek nodded. "We fight him, grab whatever is connecting him to Ryluth, destroy it, and then kill him while..." Haldrek paused as if he didn't want to say the next part. "While our dragons fight Ryluth."

I squeezed Haldrek's hand to comfort him. I knew why those words terrified him. As much as I relied on Rhaegos, Haldrek relied even more on Teminth. I'd seen how weak he'd been in Fargo without Teminth's aid. If we were going into this fight without them...

"We can do this." Henry turned and began walking further into the mountain. "I doubt they would have led us here if they weren't confident in our ability to fight Rorik."

Chapter 26

Henry led us through the tunnels, only pausing a couple of times when I assumed Syralgos was helping him. After what felt like hours, we came to a much larger room that expanded out, far above our heads. It felt familiar, yet I knew I'd never been here before.

You have been here before, little one. Just not in this realm. This is the place where Rorik tried to kill me while his followers tried to kill you and Henry.

As soon as Rhaegos said that, I remembered the room. Now it was mostly dark, only lit by a pale light in the distance. My sense of time was all messed up, but even so, I knew it should still be day. The glow reminded me of dim moonlight, but from a different angle. It made everything feel off.

"Is anyone else creeped out by this room?" Henry unsheathed his sword. "Syralgos is not happy here."

"Agreed. Teminth told me to be on alert as soon as we entered. There is something strange about this room." Haldrek gestured for me to get behind him, and while I appreciated his protectiveness, I wondered how much it would help if we were attacked.

"This is the place where Rorik attacked and tried to kill Rhaegos. Not in this realm, but in a parallel one. I'm guessing maybe there is a magical residue remaining, or maybe moving between the realms?"

"Possibly. It wouldn't surprise me that any place where a dragon dies, or nearly does, would be affected by it." Haldrek pulled out his sword and cast a small orb of light into the air as high as he could. I gasped as it revealed just how large the room was. No wonder this had been the place where Rhaegos and Ryluth had confronted each other. It was massive, easily fitting both if they had chosen to transform into dragons.

Rhaegos laughed. *It is not that large. But yes, a cavern like this is made with dragons in mind.*

"How much you wanna bet this is where Ryluth naps?" Henry's voice was soft, but I could tell he was planning something with that comment.

Haldrek turned to him. "What are you thinking?"

"Dragons have to rest, don't they? At least their physical form?"

"Sometimes." Haldrek hesitated for a moment. "What *exactly* are you thinking?"

"We see if we can bring the fight to Ryluth. Attack him when he's sleeping." Henry began sneaking into the room, disappearing as he edged along a group of boulders.

A huff and mild panic entered my thoughts as Rhaegos spoke. *That child has Jaari's impulsiveness, that is for sure.*

Before I had a chance to respond, Haldrek moved after Henry.

"Hold on." Haldrek carefully cast another ball of magic light, sending it away from us, but at an angle that would allow us to see more of the room. The light bounced off a wall in front of us, illuminating a few scales before being snuffed out.

The rumbling of a dragon's voice, one I could only imagine was Ryluth, made me stop cold. Even Rhaegos seemed to hesitate in my mind.

A responding rumble came from Haldrek, much to my surprise. Before I could react, he dropped to the ground. Something pushed me down as well, seconds before Ryluth's tail swung heavily over our heads. It crashed into some nearby rocks, then swung back.

"Ina!" Haldrek grabbed my hand, pulling me inside a stone crevice as rock chunks tumbled over us. Ryluth's voice boomed again, but I couldn't understand what he was saying.

He's ranting about how he will destroy you all. He doesn't know Haldrek is the only one who can understand him.

Ryluth lunged for the space Haldrek and I had tucked ourselves into, smashing into the rocks as Haldrek pushed me away, out of Ryluth's range.

Run, little one. Against the edge of the room.

I did as Rhaegos said, pulling my blade out just in case. One of Ryluth's wings nearly clipped me and I swung, nicking the flesh around his claw. He howled and pulled back as I ducked under another ledge. Unfamiliar human voices joined the fray as I tried to find either Haldrek or Henry in the shadows. No sign of bluish light told me they were alive, even if they were still hiding from Ryluth.

"You dare defile the great Ryluth's place of rest?" A man's voice, unfamiliar to me, echoed from the center of the chamber. I saw a staff rise, its gem casting out a bright, garish light.

The light dimmed before spreading out, causing both men and dragons to howl.

No!

An intense, searing pain radiated from my chest and I screamed in pain, crumbling to my knees as Rhaegos's presence was ripped from me. An emptiness followed as I rolled to my back, vaguely aware of what was going on around me.

"Fool! What did you do?"

"I cast their dragons—" The man's response was cut short with a grunt. I knew I'd see at least one ghost before I left this chamber.

"You sent all the dragons out of this realm! Including Ryluth! Do you know how long it took me to bring him here?"

As much as my body ached from Rhaegos's forcible removal, I had to laugh on the inside. Rorik was pissed. One of his men had completely screwed him over, and that mistake could be used to our benefit.

The man Rorik had stabbed groaned for a moment longer, and a light blue spirit rose from him.

"You may have been an incompetent necromancer, but I still have a use for you yet." Rorik raised his staff, dragging the man's body upright through some kind of necromantic magic. He groaned once more, but now as a zombie.

"The rest of you, keep looking for them. Kill them. They'll be weak and it'll make our task all the more easy." I stayed still, watching as Rorik hurried from the room. As soon as he left, the men scattered. I knew I needed to push through the emptiness, the weakness I now felt.

Pulling myself up, I locked eyes with one necromancer as he charged me, using his staff like a spear instead of a wand. Interesting. I blocked him with my blade, throwing my body weight into the attack and cutting most of the way through it. As he yanked back, the staff snapped, releasing my blade, and I swung once more, hitting him in the arm, then jamming my sword into his chest as I began to feel stronger again.

"Ina! Behind you!"

I spun around at the sound of Henry's voice and nearly collided with a man who grabbed for my hair. I ducked away and took a swipe at him, making him back off.

"I will not fail my lord Rorik. You will perish this day, wench." He lunged with his staff and I grabbed it, ignoring the spiky pain in my hand as I stabbed him with my sword. The necromancer howled and stumbled away as I shoved him off my blade. Before he could react, I yanked the staff from his hand and tossed it to the ground. Just as he reached for it, Haldrek's sword sank between his shoulder blades. The necromancer slumped to the ground, his ghost slipping between Haldrek and me.

I pulled Haldrek through the apparition and hugged him, letting his solidness comfort me in Rhaegos's absence.

"Are you all right, Ina? Did you get hurt?"

My hand stung from the staff, but I shook my head. "I'm fine, just a little shaken up from..."

"From the spell the necromancer cast?"

I nodded. "Do we know where they went?"

Haldrek hesitated before answering me. "Not really. He could have cast them any-where."

Fear crept up my spine as I wondered if they'd been sent back to Fargo. As little as I cared for my former home, no one there deserved to have dragons raging above them. Especially not Ryluth.

"I wish there was a way to figure out where they went."

Labored steps caused Haldrek and I to turn as Henry made his way over to us.

"What the hell was that? I felt like I was getting my guts ripped out or something."

"One of Rorik's necromancers cast a spell, dragging our dragons away from us and into another realm." Haldrek's voice was somber as he answered. "On the one hand, it kept Ryluth from killing us. On the other..."

"We're weaker now. Less durable," I whispered. Even though Rhaegos's presence had helped me often when I was in physical stress, her presence during time of emotional weakness is what I missed more. I felt less stable with her gone.

Henry nodded. "When we defeat Ryluth and Rorik, they should come back? Right?"

"It is possible. It would depend on what realm they went to. Whether they are still self-aware."

"So there's still hope." Henry straightened up. "We've killed all the necromancers and zombies in here. I want to say Rorik ran away through that entrance." Henry pointed to his right. "Let's go kick his ass."

We slowly made our way through a much smaller hall that wound its way through the mountain. Without Syralgos, Henry was less confident about which way to go, so we kept a glowing orb above us to look for clues. At this point, if we confronted anyone, it wasn't exactly a surprise that we were here. I noticed there were barely any signs of people staying in these tunnels, or any of the alcoves that branched off them. If Rhaegos had still been with me, I would have asked her what she thought.

"This feels like Fargo once again." Haldrek grumbled, stretching out his shoulders. "I don't like being without Teminth."

Henry chuckled, and I couldn't help but smile. Technically, it wasn't funny, but there was a twisted humor in our misery as well. In some ways, this was exactly like being in Fargo. Once again, we'd been tossed into an unpleasant situation because of a power-hungry necromancer. I wondered if Henry and I were more adept at being without our dragons because we'd grown up outside of Sethys.

"Welcome to the world of living without dragons." Henry spun around to face us. "Not that I minded having Syralgos around. I hope she'll be back when we destroy Rorik and Ryluth. But this doesn't feel much different from when I was growing up."

Haldrek didn't respond, and I could tell he was taking this harder than either Henry or me. I took his hand in mine and squeezed it.

"We'll be fine, Haldrek. We were able to fix things in Fargo. We'll be able to fix things here, too."

He rubbed the back of my hand with his thumb in response and said softly, "I'm not worried about whether we'll be able to fix things. I believe we will. But what sacrifices are we going to have to make to fix what Rorik has destroyed?" Suddenly, he hugged me tightly, lifting me off my heels. As I wrapped my arms around his neck to keep my balance, he whispered, "I love you, Ina. I don't think you know how much I appreciate you. How much better things are when you're by my side."

I stared at him as he let me go and I dropped back on my heels.

"I promise we'll deal with Rorik once and for all. When we do, when this whole entire threat is over and we're safe, we'll return to Drattüjert and celebrate. And for far longer than we did when we became High King and Queen."

The wetness in his eyes made me want to hug him once more. This was a side of Haldrek I'd rarely seen. He was terrified.

"We'll get back to Drattüjert." I gripped Haldrek's hands, trying to comfort him. "All three of us." I glanced over at Henry, who was watching the scene awkwardly. "You can meet Eero and see Mattie again and meet her family." Turning back to Haldrek, I smiled. "I trust you, and I trust that this isn't the end of our story. Not by a long shot."

Haldrek wrapped his arms around me and, after a moment, his hug became more relaxed.

"Thank you, Ina." He looked over at Henry. "I apologize. My fears got the best of me."

Henry shook his head and started walking again. "It's fine. I think we're all on edge. This is the championship game, you know?" He laughed. "It's been a while since I've used football analogies."

Haldrek laughed softly as well. "I don't exactly understand what you mean about this football, but I'm assuming it is a Fargo thing."

Henry nodded. "It's a sport. Lots of running around and throwing a ball to score points. There's a ton more to it than that, but the championship game is where you face your toughest opponent. Only one of you will win. So right now is like the moments right before the championship game. The team has come so far, but we're still not there yet. And there's always the worry that this might be the time you don't win. The time when you're risking everything."

"That I understand." Haldrek nodded slowly, still holding my hand. "I think we're near the end, too. At this point, either Rorik wins or we do. I'm going to do everything I can to make sure he doesn't."

"Agreed." Henry and I responded at the same time. The conversation lulled as we continued to walk, slowly making our way down the tunnel as it angled lower into the heart of the mountain. After a little bit, Henry said, "When all is said and done, I hope to see my mom again. If she's still alive. And if I have the chance. But I also know that it might be a while before that happens."

"Why?" I glanced between him and Haldrek.

Henry glanced back at me before turning his attention to where we were going. "Because of who I am. I might be half-Lohikärran, but I'm also half-Norycian. Add in the fact that the Emperor was my mom's dad..."

"Means Henry will probably be staying in Drattüjert with us for a while until we and whoever is in control of the Norycian empire figure out some kind of peace."

I stood there, stunned. I knew that Henry was connected to both the emperor of Norycium and the former High King, but I'd never thought about the implications of that.

"Ina?" Haldrek tugged me forward, and I pulled back.

"Are you going to put him in the dungeon when we return to Drattüjert? Like the imposter?"

Haldrek shook his head. "That wasn't my plan. Henry will be restricted to the palace, but he'll be given privileges as befit his status."

"Like what?" I glanced toward where Henry had been standing, but he was gone now. Why wasn't he more upset about this?

"Ina, not now. I promise Henry won't be left in the dungeons. Like he said earlier, depending on who is on the throne in Norycium, Drattüjert may be a safer place for him."

"It'll still be a prison, Haldrek."

"Would you rather me let him just wander wherever he'd like in Lohikärra?"

Before I could respond, Henry came hurrying back.

"Hey, Ina, I'll be fine in Drattüjert. I trust you and you trust Haldrek, so I'm not worried. But that's not important right now. You two need to see this."

Haldrek and I immediately straightened up, following Henry further down the tunnel until it flattened out. Around us, sconces with torches in them made the small space feel incredibly bright. A large archway stood in front of us and, despite nothing blocking us from going in, the air felt thicker and heavier. On the other side, the sound of chanting echoed, bringing goosebumps to my skin. Whatever was in there felt nothing like any of the other chambers we'd been to.

"What's in there?" My voice squeaked as I stepped back.

"I don't know, but that sounds like Rorik." Haldrek stepped forward and panic flushed through me, images of him dying flooding my mind.

I grabbed his hand. "We should be careful, just in case. I don't want a repeat of Ryluth."

Haldrek grimaced and nodded.

"Should we slip in together? Stay along the edge until we know what's going on?" Henry stepped forward, gingerly touching the darkness. Now it almost looked like a thick fog. "There doesn't seem to be anything strange about the air, other than it being darker than normal. I can go in first. I promise I won't go running off again."

"Fine." Haldrek gestured, moving so Henry could slip ahead of him.

As Henry entered through the archway and disappeared into the darkness, I looked at Haldrek.

"I'm sorry for getting upset."

"It's fine. He's your friend. It's something we can deal with once we return to Drattüjert." Haldrek paused. "I love you, Ina. In case anything happens when we go in there, I want you to know that."

"I know. And I love you too." I took a deep breath to calm my nerves. Seeing Haldrek anxious didn't help me at all.

Henry popped his head out from the heavy darkness. "Are you two coming? Or do I need to pull a repeat of the last chamber?" He grinned impishly.

"We're coming." Haldrek grumbled, grabbing my hand. Without another word, we hurried into the ominous room before us.

Chapter 27

The fog at the archway had been an illusion of some kind. As soon as we passed through it, the air became clearer, although still dark and carrying an ominous weight.

Henry grabbed my free hand, pulling all of us around the edge of the room. When we made it to a spot where we could see Rorik, we stopped. My chest was frozen with fear.

In the center of the room, Rorik was levitating a few feet above the ground. In his right hand, he held a large staff with an ominous green gem at the top. It glowed brightly, as if channeling magic to his body.

"What in the name of the dragons?" Haldrek's voice was barely a whisper, his shock clear.

"It looks like Rorik has leveled up. He's now the final boss." Henry's voice was just as quiet, but there was no fear in it.

"This isn't a video game, Henry. We're not going to respawn if he kills us," I continued, staring at Rorik in horror. While he'd always been wearing robes over his armor every time I'd seen him, now they were longer and floating around him. Just like in the vision the Vollr had given me. My attention was drawn to a few more shapes on the ground. More bodies. They also wore black robes, and I assumed they were some of his followers.

"Did he...?" Henry's attention was now on the bodies as well.

"I don't know if he killed them as much as he took their life force to make himself more powerful." Haldrek shuddered. "He truly has turned himself into a monster."

"How do we fight him?"

"We need to find out what's giving him that power." Henry gestured to Rorik's staff. "I'm thinking that's a good start."

"Didn't the dragons talked about a relic or talisman?" I asked.

"Would the staff be a relic? Like your weapons? Passed down or made from something ancient?"

"Possibly. But is it giving Rorik his connection to Ryluth? That's the thing we want to destroy." Haldrek shifted slightly to get a better view, then stopped as Rorik's chanting ceased. Rorik swung his arms, adding a few more inches to his levitation, then began chanting again.

"So maybe we fight, going after his staff, but also seeing if there is something else?" Something on an altar of some kind, reflected light from Rorik's gem and I stopped, focusing on it. "What if the staff isn't the only thing that needs to be destroyed?"

"That's also a possibility," Henry murmured.

I pointed to the table where I'd seen the light reflected. "There's something on that altar Rorik is focusing on. It looks important."

Henry grinned, and I could tell he was thinking of something. "One of us should go check it out while the other two distract Rorik."

Haldrek and I glanced at each other for a moment before he nodded. "See if you can figure out what is on that altar." He looked up at Henry. "You ready to start antagonizing Rorik with me?"

Henry grinned widely. "Like you even have to ask."

Haldrek moved around me as I squeezed up against one of the rocks we'd been hiding behind. Without a word, he grabbed Henry by the shoulder, and they began moving to the left side of the chamber.

I took a deep breath and began sneaking behind rocks on the other side, doing my best not to be loud. It was impossible to be silent, but Rorik's chanting was noisy enough to drown out most of the crunching beneath my feet.

As soon as I was on the opposite side of the room, Henry tumbled out from his hiding spot and launched a rock at Rorik's head.

"Hey asshole, your singing sucks!"

Rorik went silent and turned to where Henry was doing some kind of ridiculous mocking dance.

"You fool! You know nothing of my power or what I do!" He cast a spell from his staff, which Henry dodged easily.

"Or perhaps you aren't as powerful as you want people to believe," Haldrek's voice boomed from near where we'd been standing before. "What's going to happen when Ryluth returns? Will he consume you too? You'll be nothing once more."

Rorik spun to face Haldrek, his robes floating around him like a ghost. "Silence! I am the most powerful necromancer Lohikärra has ever seen." He cast another spell at Haldrek as I hurried closer to the altar. It hit Haldrek's shield and made him stumble backwards.

"Are you so sure about that?" Henry moved back toward Haldrek and flung a dagger at Rorik. It landed within Rorik's robes and he hissed, twisting to keep his focus on Henry.

"I AM THE HEIR OF RYLUTH! My power is unmatched!" Another blast of magic caused Henry and Haldrek to jump away. The spell hit a rock, but instead of exploding, the rock turned into a pile of sand.

Haldrek straightened up, slamming his shield and sword together. "I am Haldrek of Andrattür. High King of Lohikärra and Wiglaf's Heir! You are not the first necromancer I have destroyed, and you will not be the last."

Rorik began laughing as he turned his complete focus to Haldrek. "You have always been a noble fool. Ever since we were children. If you are truly Wiglaf's Heir, fight me now."

He pulled up magic with his free hand and cast it at Haldrek. As Haldrek blocked it with his shield, another blast of necromantic magic grazed his face. I flinched as he grunted.

"You missed, Rorik. And he's not the one you should be focusing on." Henry's voice drew Rorik's attention as I hurried behind the altar. Rorik was only a few feet from me, but with his attention focused on Henry and Haldrek, I had time to figure out what exactly was the source of his power.

"You two are meddlesome. If it weren't for my sire's demands, I would crush you both and raise you as my slaves."

"I'm pretty sure Gustav isn't in a place to demand anything anymore!" Haldrek shouted, taking a swing at Rorik's robes. Henry pulled in closer as I tried to find what I'd seen before. There were plenty of bones and tarnished jewelry on this altar, remnants of earlier sacrifices. None of them would have reflected light.

"Ryluth is my sire now. I have cast off my human weakness and taken on his power instead."

"So you think you're a dragon now?" Henry started laughing as a glimmer of reflected light caught my eye.

"Silence, you fool!" Another blast of magic nearly hit Henry and blasted nearby rocks as I touched the smooth scale in front of me. Pitch black, but shimmery at the same time, I had no doubt it was one of Ryluth's. This had to be what was connecting Rorik to him. Henry grunted as he dropped to the ground and tried to knock away debris.

"You are the only fool in this room, Rorik! Your destruction is imminent." Haldrek lunged for him once more, only to get tossed back. The blast of magic hit Haldrek's shield, blowing it to smithereens.

Freya's Menace warmed in my glove as I raised it above the scale.

"This ends now, Rorik." I stood up, slamming my blade into the scale and shattering it into hundreds of little shards. As the scale broke, plumes of magic exploded outward. That wasn't normal.

"No!" He spun around, howling with anger.

I looked up in horror, only to have a massive orb of black magical aether hit me square in the chest. Freya's Menace went flying as I was lifted off my feet and backwards, slamming into the wall, my neck snapping against a jagged rock. As soon as I heard that sound, I knew something bad had happened.

"Ina! No!" Haldrek's voice sounded distant as my body fell to the floor and a terrible darkness overcame me.

Chapter 28

I opened my eyes to find myself still in the cavernous room, but feeling strange. Less fatigued, less scared, just confused. And empty. After a few moments, I realized wherever I was, not only was it lighter than before, but it was also deathly silent.

Where was Haldrek? Where was Henry? Had Rorik run off again? Did they chase after him? Henry might, but I doubted Haldrek would leave me alone.

"They're not here, thank the dragons. I don't need to kick my son out of the Realm of Ghosts again."

I sat up and spun my attention to the young man walking out of the shadows. He bowed to me.

"Hail, High Queen of Lohikärra. Welcome to the Realm of Ghosts. And here I thought I'd only be saying that once. To my mother."

Immediately, I knew who it was. "Jaari? Kalleson? I'm not... I mean... this can't be the Realm of Ghosts. I've been to the Realm of Ghosts before. This feels different."

"That's because you are actually dead this time. All the other times, your body was still alive when you moved through this realm. And while I am Jaari, I prefer Jaari the Elder now. Since I have a son who was technically named after me." He grinned widely.

I sat there, shocked, as I tried to take in everything he'd said.

"This isn't... I can't be dead. I have to fight Rorik. Henry and Haldrek..."

"Will fight him in the Realm of the Living. My cousin and my son are both capable enough fighters. Come." He held his hand out and, in the blink of an eye, he was in front of me.

I scrambled to my feet, not taking his hand. For some reason, I felt like if I touched him, I would be stuck here. Wherever here was. Realm of Ghosts made sense, but I couldn't be dead. Rorik's magic had only knocked me out, right?

Jaari shrugged. "Suit yourself. If you've been to the Realm of Ghosts before, you are either very unlucky, or you're related to Ingmar Svanunge."

"Technically, both, I guess. Wait, you don't know who I am? I thought you just said—"

He laughed. "Of course I do, Ina of Svartån. I mean to jest. You look like a female version of your father. Plus, your presence is familiar, similar to my mother. Noble and stubborn. You have the bearing of a High Queen, even if you're unsure of it still." He began walking away, gesturing for me to follow. "I need your help. While your husband and my son fight Rorik in the Realm of the Living, you and I need to fight him here. Otherwise, we'll be here for a while. The longer we are, the higher the chance of Rorik turning you into one of his undead. Which I don't think anyone wants."

I hurried after him, realizing now the room wasn't exactly like the room where Haldrek, Henry, and I had been fighting Rorik. My mind went back to when my father had died and Rorik had pulled his dragon from him. Immediately, I glanced at my hand. Everything seemed fine.

"Give it a few hours. Your body in the Realm of the Living hasn't started decaying yet." Jaari's voice echoed from the next room over. I ran to keep up with him.

"Wait. If you've been dead for decades now, why aren't you rotting away?"

Jaari stopped and turned around. "My dragon, Visalth, is still with me. No one ever did my rites after I died, so we were never separated. That is of little importance." Jaari started walking again. "Right now, we need to figure out where Rorik's ghost is. With all his necromantic machinations, he's pulled himself into two separate realms, the rotting magical flesh mage you were fighting in the Realm of the Living and its ghostly counterpart here. It's part of what is making him so difficult to kill. That and Ryluth. Visalth is pissed he can't help his kin with that fight."

"How are we going to destroy Rorik once we find his ghost?"

"I don't know exactly. Visalth mentioned a token of some kind, but I don't have any clue what Rorik would be carrying on him."

"His pendant, maybe?" I thought back to the previous fight as my memories began to piece themselves together. There had been a scale on the round altar behind Rorik. I had been certain it was what connected Ryluth and Rorik. Even Haldrek and Henry had been certain it was important. As they had fought Rorik's remaining necromancers, I had snuck over to the shrine and attacked it with my sword. When it shattered, it had done something else. It had—

"Reinforced the bond between Ryluth and Rorik, but in a way that wasn't beneficial to Rorik." Jaari squatted behind a large stone and gestured for me to kneel next to him. "I saw when that happened. No idea how it did what it did, but it affected this realm as well."

"You need to stop reading my mind." I grimaced as I hid behind the rock.

"You sound like my mother." Jaari grinned, and I looked away, trying not to see Haldrek in him. Whatever genetics they all had were strong. Jaari laughed, but didn't respond.

Instead, he said, "I sense this battle with Rorik and Ryluth isn't just a small skirmish. Visalth tells me this is a vast battle for not just Sethys, but for many other realms as well. What happens here will affect the living, the dead, and the dragons. Just like when Bjornulf and Freya killed Ryluth for the first time. It affected multiple realms in ways I doubt they ever knew."

I spun around in surprise. "What?"

"It makes more sense that way, too." Jaari kept talking, as if trying to make sense of his thoughts. "Why else would Rorik become a necromancer? Combine himself with Ryluth? Why would Ryluth tolerate a puny human? There is more at stake here than just the Realm of the Living."

"They both want power? And glory?"

"Yes." Jaari turned to face me. "What is more powerful than life and death itself? The dragons? Not quite. As powerful as they are, they still live and die like the rest of us. But if someone had power over life, death, and the dragons? All the sentient races of Sethys would tremble in fear before them."

"So ultimate power and glory?"

Jaari nodded. "At least as far as someone like Rorik can comprehend. Or Ryluth. They both want that." He shifted away from me, watching something on the other side of the boulder. After a moment, he gestured with his head for me to look at what he'd been watching.

I moved around him and looked down. Somehow we were on a ledge, and I could look down at where Haldrek and Henry were fighting. Both were fiercely attacking Rorik's new ghastly manifestation, but every time they'd knock him down, he'd rise again. They were getting worn out.

"We need to help. They can't do it alone and neither can I." Jaari's voice became less light, more worried.

"We need to find the talisman that ties Rorik and Ryluth." I watched as Rorik swung around, blocking one of Haldrek's attacks before casting a spell to knock Henry off his feet. All the while, his pendant swung around his neck. In my mind, I realized that was the key to this whole thing. It had never been the dragon scale.

"My queen?" Jaari's voice brought me out of my thoughts as a shadow moved over us. Suddenly, the entire realm shuddered and I fell to my knees, nearly skidding off the ledge. I kicked my leg out instinctively to stop myself, but much to my surprise, it floated instead of dropping off the ledge.

"Ina!"

I looked up at the shadow above us and gasped. Above Jaari and me, there was a large ghostly vision of Rorik. Its bright green eyes stared down at me as terror flooded my body.

"Now is the time for your destruction."

Chapter 29

I scrambled to my feet as the ghostly lich-like embodiment swung one of its heavily armored hands at me. Jaari ducked and I wondered what his plan was, or whether he even had a plan.

My plan was to keep the Rorik-lich from hitting me. It swung again and I rolled away, pulling out Freya's Menace and righting myself. The chamber we were in was different now; I couldn't see Haldrek or Henry fighting. The Rorik-lich floated toward me, darkness emanating from it as I kept my distance. In the background, there was rumbling and thunder as something collided out of sight, followed by the shriek of a dragon.

"You have tormented me long enough, Ina of Svartån. I will rejoice when I consume your soul." Rorik's lich voice crackled even as it boomed deeply. It partially sounded like Ryluth, but it also sounded young in a way I couldn't describe. Like Rorik wasn't sure how intimidating he sounded and had decided to say something more threatening.

"Are you going to consume my soul or is Ryluth? Last time I checked, he was the only one capable of doing that."

The lich swung at me with his staff, and I blocked it with my sword. The crystal head of the staff shattered as my blade hit it, throwing bright light and blinding me momentarily. Rorik's lich pulled away from the light and, for a moment, I saw three dragons flying, attacking one larger, tattered dragon. The larger dragon flung his wing around, knocking the nearest to him into a downward spin.

As quickly as the vision appeared, darkness consumed it. I was met with Rorik's ugly, rotten mug in my face. I stumbled back, striking his face with the armor on my left glove. The flesh clung to it as I recoiled, watching more reappear on his face.

"You can't destroy me that easily." Rorik's laughter was jagged and ended with a cough. He spat up something disgusting as I moved out of the way.

"Neither can you." Jaari's voice jumped from the shadows, taking Rorik's attention away from me. I used the opening to attack, slicing my blade across Rorik's arm and watching in horror as it dropped to the floor and fell through as if going through water. A new, more mangled arm grew in its place and I ducked as a scattering of green light burst from it.

Jaari rolled away as Rorik cast a spell from his broken staff, barely dodging the magic.

"You think you two can defeat me? I have the power of a dragon coursing through my veins now. I am immortal."

"Since when? The dragons aren't even immortal." Jaari popped up next to me as Rorik spun to face us. His pendant caught my attention once more. It was covered in something black, almost if tarnished, and moved with its own power. That had to be the connection to Ryluth. It had to be.

"We need to figure out how to knock him down a few stones." Jaari and I both ducked and rolled as Rorik cast more magic from his mangled staff and arm. "We can't keep hacking off his limbs."

"We need to get at that pendant. The sooner we do, the sooner we can kill him and the dragons can take out Ryluth."

"How are we going to do that? We have to kill Rorik in two realms at the same time the dragons go after Ryluth."

A large blast of green magic electrified the air between us. I rolled to the left and Jaari rolled to the right. Rorik swung at him as I lunged for the staff in Rorik's hand. Even if lopping off body parts didn't kill Rorik, it definitely slowed him down. He howled as my blade sliced through his wrist. His hand and the shattered staff still gripped in it sank through the murkiness beneath our feet.

Rorik swung back at me, his hand regrowing with the staff once more. This time, both were far more shriveled than before. "You wretched wench! I will feast on you!"

"Feast on this, asshole!" Jaari launched a dagger into Rorik's back, then disappeared into thin air as the lich turned around. He reappeared next to me.

"You have a plan yet, my queen?"

We needed to get the pendant. And destroy it at the same time as Haldrek and Henry. Images rolled through my mind of who was fighting in each realm. Thoughts of how to coordinate our attacks. Then it all clicked together. I knew how we were going to win.

The lich swung around once more, and we ducked once more to avoid its magic. I swung my blade where I assumed its leg was and was met with another howl as my sword cut through, dropping another body part into the mire below.

"You really think you can defeat me like this?" The lich laughed again, coughing up more of whatever was inside of it.

"It's worth a shot!" Jaari flung another blade at the creature. It shuddered and stilled for a moment before swinging to grab him.

Instead, Henry's dad disappeared and reappeared next to me. "Quickly. Plan."

"Visalth goes to the dragons. You go to Henry. Tell Henry they need to focus on the pendant in their realm. I'm going after it here."

"Got it." I ducked and Jaari disappeared as the lich's hand slammed down where I'd been standing.

"You need to fight harder than that, you corpse bum!"

Rorik the lich swung at me with his free hand, and I slashed through it with my blade. As he howled, an orb of green magic slammed into my head. I grunted as I went flying into one of the rocky walls.

"Now you are mine!"

I rolled away as he grabbed for me, but I couldn't gain purchase with my hands or feet in the mire where I'd landed. The ground was softer now, and I wondered what kind of magic Rorik had been lobbing at us. Instead, I sank my fingers into a piece of rock as he grasped for me again, pulling myself upright. The ground grew more solid, and I planted my feet on the base of two broken rock formations.

"You haven't won yet." I sliced Freya's Menace into his neck, and even though it didn't go through, my blade cut the metal chain holding the pendant around the lich's neck. It dropped into my hand as the creature howled once more, slamming me against the opposing wall.

I opened my eyes in time to see Jaari jump into the air, a dagger in each hand, and plunge them into the Rorik-lich. Black tendrils wrapped around him as he struggled to keep stabbing the creature.

"Now, Ina!"

I slammed the blackened pendant with the edge of Freya's Menace, more afraid I wouldn't have enough strength than of cutting open my own hand.

Neither happened. The pendant shattered as if made of glass and a high-pitched shriek echoed through the chamber. I dropped my sword and the remnants of the pendant, plugging my ears as much as I could. Vibrations from the shriek coursed through me as I curled up against the now-solid floor.

When the shrieking finally stopped, the lich began howling, and I looked up at it, now covered in wispy black chains and fighting to escape them.

"Send it to Lyrroth!" Jaari's voice boomed over the howls, and I turned to see him flat against the floor as well.

Wait. Rhaegos's voice stopped me. *You cannot do the death rites here.*

My relief over her return and my exhaustion fought as I collapsed completely. The lich continued to fight, but I knew what was happening as I watched chains encircling it, tighter and tighter.

"What are you waiting for?" Jaari scrambled to his feet, making his way over to me. I ignored him as the chains silenced its howls. I knew what was going on, how this was going to end. As soon as the lich went silent, a boom exploded and I flinched. Jaari tackled me as the room shook, pressing both of us against the floor.

When the shaking stopped, I heard Rhaegos once more. This time with a sound I'd never heard from her before. Disbelief.

He's actually gone. The void consumed Ryluth.

Jaari slowly got off me and I sat up, staring at the now empty room. The lich was gone as well. Destroyed by whatever magic had also destroyed the imposter Cassius.

"Ina?"

I turned to Jaari as concern crossed his face. Before I could respond, my eyes closed, and I passed out.

Mumbled voices brought me back to consciousness, as well as someone's grief-stricken sobs in the distance. While not loud, the crying was guttural and my heart ached to comfort the person. Opening my eyes, I turned my head and saw a ghostly vision in front of me. Haldrek held my limp body in his arms, sobbing into the chainmail covering my chest.

"You can't be dead, Ina. Come back. Wake up, please. Wake up."

Henry stood behind him, eyes wide with panic and mouth slightly ajar, as if trying to think of something to say.

"Haldrek...I—"

"No." Haldrek turned away from my body. I could feel the rage emanating from him. "Let. Me. Be."

Henry nodded and stepped away, silent.

I rolled to my knees and crawled to the vision, hoping I could reach out to Haldrek, comfort him somehow. Figure out a way to return to my body. Instead, the vision disappeared as I reached out for it.

"I'm sorry, Ina."

I spun to see Jaari standing before me, head bowed and hands crossed solemnly in front of him.

"What?" My mind was spinning. I couldn't think of anything else to say. Fear sank into my heart as I realized what he might be apologizing for.

"I'm sorry. It is always a difficult thing to see the grief of our loved ones in this realm. You made a noble sacrifice, much like Tenelth and Beroan of old. I doubt I could have defeated Rorik's lich alone."

"No!" I scrambled to my feet, looking for an exit. There had to be a way out. I was too young to die. This wasn't how I was supposed to go. I thought back to the visions the Vollr had given me. None of them were set in stone, but I'd seen myself, old, with Haldrek and our family. Had I'd really lost that?

Tears flooded my eyes, and I dropped back to my knees as I wept. This couldn't be happening. I'd been to the Realm of Ghosts numerous times, and *this* was the time I got stuck here?

"Is there anything I could have done to change this?" I looked up at Jaari, but his expression was grim and sorrowful. "I've been here before, and I could always leave. I don't want to be dead. I want to be with Haldrek. I want to be with Eero."

"I'm sorry, Ina. If there was a way to escape the Realm of Ghosts, I would have done it decades ago. I would have followed Victoria to any realm she chose. Unfortunately, for most people, once they arrive in the Realm of Ghosts, they don't have a choice. Most people do wish they could return to their loved ones."

"But—"

"But Ina is different. She is a Svanunge and an heir of Ottkatla." The tapping of dragon claws on stone preceded Rhaegos's appearance. It surprised me to see her here. Had my rite already been performed? Was this what happened when a haldraga and their dragon were separated?

"Rhaegos?" I squeaked as she stood next to Jaari.

"I am still with you, little one. Do you really think Haldrek has already done your death rite—or let Henry do it?"

I laughed uneasily and shook my head.

"How is Ina different?" Jaari glanced between me and Rhaegos.

"As an heir of Ottkatla, Ina can move between the Realm of the Living and the Realm of Ghosts at will. She also has one opportunity in her lifetime to return to the Realm of the Living with no consequences."

"I do?" I wiped the tears from my face, eager to return to Haldrek and the rest of my loved ones in the Realm of the Living.

Rhaegos held her hand up. "While I said there would be no consequences, I meant long term. If you choose to return to the Realm of the Living, your body will still feel the effects of its injuries. You will feel the results of your healing body upon your return."

"I can handle a little pain."

Rhaegos raised her eyebrows at me. "It will be more than a little pain."

"Will it be worse than when I electrocuted myself while killing Seirye?"

She laughed. "Perhaps. If you could handle that, I suppose you will be able to handle your spine healing itself."

I shuddered. So that's what the crunch had been. Another thought popped into my head. One about my father.

"Did my father have this option? After the Battle of Drattüjert?" Part of me wondered what it would have been like to see him again while he was still alive.

Rhaegos nodded. "He was well aware. But he also knew that accepting his death could trigger bringing you here to Lohikärra. As it did."

That revelation hit me hard. My dad could have come back to life, but instead he stayed in the Realm of Ghosts so I could come to Lohikärra. If he had even chosen to come back to life after the battle, how would that have complicated things once I was here? I groaned, my mind spinning.

"Do not think of the decisions of the past too hard, little one. There is nothing you can change. Only the future."

I looked up at Rhaegos and Jaari. He bowed his head respectfully.

"If you choose to stay in the Realm of Ghosts, I will stay with you until you reach Mirroth."

"And if I choose to return to the Realm of the Living?"

"Then I will guide you there, little one. It is your choice to make." Rhaegos smiled somberly.

I turned back to Jaari. "If I return, would you want someone to do your rite, finally?"

He glanced at Rhaegos, and she raised an eyebrow. Shaking his head, he said, "I'm content to stay for a little while longer. A couple of decades is a short time in the grand scheme of things." A smile lit up his face. "Plus, it gives me a good chance to see Victoria again. And get to know my son more. Even if they aren't aware of my presence."

I got it. "Then I'll let them know when I see them again." Turning back to Rhaegos, I smiled. "I want to go home. To Haldrek and to everyone else."

Rhaegos smiled widely. "Then I will take you there." She held out her arms for an embrace and I ran to her, squeezing tightly. As soon as I closed my eyes, a bright flash of light enveloped me and I knew I'd made the right decision.

Chapter 30

As soon as the bright light faded, a searing pain shot down my neck and along my spine, branching out to the rest of my body like a wave of fire and needles piercing me from head to toe. For a few moments, I braced as the pain rushed back and forth across me.

This was worse than when I'd electrocuted myself.

When it finally faded, I gasped, sucking air into my still-burning lungs as my eyes opened.

"Ina?" Haldrek's voice was faint with disbelief. He knelt next to me, my body cradled in his arms. His eyes were red, his tears soaking his beard. Behind him, Henry stood, eyes wide with shock.

"I'm here. I'm alive. Again." My throat burned with every word, and I started coughing, setting off a terrible headache. Henry ran out of my vision as Haldrek caressed my cheek. He leaned down, pressing his forehead against mine, sobbing in relief. A few of his tears hit my cheeks and I started crying, too.

"Thank the dragons. I don't know what I would have done if..." He shook his head and kissed my forehead. "I'm not going to think about that. You're back. You're safe."

"Rhaegos gave me the option to return." I coughed again and took a drink as Henry brought a waterskin to my mouth. The water wasn't the freshest tasting, but it felt glorious on my throat as I swallowed. "She said I could leave the Realm of Ghosts once without consequence because of Ottkatla. Being her descendant or something."

Haldrek nodded. "I won't question it. I'm just glad you chose to come back. We defeated Rorik and Ryluth. We're safe."

I nodded, feeling my neck bend back and forth like nothing had ever happened, and smiled. "You think I would leave you and Eero if I had the choice? Never." I sighed and took another sip of water. "I think attacking Rorik and Ryluth in three different places is what worked. Jaari and I fought Rorik's lich in the Realm of Ghosts."

"So I *did* hear his voice telling me to go after the pendant."

I nodded again. "We needed to attack at the same time. And... Jaari said he couldn't have fought the lich by himself." As I took another deep breath, I realized my death had needed to happen in order to defeat Rorik and Ryluth. The gravity of the thought terrified me, as well as how much I'd risked to protect my loved ones. No one else could have fought Rorik in the Realm of Ghosts and returned to the Realm of the Living.

"How are you feeling now?" Haldrek stroked my cheek again, and the intense desire to just stay in his arms overwhelmed me. "Are you numb, or are you able to walk?"

"I'm not numb." Wiggling my foot, I was able to move it across the ground an inch or so. I flexed my fingers inside their gloves. Slowly, with Haldrek's help, I tried to sit, but my body was heavy. I barely had the strength to hold myself up. "Fighting in the Realm of Ghosts took a lot out of me, though, I think."

"Also coming back to life," Henry murmured. "That's not something that happens every day."

I had to laugh. Of course it wasn't. But how much of my life had been regular, normal everyday events? Especially since coming to Lohikärra?

Haldrek shifted his hand under my body and gestured to Henry with his head. "I'll carry Ina. You take her sword. I trust you enough to not do anything terrible with it."

Annoyance flashed across Henry's face as he picked up my blade. "I would never do anything to harm Ina or her loved ones. There's been enough violence and villainy for all our lives."

"I agree. My comment wasn't one of reluctant trust. I see you now as an ally. And I can see why the dragons do as well. You have my complete gratitude, Henry." As Haldrek stood up, I wrapped my arms around his neck and braced myself, hoping my strength would return quickly. The sooner this experience became a memory, the better.

"Thank you." Henry looked around the empty room. Every necromancer's body, including Rorik's, had disappeared. Part of me wondered how much of that had to do with what had happened in the Realm of Ghosts and the Realm of Dragons. "Since we completed our quest, should we leave this place? As much as I'm not looking forward to meeting up with Aallotar and the others, it's not nearly as bad as being in here."

Haldrek laughed. "Let's go. As a token of my gratitude, I can keep you under my protection as High King. Though after word of what we just did gets out, I doubt there will be many Lohikärrans who will want to kill you."

"Even Aallotar?" Henry raised his eyebrows in disbelief.

A grimace crossed Haldrek's face. "Don't worry about Aallotar. She is my cousin and loyal to Lohikärra. If I say you are my ally and under my protection, even she won't come after you."

Henry's expression told me he wasn't completely certain, but he nodded.

"Then let's head out. I never want to see this place again."

We traveled along a few unfamiliar but rough-hewn hallways for what seemed like hours. While I didn't see many spirits directly, there was always a light blue haze in my periphery, signaling that we weren't alone. I made a mental note to return—or have someone return—once I'd regained my strength. Henry led the way, guided by his dragon. Haldrek didn't seem worried, so I dozed off a time or two in his arms, only to have him gently nudge me awake. I didn't blame him. I knew it would be a long time before he'd feel comfortable with me sleeping. It would be a long time before I'd be able to doze off without worrying about slipping back into the Realm of Ghosts.

When we did reach an entrance to the outside world, soft morning light flooded in. I tried to think of how long we'd been inside the mountain, but all sense of time still felt blurred.

Haldrek stopped for a moment, then laughed. "Hail, Aallotar! We've defeated Rorik the necromancer and Ryluth."

Aallotar stared at us for a few moments, the creases around her face lessening as she smiled. Her smile disappeared as her focus reached Henry, and she gestured for some of her warriors to grab him.

"Hey! I'm *not* the enemy!" There was shuffling out of my view and Haldrek stepped in front of Henry.

"He is under my protection, Aallotar. Call back your warriors."

"He didn't betray you?"

Haldrek sighed in frustration. "No. If he had, I would have killed him myself. Instead, he fought courageously against Rorik and his necromancers, even risking his life a few times to protect Ina and myself. Tell your warriors to stand down."

Aallotar stared at him a moment longer, then waved for her warriors to give us some space.

"Why didn't you go to the entrance at the top of the cliffs? I assumed—" Aallotar shook her head and sighed. She nodded to one of her warriors and the woman disappeared.

"I'm guessing this one is closest to where we fought Rorik. It's the one Henry and Syralgos led us to. And it saved us time."

"You were never worried that Henry was leading you into a trap?"

"Like I said before, he has proven himself trustworthy. If you're here, I'm assuming you followed shortly after us?"

Aallotar nodded. "I waited as you asked, though. My warriors and Gunner's are setting up the war camp as we speak." She turned her attention to me. "What happened to you, my queen?" Her tone irritated me. Even if she wasn't openly derisive, I could still tell she thought I hadn't held my own.

"I died, destroyed Rorik's lich with your uncle Jaari, then returned to the Realm of the Living."

Her expression changed to one of surprise as she looked at Haldrek. He nodded. "There is no question in my mind that Rorik killed Ina during our battle. I held her body while she was dead and was there when she revived."

"No one can bring themselves back from the dead, cousin."

"No one except Ottkatla's heirs," I snapped. My fatigue was making me irritable. What did Aallotar think? That I would lie about dying and coming back?

Aallotar opened her mouth, but Haldrek shook his head. "I am tired, cousin. If the camp is secure, is there a place for us to rest? The last however many hours have been exhausting."

She glanced at Henry for a moment, then nodded. "My warriors and I will return to camp with you three. Were there any other necromancers left after you killed Rorik?"

Haldrek shook his head, and I focused on Aallotar.

"There are plenty of spirits, however. We'll probably need a sattar of priests to send them all to their respective afterlives."

Aallotar nodded. "I'm sure we can find some. We don't want any more undead popping up." She turned with a gesture and Haldrek followed her out, with me still in tow.

The path from the cavern wove its way through the forest and along the riverbank. By the time we reached the valley, it was filled with tents and numerous warriors.

As we entered, I didn't have to look to know everyone was watching us. I leaned my head against Haldrek's chest, trying to fight off my own exhaustion.

"We're almost to a place where we can rest. All three of us."

"I appreciate your protection, Haldrek." Henry's murmur made me open my eyes. I noticed he kept a close step to Haldrek and an eye on the warriors watching him. With a sigh, I hoped one day things would be less tense.

Once inside the tent, Haldrek laid me down on a cot and gestured for Henry to take the other one.

"What about you?" Henry stopped in surprise.

"I'm the High King. If we need another cot, they'll bring me one. For now, I'm fine." He sat down on the ground next to my cot, pulling his helm off. I smiled, brushing a few strands of his hair from his temple. I was exhausted, but having him near me, knowing we were finally safe from Rorik, gave me energy.

"You should rest too, Haldrek. It wasn't like you weren't fighting either," I whispered as Henry laid down on his cot. I stroked Haldrek's cheek and ear, savoring his nearness.

"I'll be fine. Teminth has been helping me and we are the least injured of our party."

"It doesn't mean you shouldn't rest."

He took my hand and kissed it. "In time. For now, I'll be fine."

Footsteps at the entrance of the tent took my attention away and a handful of healers came in along with Aallotar. She stood grimly watching the scene as Haldrek stood up and made his way to a stool between me and Henry. As I glanced Henry's way, it surprised me to see joy light up his face. He apparently knew the healer attending to him, and I was glad to see him happy again

"Once the healers are finished, what would you have Gunner and I do with the Blodnar man?"

My attention turned to Haldrek and Aallotar's conversation, even as a healer began removing pieces of my armor and checking me for injuries.

"Henry is to have his own tent. Let him rest. If he needs further healing, make sure he gets it. He is our ally."

"He is your ally. With all due respect, Haldrek—"

"He is an ally of Lohikärra and those who are loyal to it. While that cannot be said for most Blodnar, that can be said for Henry. Understood?"

Aallotar was silent for what seemed like ages before asking, "Do you wish to give him the same *liberties* as the rest of the warriors?"

Haldrek sighed. "Within reason." He turned his focus to Henry. "As much as I trust you, Henry, as a member of the Blodnar—Norycian—imperial family, until there is peace between our two peoples, I cannot let you roam free in Lohikärra. Not that it would be a wise idea, anyway."

Henry nodded, and I noticed the healer tending to him seemed more interested in the conversation than the healers tending to me or Haldrek.

"So I am to be a political prisoner for the foreseeable future?"

"Unfortunately, yes. When Ina and I return to Drattüjert, you will be returning with us. But I am already planning on opening communications with whoever is in charge in Norycium now. If it is your mother, then we may be able to agree to peace quickly."

"And if it's my uncle, I may be safer in Lohikärra than Norycium."

Haldrek nodded, and Aallotar cleared her throat.

"Do you think it is wise to suggest peace so quickly, cousin?"

He turned to her with a grumble. "This war started because of a miscommunication and two old men wanting vengeance. You and I have both seen what that desire for vengeance has done. I am tired of war, Aallotar, even if you aren't. I want peace. Not vengeance. The dragons have charged me with restoring Lohikärra, and I can't do that if it is still at war. If Henry's mother's disappearance was the reason this war started in the first place, I doubt she'd want to continue it."

"And if she does? If she demands payment for the Blodnar who died invading our lands?"

"Then we will fight. But if there is no fight to be had, I won't start another one."

Aallotar remained silent for a moment, not looking at any of us. Once the healers were done—even the one who lingered beside Henry—Aallotar nodded.

"Fine. But don't say I didn't warn you." With that, she spun and left the tent. The healers waited a few moments before leaving themselves.

Once the three of us were alone, Haldrek sighed.

"I'm sorry for causing you this grief," Henry's words were barely audible, his attention on the tent opening. A cool autumn breeze made its way inside.

"It's fine." Haldrek looked outside as well. "As much as I understand Aallotar's desire for vengeance, she will need to bridle it. I wasn't lying when I said I was tired of war. I believe most people here are tired of it."

"Here's to hoping Henry's mom is in charge and not her brother," I whispered. Knowing Victoria—Mrs. Pollard, as I always remembered her—I doubted she'd want to keep fighting, regardless of her current feelings about Lohikärra.

Henry nodded. "My uncle is a crazy man. I think he would keep fighting just to cause more bloodshed."

"Good to know." Haldrek kept his attention on the entrance. "By the way, you seemed familiar with the healer who was tending to you."

Henry coughed, his face turning bright red. "We know each other, yes. He is a friend. I helped his village when some of the young women—including his sister—were kidnapped by Rorik's thugs."

Haldrek nodded, but said nothing. I thought I saw a slight smile on his face.

"Henry? Your friend? Is he a friend like Alex?" I tried to be as discreet as possible, but the hint of a possible new romance was just the light-hearted thing I wanted to hear about.

Henry laughed, then groaned. "Kinda? Maybe? I don't know. It's going to depend a lot on what happens in the future." He gestured to Haldrek. "Or how open people are to, you know..."

Haldrek shrugged. "I personally don't care about what is going on in other people's beds. But I can't speak for others. There are probably thegn lands that care more about that kind of thing, but as High King? Lohikärra has far more pressing issues than who is sleeping with whom."

As he straightened up, stretching out his shoulders, a couple of women stopped at the tent opening, their hands full of food and drink. My stomach grumbled, and I realized just how hungry I was.

"That is what I care about most right now." He waved the women in, and in short order a table sat in the open space between us all, with plates of food covering it. As soon as the women disappeared from the tent, Haldrek smiled and prepared a couple of plates for both Henry and me. When he sat down, he took his own plate.

"Now let us eat and drink. To our health, to our futures, and to keeping Lohikärra safe."

Chapter 31

Long after we finished eating and as we rested, I felt a warm sensation on my chest. I opened my eyes to see Haldrek and Henry both still dozing, the tent quiet.

Pulling my pendant out from underneath my tunic, I opened it to see a familiar face. Henry's mom.

"I'm glad to see you are well, Ina. I don't think either of us expected to see each other in this realm. Or world." Her laughter made me smile.

"No, not at all." I tried to blink away the fog of sleep. "How are you? I know Henry was worried about you."

"I am... I'm fine." She glanced away from my focus for a moment, her smile disappearing. "Normal Norycian politics, that's all. Is... I'm assuming Henry's safe?" Her attention returned to me.

I nodded. "He's resting in the cot next to me." Quickly, I took my pendant off and angled it so she could see him. A muffled gasp came from the pendant as Henry shifted in his cot.

"Who are you talking to, Ina?" Haldrek's eyes opened as he sat up near my legs.

"Henry's mom. She called me on my pendant."

"She *what?*" Haldrek grabbed the pendant from my hands and stared at the glass.

"Hey!" I grabbed for my pendant, but my stomach muscles spasmed.

"Is that how you treat your wife?" Mrs. Pollard's voice turned cold, a tone I'd rarely heard her use before.

"How did you figure out the dragons' magic?" His expression darkened with distrust.

"The goddess Rhaegaia taught me how to use these communication pools. Though you would probably know her by the name Rhaegos."

"*Rhaegos?*"

Your husband would do well not to shout my name with that tone of voice. Rhaegos's gentle chastisement came with a sense of amusement from her. She might have been annoyed at Haldrek for the moment, but I sensed she was entertained by the situation as a whole.

"Haldrek, Rhaegos has spent time with both Norycians and Lohikärrans. She just told you to chill."

He turned his attention back to me, eyes wide with disbelief. For a moment, I thought he'd snap at me. Instead, he looked down at the pendant. "How... I've never heard of the dragons' magic being used outside of Lohikärra."

"Then your information gatherers have been failing you, High King Haldrek. Though we Norycians may not worship the dragons as you Lohikärrans do, we still do honor them in their human forms. And they bless us in return."

Haldrek scowled. After a few moments of stony silence, Henry's mom cleared her throat.

"If you don't have anything to say to me, would you please return your wife's pendant to her?"

Without a word, he handed the pendant back. Henry's mother smiled. "Though part of my reason for calling is to open lines of communication for peace, I will say this. If your husband ever treats you as anything less than the High Queen that you are, Ina, you are always welcome here in Norycium."

Haldrek's eyes widened, and Rhaegos started laughing in the back of my mind. I tried to conceal my amusement as I said, "Haldrek is a good husband. I think we are all still tired and on edge from fighting the necromancers."

Henry's mom nodded, amusement lighting her expression. "Well, I am glad you all are safe then and have resolved that situation. I feared that if Rorik overwhelmed Lohikärra, he would set his eyes on Norycium next."

Haldrek huffed and muttered something about how Rorik never had a chance at winning. I nudged him with my knee, keeping my focus on Henry's mom.

"Well, Rorik is dead now and we're hoping for a time of peace. That said, I had a question. Something I'm curious about now."

"Yes?"

"Are communication pools using dragon magic common in Norycium? If so..."

Henry's mom shook her head. "The one I am speaking to you from is the only one I know of. Rhaegaia and Jaari helped me secretly build it years ago, back when Jaari and I thought we'd be the ones to bring long-lasting peace to Lohikärra and Norycium." She sighed. "I have just finished restoring it. Being Empress means I have little time for personal projects, I'm afraid."

A thud and movement out of the corner of my eye took my attention away from her. Henry grunted on the floor as he tried to sit up.

"Mom?"

Immediately, Mrs. Pollard's eyes became glossy with tears. My chest tightened up as well. Henry scrambled over to my cot, peeking over my shoulder and laughing in relief.

"Henry, you're well?"

He nodded, and I felt some wetness on my shoulder. Haldrek straightened up and looked slightly chastened.

"I'm fine, Mom. Ina and Haldrek have been good friends. I don't think I'd be here if it wasn't for them. How are you doing? You said you're Empress now?"

Mrs. Pollard nodded.

"What about—"

"Don't worry about your uncle. We had a nice long chat after what he tried to do to you. He decided to *retire* from being emperor and let me rule instead."

Haldrek raised an eyebrow and even I knew there hadn't been a peaceful transfer of power between Henry's mom and uncle.

Victoria is a wise and just individual, but she's not a person to be underestimated, either.

"Since he is no longer in power, it is up to me to repair what he and my father have damaged over the years, including the relationship between Norycium and Lohikärra. A relationship that Jaari and I tried to foster." There were a few moments of silence as we all thought about what had happened over the last twenty years, both here in Sethys and on Earth.

"Haldrek?" Mrs. Pollard's voice broke the silence and Haldrek looked up. "As the Norycian Empress, I wish to open true peace negotiations with you, the High King of Lohikärra. Do you accept?"

Haldrek moved so he could see the pendant's face as well. "I accept opening peace negotiations with Norycium. Much has happened in these past twenty years, so it may take time to find agreements that benefit both sides."

Henry's mom nodded. "That is to be expected. As a gesture of my goodwill, I've already signed and sent out documents ordering all Norycian soldiers back within our borders." She paused, and I wondered what else was on her mind. "In return, may I ask something of you? As a favor from one parent to another?"

Haldrek went pale. "How did you know—"

"We both have information gatherers, Haldrek. We are both leaders of great countries. Playing the fool doesn't look good for either of us."

He grimaced. "Fair enough. You already know I'm willing to do what I need to keep my family and my people safe?"

She nodded. "As am I. Which is why I'm asking you and Ina to keep my son safe. He may be an adult now, but he is still my son. This I ask because I am no fool. I know there are many people in Lohikärra who won't see him as Jaari's son, but solely as mine. I nearly lost Henry to my brother. I won't lose him again."

Haldrek nodded. "I understand. As it is, I've already placed my protection as High King over him. He has proved himself an ally of Lohikärra, and I won't ignore that."

"Thank you." She shifted a bit, as if trying to get a better view of Henry. "I thank the deities above, be they human or dragon, that you are safe, my child."

Henry grinned. "There were a few dodgy points here and there, but yeah, I'm with friends now. People I know I can trust." He glanced up at me and Haldrek.

"Good. I should let you go now then. At least to rest. Hopefully, one day, we'll be able to see each other in person again." She paused to wipe her tears. "I love you, Henry."

"I love you too, Mom." Henry choked up, and I noticed him trying to blink back his tears as my pendant went black.

As he returned to his cot, a lump in my throat made it hard to speak. Instead, I looked at Haldrek, hoping he'd have words of comfort. His eyes were teary too as he nodded, glancing out at the darkening sky beyond our tent.

"Today is the end of an era. Rorik is gone, as is Ryluth. Lohikärra will finally have peace for the first time in years. We should rejoice in that, as strange as it may seem right now. I think I speak for each of us when I say I'm looking forward to what tomorrow brings."

Chapter 32

It was several weeks later before we were able to return to Drattüjert. Despite the snow covering everything when we arrived, I was glad to be home. I couldn't contain my tears as Haldrek and I were reunited with Eero, who seemed to have doubled in size since I left.

While the healers had done well while we were in camp, all of us—Haldrek, Henry, and myself—were still recovering from our injuries, even after returning home. I had aches and pains which could only be attributed to my body healing from my time in the Realm of Ghosts. Even Senja's magic could only do so much. She recommended I take time to let my body heal. Which meant I was content to stay in Haldrek's and my quarters and snuggle Eero for as long as I could.

One night after our arrival, I woke up to the sound of Eero fussing. As I entered the small alcove where the wet nurse still stayed with him and her own child, she looked up at me in surprise.

"He's just hungry, I think. Hasn't had any screaming fits like before."

"That's good." I sat down on the floor and closed my eyes. Even though it was the middle of the night, I was awake now and wanted to spend what time I could with him. "Any new scratches?"

"None, my queen. Even the large ones disappeared right around the time you and the High King would have been killing the necromancer."

"I'm glad. That is good news indeed." Opening one eye, I watched as he ate hungrily, trying not to be weird, but at the same time savoring the moment. My nightmares had gone away, but the conversation between myself, Rhaegos, and Jaari was still etched in my mind. I knew how close I had been to not being here at all, so now every moment was precious.

After a bit, Eero finished feeding and fell back asleep. The wet-nurse offered him to me and I stood up, gently taking him in my arms. I was awake, so I might as well let her sleep. Slipping out into the antechamber, I quietly made my way past a few sleeping servants and over to my favorite window bench. A slight breeze blew outside, but the fires were still warm enough to keep me comfortable. Even at this late hour, I could hear whispers of the night guard keeping watch over the city and noise from a nearby tavern, sounds that now brought me peace.

"Ina?"

I jumped at the sound of Haldrek's sleepy voice and I looked up to see him standing next to me. A few of the servants stirred in their sleep, but no one woke up.

"You should be sleeping, Haldrek."

"So should you." He sat down on the bench across from me, leaning against the wall. "Did you have another nightmare?"

I shook my head. "My body decided it was awake. So I wanted to snuggle Eero until I grew tired again."

"You know we have nursemaids for that," Haldrek teased.

"I know. But after spending so much time away from him, I want this." I tucked Eero into the crook of my arm and gestured at the three of us with my free hand. "This is what I came back from the Realm of Ghosts for. I'm going to relish it while I can."

"Very well. I suppose it isn't the worst thing in Sethys." His soft laughter made me smile.

"It's not. Plus, I figured coming out here would let you sleep some more. You were still up and dealing with court matters when I went to bed."

Haldrek nodded. "I had to meet with some of the thegns and thegn-heirs whose loyalties had been with Rorik. Decide what punishments needed to be doled out. Who was deserving of mercy and who needed justice."

"And?"

"It is all squared away. The thegns who supported Rorik mostly did so out of cowardice. A few, including Lansiranikä, were found dead within their thegn halls, so their heirs came to pledge their loyalty."

"You didn't..." That news was surprising to me.

"I did nothing. But I think their ties to Rorik ran deep. When he and Ryluth were killed, it triggered some kind of magic. At least that's the best explanation I can come up with. Kotkel muttered a comment when he swore his allegiance, making that explanation seem more sound."

"What did he say?"

"He said he didn't wish to make the same mistakes his father did by turning his back on Lohikärra and the dragons. Given Kotkel's past interactions with me concerning his father..."

"He wouldn't say that if he thought you were to blame for his father's death."

Haldrek nodded. "All of that is in the past now. All twelve thegns and thegn-heirs have sworn their allegiance to us by the dragons. Lohikärra is officially at peace."

"What of its neighbors?" Henry was still very much a political prisoner, but during the few times he had come up to visit, I could tell Haldrek had given him significant liberties within the palace. I also watched as Jaari's ghost followed Henry around, seemingly to keep an eye on him.

"Victoria has sent envoys. From what I've been told, they should arrive in a few days. I've also sent information gatherers into the Blodnar empire to make sure her claims about calling back Blodnar soldiers are correct. So far, it seems that way." He leaned forward, stroking Eero's head gently as our son snored away in my arms. "I am curious to see what the envoys have to say, but if the news is promising, I look forward to creating a peace treaty with her. It'll be the next step in restoring Lohikärra."

"That is good news. I think Henry's mom will be a much better ally than either her brother or father could have been."

"There certainly is potential for that. I hope we come to an agreement soon. Once that is achieved, Henry will be free to go wherever he pleases. Though I'd probably advise him to stay away from Heidrunefoss for the time being. Aallotar is still not happy about how I've treated him."

I sighed. Aallotar's anger was justified, given everything the Blodnar had done to her family, and part of me wondered if she now hated me for my connection to Henry. Still, I hoped her animosity would ease one day.

"Don't worry, Ina. As long as he is under my protection, Aallotar knows better than to do anything stupid. Even once he isn't, she knows we consider him our ally, and that has considerable weight in and of itself." He leaned forward once more and kissed me on the forehead, sending a wonderful tingling sensation down my body. "I promise to do right by Henry. As a token of my gratitude to him for keeping you safe when I couldn't."

"Thank you. I'm glad for that. He's always loved this world, and Lohikärra, even if just in the video games."

Haldrek laughed softly, kissing me once more. "If we ever go back to Fargo, you'll have to show me those video games."

"Eh, the real Lohikärra is so much better. In my opinion." I pulled him closer for another kiss, letting him brace himself against the wall behind me.

When we finished, he smiled. "Then let's return to bed. Lohikärra has a bright, beautiful future ahead and we will embrace it in the morning."

The Lohikärran Chronicles

A mysterious young woman, an elven invasion, and the tokens of the High King
Haldrek Rodreksson has known his entire life where his future lies and what is expected of him. But on the eve of battle, soothsayers show him three visions of a different future: a mysterious young woman, a new invasion, and theft of the High King's tokens. Visions which make him question his future and that of his homeland, Lohikärra.

When the capital of Lohikärra falls, Haldrek's world is thrown into disarray and he must scramble to keep the young woman from his visions safe.

Injured, weaponless, and with little support, will Haldrek be able to save the woman and change the visions he was given? Or will he, his homeland, and his loved ones fall to their enemies?

Lohikärra was just a game. Until it wasn't.

Ina Svanunge lives in North Dakota, avoiding attention and counting the days until she's free of her abusive mother. But when she and best friend, Mattie, sit down to play the newest release from their favorite video game series, they find themselves in the game's world, Lohikärra. Only it's not the game - Lohikärra is real.

Once there, Ina finds out her long-absent father was a powerful thegn - and she's his rightful heir. Unfortunately, she isn't the only one claiming his title, and the others are more than willing to kill her for it. On a journey across Svartån, Ina must fight for her birthright or risk rejection from the world she has long wished to be part of.

Will Ina be able to claim her rightful title with help from Mattie and their handsome new friend, Haldrek? Or will she end up dying in a foreign, unforgiving land?

<u>Thegn of Svartån</u>
She will be Thegn of Svartån. If Svartån still exists.

Ina Svanunge is the rightful thegn-heir of Svartån, but she must fight to lead and protect her new homeland's people, even as she's still learning how to do both. Can she learn to lead and bring her people together before they are brutally conquered?

An invasion from the Isillas elves - Svartån's most ancient enemy - looms imminent and Ina's first priority is to prepare her new homeland's defenses. Which would be easier if not for the deep hatred held by many of her subjects against their half-elven neighbors. With the Isillas at their doorstep, Svartån is fractured and in need of a leader to unite it once and for all. Racing to improve not only her fighting and leadership skills, she finds herself out of time when the Isillas attack and endanger not only Svartån, but those closest to her.

Weakened and alone, will Ina be able to protect Svartån from the Isillas? Or will she both lose her hard fought title and risk the destruction of Svartån?

<u>Queen of Drattüjert</u>
Old enemies. New challenges. Ina is thegn, but can she be queen?

It's been almost two months since Ina Svanunge officially became the Thegn of Svartån. With the Isillas conflict behind her, she must now aid her fellow thegns against an even bigger threat: the Blodnar Empire from the south.

Lohikärra will never be whole without its heart: the capital city of Drattüjert still under Bloodnar control. Ina and her fellow thegns have a plan to take it back, but there are traitors amongst their ranks bent on obtaining their own power and glory. The last thing Ina's beloved country needs is the emergence of a necromancer bent on destroying both Lohikärra and its dragons entirely.

When traitorous calamity strikes, Ina and Haldrek are forced into a race against time to save their loved ones, Lohikarra, and even Ina's hometown Fargo. But the cost could be Ina's life.

Lady of Lohikärra
With great power comes great responsibility. And greater enemies.

Fully embracing Lohikärra as her new home, Ina has taken her place alongside Haldrek as High King and Queen. But Lohikärra is a broken country on the verge of civil war. Respected by some, despised by others, Ina must rebuild the capital city of Drattüjert while Haldrek rebuilds Lohikärra.

When Henry, an old friend from Fargo, arrives in Drattüjert offering a solution to all her problems, it'll either be her saving grace or too good to be true.

Will Ina figure out which before it's too late? Or will fractured loyalties cause her to lose everything she holds dear?

Heart of Lohikärra
What would you risk to protect those you love?

Life is good now for Ina and Haldrek. The war with the Blodnar is nearly over and the birth of Lohikärra's new Aethling - their son, Eero - is a sign of more peaceful and prosperous times to come.

Even so, the necromancer Rorik is still loose and his power grows. When rumors reach them of an ancient dragon being brought back to life and people being kidnapped by Rorik's followers, both Ina and Haldrek know they need to quell Rorik's machinations. Haldrek sets out to confront him, leaving Ina and their newborn son within the protection of Drattujert's palace and its dragons.

But when dragon magic begins to fail, a new prophecy is revealed, and Rorik's dark magic is felt deep in the palace, Ina realizes she can't wait for Haldrek to save the day. Along with an old friend, she will have to confront Rorik once and for all. Even if it means risking the future she has desired her entire life.

About the Author

L. L. Nelson is a full-time librarian, history buff, and author of numerous stories and poems. In short, she is a word nerd with a passion for poetry, fantasy, historical fiction, and just a little bit of romance. She's been creating worlds and figuring out the 'what ifs' in her stories since she was old enough to read the words 'Egg Roll King' on a local Chinese restaurant sign in 1992.

In college, she took all the creative writing classes she could to feed her need to write. This gave her enough credits to graduate with a minor in English and the ability to second guess her work like a true writer. It also introduced her to a variety of genres and their tropes that she now uses in her stories and poetry.

As a librarian, L. L. Nelson has honed her research skills to a science. (A library science.) This has given her mad talent when it comes to finding obscure facts to use in her stories and poetry. (Like the fact that the Vikings used rap battles as a form of combat.)

When not dealing with her scripturient nature, L. L. Nelson is a mom, inventive cook, wannabe linguist, and dreams of being not only a 'word traveler' but a world traveler. Fortunately, she lives in Southern California with her husband and kids, so she can go to Disneyland once a year and pretend that she's actually traveling around the world, even when she isn't.

Love it?

Love it?

Leave a Review!

Did you enjoy *Heart of Lohikärra*? If so, I would be delighted if you left a review. (If you already have, thank you so much!) As a new author, book reviews are golden. You can leave reviews wherever you purchased the book, Goodreads, or other places as well. Book recommendations on social media (Youtube, Instagram, Twitter, TikTok, etc) is also awesome.

Follow me!

Website: https://www.llnelsonauthor.com/
Newsletter: https://www.llnelsonauthor.com/newsletter/
Facebook: https://www.facebook.com/llnelsonauthor
Instagram: https://www.instagram.com/llnelsonauthor
TikTok: https://www.tiktok.com/@llnelsonauthor

Acknowledgments

My utter gratitude goes out to a whole host of people, without whom this book would have taken a lot longer to write. Among them are the *many* friends I've made at the various 20Booksto50k conferences I've gone to since 2021 (especially Meryl Yourish and Cady Hammer), my editor for this book—Karie Crawford, my fellow mom writers, and of course, my family. Your support and help have been priceless.